COVALENCE

SAMANTHA MINA

COVALENCE

BOOK 4 OF A SERIES

For Alexandra Smith
who never once for a single moment
ceased to believe in my dream.

PRONUNCIATION GUIDE

Acci: *"AX-ee"*
Arrhyth: *"AR-hith"*
Buird: *"Bird"*
Comat: *"Kaw-met"*
Ichthyosis: *"Ik-thee-OH-sis"*
Leavesleft: *"LEEV-ssleft"*
Lechatelierite: *"Luh-shaht-LEER-ahyt"*
(rhymes with "light")
Nuria: *"NER-ee-ah"*
Qui Tsop: *"Key Sop"*

NORTHWESTERN HEMISPHERE OF SECOND EARTH

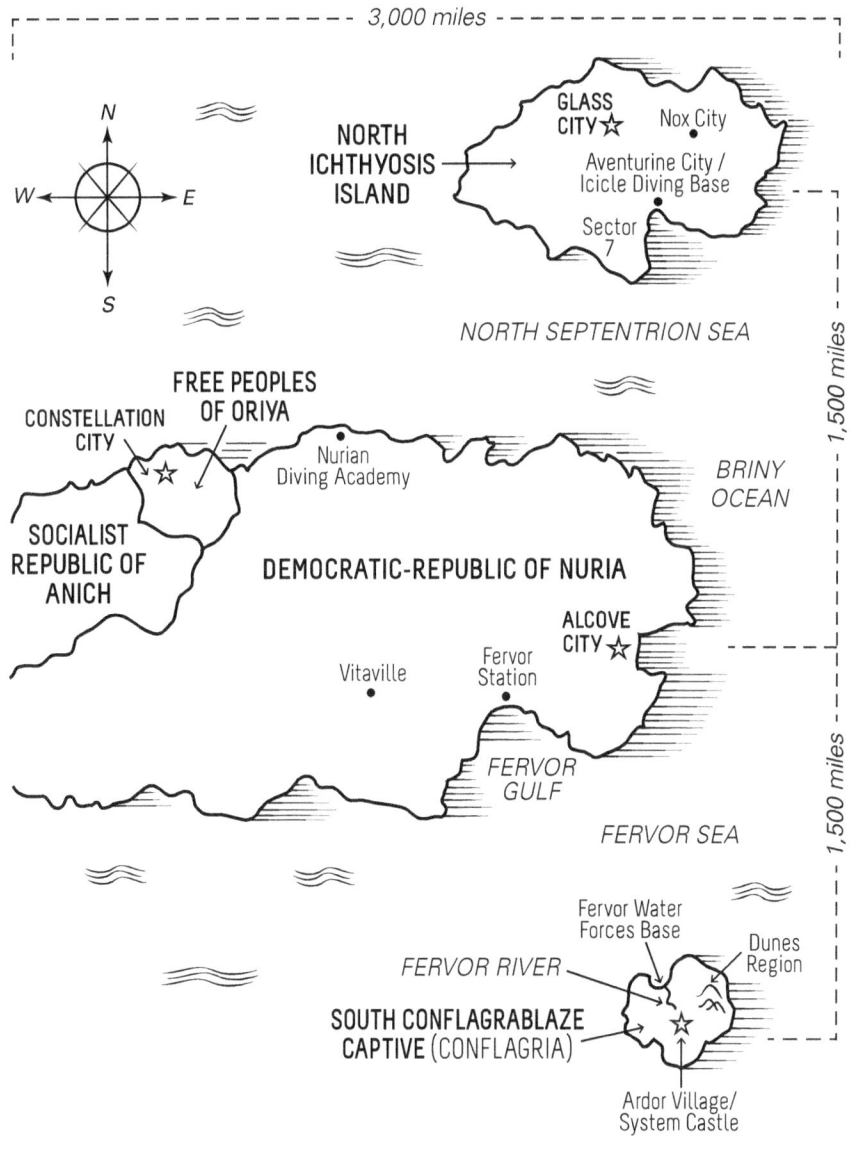

PART I
THE MAGIC WARS

Your name and your deeds were forgotten
Before your bones were dry,
And the lie that slew you is buried
Under a deeper lie;

But the thing that I saw in your face
No power can disinherit:
No bomb that ever burst
Shatters the crystal spirit.

—*Excerpt from* Crystal Spirit *by*
George Orwell, Autumn 1942

QUI TSOP LECHATELIERITE

June twenty-first of the ninety-fourth age, seventh era. The summer solstice.

"Mrs. Tsop?" An orderly appeared in my doorframe. Nurians liked using my maiden name, probably because 'Lechatelierite' was too much for their lazy lips. "You have a visitor."

I'd only heard those words once since going inpatient, here at the Alcove City Hospital. Scrunching my lids shut, I growled, "Is it that Leavesleft woman, again?"

"No, ma'am," came a young female voice, accompanied by light footsteps.

I opened my eyes.

"Hello, Mrs. Lechatelierite," she pronounced my last name fluidly, as no Nurian could. "I'm Scarlet July, the former Second Commander of the Nurro-Ichthyothian Diving Fleet and the current Leader of the Conflagrian Red Revolution." Her Ichthyothian was perfect, without a trace of an accent. "Pleased to meet you."

Flabbergasted, I beheld Scarlet July's delicate frame, disheveled hair, striking gaze and flushed cheeks. I'd heard a lot about her, but never even saw a picture of her before. My husband met her in January when she came to the Nurian Trade Centerscraper to ask to borrow a ship. Finis came home that night reeling about how 'our damnfool of a son lost his mind over the likes of a scrawny, hyper-emotional, barefoot fire-savage.'

Without waiting for a response, Scarlet boldly reached forward and took my cold bluish hand in her warm tiny one. She didn't shake it, but held it for just a moment, gently, tenderly, brushing my knuckles with her thumb. Then, she hopped into the seat by my bed, feet dangling.

She was a warrior? Impossible. I couldn't picture her sailing the Septentrion into battle, clad in a diving suit and brandishing a sidearm. The very thought of her shooting things and blowing stuff up seemed downright laughable. Cease was physically little too, yet everything else about him—his demeanor, posture, voice—bore an undeniable aura of authority and power. His presence could fill a whole room. But, Scarlet?

Scarlet cocked her head like a Nurian cardinal, staring openly at the woven cap concealing my balding scalp.

"What do you want?" I asked, frostily.

"The same things you do," she cooed, softly and dreamily. "Family. Life. Hope. A new beginning."

Ugh. So, she was one of *those* people who got all poetic and ethereal when asked a simple question, rather than just answering directly. Was that how she got Cease under her spell—by spinning a web of mystical words?

"Maybe, the news I'm bringing you today will help fulfill some of those desires," she went on, green eyes glistening.

I gave her a sour glower. "*Your* people are the ones who took all those things from me, *Scarlet July*," I spat her hateful mage name.

"Ma'am, my people aren't to blame for your losses."

"Is that so?" I growled. "Then, please, do enlighten me, Miss Red Leader, who is?"

She bowed her head, momentarily closing her eyes. "Me."

My heart leapt into my throat. "What?"

"Mrs. Lechatelierite," she trembled, "I-I'm the one who designed the incendiary that the System used on the Nurian Trade Centerscraper."

"You," I sat up straighter, "you dare call yourself an Ichthyothian diver, you demon-eyed, barefoot, barbaric, third-world fire-sav—"

"I was deceived," she cut across me, "by a double-agent. I believed the bomb was meant for the System Mage Castle. War leaders like your son and I, we're human beings; we're fallible. I made a mistake, trusting Ambrek Coppertus. I ask you to please forgive me."

"Is that why you came here?" I seethed. "To clear your guilty conscience after stealing my whole world?"

"Only partly, ma'am. There's a lot more you need to know. I want to be upfront with you, about everything."

"Get out. Now!"

"No," she bluntly objected, "I'm not finished. You deserve to know the truth, all of it. The truth about Cease and me—about *us*."

"I already know about that!" I raged. "My son loved you more than he ever loved the ones who brought him to this earth! And, now, he's gone, leaving me all alone, without a family!"

"That's not true; you still have a family."

I snorted, "Who, you?"

"No," she whispered, "your grandson." And, with that, she placed a hand on her belly.

I felt as though hit upside the head with a slab of ice. My lips parted as I beheld her birdlike body, carrying the sole continuation of the Lechatelierite bloodline. She was a *child*, for heaven's sake! A child having a child!

"Wh-when?" I sputtered.

"February twenty-fifth."

I looked away suddenly, as though slapped. I doubted I'd live that long.

Scarlet seemed to crumble beneath the weight of my silence. Fearfully, she breathed, "Do you think you could love your grandkid, even if he's half-Conflagrian?"

I realized I couldn't see anymore, so much my vision was distorted by tears. I couldn't believe it. My son—*my* son—was having a son of his own. But, alas, he'd never know. He'd never get the chance to hear his boy's first words, nor hold his hand as he takes his first steps, nor sit him on his lap to tell war stories, nor watch him grow up in his likeness...

Brazenly and wordlessly, Scarlet slid from her seat and placed her thin arms around me, leaning my face against her bony shoulder. I didn't have the strength to resist. My arms hung limply at my sides as she enveloped me.

"I can't help but think that you've had so much more of Cease than me or my husband," I choked, tears soaking into the fabric of her outrageous costume.

"I know," she stroked my back, "life hasn't been fair to you, nor any parent of a base-raised soldier. But, Cease brought justice to future generations: he convinced the Trilateral Committee to do away with the Childhood Program, just as he promised."

I smiled, but only internally. "Finis would've been happy to hear that. But, of course, he'll never know."

"Yet, Cease did it anyway, just because it was the right thing to do."

We sat there for several minutes, Scarlet hugging me relentlessly. How this little girl had the strength to offer comfort, I hadn't a clue. Because, she was clearly suffering now, too; she also loved Cease—not just the idea of him, but *him*, his person. Unlike me, she actually knew him well.

"How did he die?" I spontaneously spouted. I knew he was killed in combat on Conflagrian soil, but that was about it. "Were you there?"

There was a painful pause.

"I was," she finally peeped.

"Are the details classified?"

"N-no." Withdrawing, her lids scrunched shut. I noticed she tended to do that when afraid, as though hiding her eyes would vanquish the horrors before them.

"I need some closure," I demanded.

She put her head in her hands.

"Was it quick? Did he suffer?" I pressed.

"Well… um… h-he was thrown into the Fire Pit by a System warrior—the same man who tricked me into designing the incendiary, actually," she croaked, lifting her wet face. "And, Cease didn't fall straight into the core, either—he landed on a ledge and burned alive, slowly, as I was forced to watch, restrained."

At once, my insides turned to molten lava. I couldn't attempt to describe how I felt, in that moment. My anguish went far beyond words.

Scarlet wiped her runny nose in her floppy sleeve. "I-I'm so sorry, Mrs. Lechatelierite, I didn't come to hurt you. I wanted to bring good news."

"I needed to know." My voice came out hollow, dead.

"He went bravely. I don't know how, but he neither screamed nor cried. He just looked up at me and smiled with his eyes and told me that he couldn't think of a better way to go than to free my people. And, that's exactly what he did. He damaged the Crystal, rescuing magekind from the System's mental enslavement. His death wasn't in vain. He single-handedly accomplished the impossible. All of Second Earth is safer because of him."

A heavy silence ensued.

"I stopped here on my way back home to Conflagria," she went on, getting up. She was hardly much taller, standing. "The Red Revolution has rekindled. But, it'll be different this time around, now that we have our magic."

"Magic," I echoed, pulse hammering. "My grandson—is he—will he have—?"

"Yes." She didn't blink. "I can feel his aura already. He has a visible frequency. Two, in fact. His spectrum is iridescent. Red and black."

My breath caught in my chest. My own grandson, a mage. I never would've thought.

"What's his name? And, please, don't say you're naming him after Cease. This bloodline has been cursed with end-names."

"Don't worry, that ended with Cease," she declared. "Our son will be Commence. Commence July Lechatelierite."

PRUNUS PERSICA

My grandfather, Ivan 'Ivy' Leaf, perched on the roof of Red Headquarters like a spindly bird, thin legs folded beneath his green robe. Face crinkling, he squinted his hazel-green eyes at the glowing horizon, where the deep brown Fervor Sea met the burnt orange evening sky. He was old, reaching his expiration. Sooner or later—probably sooner—I'd be the last of my family. No, the rest of my relatives weren't dead. But, it was just as well: they were System-supporters.

I was born and raised in Ardor Village, the very same hometown as Scarlet July, Fair Gabardine, Ambrek Coppertus and Crimson Cerise. Crimson was chosen to start training for the System Water Forces when she was eight, unlike her brother, four ages her senior. Twelve-age-old Ambrek was both proud and jealous of his little sister. Desperate to prove his worth, he began over-achieving, in both the classroom and the gym. But, no matter what he did, the System didn't seem to notice. I never understood why; Ambrek was smart, had a highly-useful powersource and was ridiculously well-built for his age.

I knew I'd never get picked for the military and I didn't care. With a peach aura, my source was my skin. I was difficult to cut or wound. While that obviously would come in handy on the frontlines, it also meant my magic offered no special fighting prowess. I was a one-man fortress, but nothing special on the offense. I couldn't rip flesh with my fingers, or crack a sub's hull with my feet, or decapitate a man with a swish of my hair, or anything like that. I was good at not getting hurt, but that was about it.

"Anapes Patrici is an *internal-organ* mage," twelve-age-old Ambrek once told me incredulously, speaking of the then-tween soldier-student who'd eventually become the Water Forces Captain. "That's about as obscure as it gets, without being declared Useless—far weirder than a skin mage, if you ask me. If *his* source is good enough for the military, then yours definitely should be."

That was my cue to remind Ambrek that I wasn't particularly interested in fighting for the System… which he always took as a sort of personal offense.

"Maintaining troops is a waste of time and energy anyway; there's no war on Second Earth," I'd argue.

I was Ambrek's neighbor and classmate, but we were never close. Most nights, we walked home together from the Mage Castle, but that was the extent of our extracurricular interaction. Unless it was a school-day, we didn't see each other at all, unless by accident. We were friendly, but not friends.

We were thirteen when the System informed us of our betrotheds' names, via in-class note. Of course, our parents knew their identities since our infant or toddler days, but *we* weren't permitted to know until the start of our teen ages. I remembered the autumn afternoon I unrolled my notice in history class and beheld the name of Crimson Vermillion Cerise. Alarmed, I quickly stowed the parchment in my pocket before Ambrek, seated right behind me, could see. When your thirteen-age-old neighbor-slash-classmate was one-hundred-seventy pounds of pure muscle, you made sure to stay on his good side. Tough skin or not, I figured Ambrek could still probably tear me limb-from-limb, if he wanted to. And, I had a feeling he'd certainly want to, if he thought I was inclined to approach his nine-age-old sister anytime soon. Crimson wouldn't receive her own notice for another four ages and I had the decency not to make any moves before then.

When school ended that day and Ambrek met up with me, he spurted without preamble, "So, who'd you get?"

I shrugged, hoping he wouldn't notice the sweat snaking down my forehead. "Someone I don't really know. She's only nine, so I'm going to wait to talk to her. It'll be a long while until she finds out I exist."

He gave me an edgy smile. "Does she have a name?"

"Yes, she does," I awkwardly deflected. "Who'd *you* get?"

He brandished his slip proudly. Scarlet Carmine July.

I cocked a brow. "Isn't she that scrawny redhead who got expelled from the Mage Castle for magic deficiencies?"

His gold gaze grew dangerous.

"Sorry, I didn't mean that as a jab or anything," I quickly added. "I'm only stating facts. What little facts are known about her, anyway—I mean, for Tincture's sake, she doesn't ever go outside." I was starting to believe that obsessive protectiveness was in Ambrek's nature. He behaved the same way with Crimson, despite the fact the girl already was a top-notch warrior—certainly capable of defending herself.

"Scarlet *does* go outside," he shot. "I see her swimming, all the time." He also was a big swimmer; I supposed he was liable to spot her down by the Fervor River.

"Okay, so, she's either locked up in her parents' cabin… or underwater. Not exactly the town socialite."

"She can't show her face because the System condemned her," he fiercely defended.

"Yeah," my eyes rolled, "because she's *magicless*."

"That's a heap of dragon dung and you know it." He clenched his square jaw. "She's got an aura like everybody else. *Brighter* than everybody else, if you ask me. The System only rejected her because they're unable to accommodate her special spectral needs."

Special spectral needs, right. "Yeah, okay, sure." We'd reached our block by then and I was more than ready to put a couple hundred feet and a few solid walls between us. "Well, see you later." I turned.

"Hold up." He caught my hood, nearly gagging me. "You still didn't tell me who you got!"

"I said it's someone I don't know."

"So, what?" His voice was low. "Maybe, *I* know her. You got to badmouth my girl; now, I get to take a crack at yours."

"I wasn't *badmouthing* Scarlet. I'm going home, now."

His hands dove into my pockets.

"Hey!"

All color drained from his face. "You bastard," he breathed.

"It's not like I had a say! The System doesn't make mistakes!"

"You better be glad they don't," he growled, "or else I'd break your face, right now." His arm muscles flexed, threateningly. "If you dare come near Crimson a *day* before her thirteenth birthday, I *will* kill you. Got it?"

"Yes, of course," I whimpered.

With that, he exhaled through his nostrils and stalked away. Trembling, I scurried along home. Little did we know, neither of us would ever actually marry our betrotheds. Scarlet would get deported by the time she was ten and Crimson would die at the hand of the Ichthyothian Diving Commander by the time she was sixteen. So much for teenage dreams.

Anyway, while thirteen-age-old Ambrek was busy overprotecting his younger sister, he didn't stop to consider that maybe Scarlet also had a vigilant older brother. At twelve, Caitiff Carpus was maybe half Ambrek's size, though he did have a mean yellow wrist and a volatile temper that clashed with his sweet singing voice.

Ambrek didn't try anything outrageous or inappropriate with nine-age-old Scarlet, though; he only wanted to pursue friendship for the time being. And, he figured the best way to facilitate that would be through her only pal, a sassy social butterfly named Fair Antiquartz Gabardine.

Fair was a hair mage and a student of Magister Risque the Blue. Headstrong and smart, she showed a lot of promise. At nine, she was placed in my spectroscopy level, becoming the youngest in the class by four ages. She was also astoundingly gifted at magical combat, so it was a toss-up whether she'd wind up a soldier or a spectroscoper.

Fair had a mahogany complexion, cotton-white hair, oil-black eyes and wore a flowing lily robe that accentuated her grace and height. Crimson was nice and all, but I'd always secretly hoped that the System would choose Fair for me.

Every Sunday, Fair came to our neighborhood to visit Scarlet. So, one such Sunday, Ambrek decided to run into her, accidentally-on-purpose. That afternoon, I was returning from the Fire Pit with my family's ration when I bumped into him, loitering on the Dust Path.

"Hey there, hypocrite," I greeted him. "How'd you feel if you saw some big guy lurking in front of your house, preying on your little sister?"

"I'm not *preying* on anyone, Prunus," he answered, distractedly. "I'm not even here for Scarlet. I want to talk to Fair Gabardine. Now go away before someone sees; both of us hanging around looks conspicuous."

Curiosity piqued, I dared to ask, "What do you want to talk to Fair Gabardine for?"

Fair bridged the top of the hill.

"She's coming. Quick!" Grabbing my torch, Ambrek pushed me behind a thorn bush, right into the splintered siding of Scarlet's cabin. If I weren't a skin mage, I would've gotten shredded. "Stay below the window," Ambrek hissed, "and don't get up until Fair's gone!"

"Hey, I'm going to need that back," I whimpered, eyeing my torch. "That's my family's fire!"

Ignoring me, Ambrek swiveled around. "Hey, Gabardine." He raised a massive bronze hand.

"Ambrek." Fair stopped and stared. "What are you doing here?"

"I was just on my way home from the Fire Pit." He waved my torch.

"Your home's right there." She pointed directly across the path from where they stood. "Now, you wanna tell me the *real* reason you're hovering?"

Oh, what I would've given to see Ambrek's expression. He got verbally disarmed by a nine-age-old! But, his back was to me; I could only see Fair's pretty face.

"I just wanted to say hi," he replied oh-so-casually, as though it were perfectly normal for a thirteen-age-old boy to go out of his way to greet the nine-age-old friend of his neighbor.

Fair blinked. "Well, hello, then." She walked around him as though he were a parked wagon, heading to Scarlet's front door.

"Wait a minute," Ambrek spurted.

Fair halted. "What, now?"

"You never told me what *you're* doing here."

What a clumsy line. I bit my tongue so I wouldn't laugh aloud.

"If it's any of your business, *I'm* here to see my best friend."

"Who?"

Fair gave him an incredulous look. "You don't know your neighbors?"

"I know the twins, Amytal Angel and Caitiff Carpus," Ambrek answered in a rather innocent tone. I never knew he was such an actor. "Blue wing mage who paints for the Ardor Art Gallery and yellow wrist mage who sings in the Castle Choir. You here for either of them?"

Fair shook her head, white hair glistening in the sunlight. "For Tincture's sake, I know who *you* are and you aren't even *my* neighbor. I'm here for Scarlet." There was a pause. "You know, Scarlet July? Amytal and Caitiff's younger sister?"

It was Ambrek's turn to shake his head. "Nope, never officially met her. Would you like to introduce me?"

Fair regarded him critically. "Why do you *want* to meet her?"

"You said it yourself; I should know my neighbors."

She shrugged. "Sure, if it's okay with Scarlet's parents, I guess."

"Prunus Persica?" a female voice sounded from directly above. Startled, my head bumped the sill's underside. Then, I peered up and saw a preteen girl with scintillating blue wings and chin-length brown hair, leaning out the window. Amytal Angel. "What're you doing in our bush?"

"Um." Oh, Tincture, Ambrek was going to kill me!

Amytal's sky-blue eyes rose to Ambrek and Fair, approaching the doorstep.

"Oh, Caaaaiiiiiii-tiiiiiiff!" she called in a sing-song voice.

"No, please don't," I pleaded. "Ambrek's going to have my head."

She stuck out her tongue then turned her back on me, wings twitching with excitement. "Caitiff, will you get the door? Fair's here to see Scarlet."

Out came a boy with platinum-blonde hair, fair skin, a lemony robe and a glowing wrist. He and I were in different grade-levels, so I only ever saw him at chorus concerts.

I always thought it ironic that the son of Coronet Regal, a throat mage who could crack a dozen clay pots with a single shout, was a singing prodigy whom mages across the island flocked in to hear. The System considered him a 'partial multi-sourced mage'—he had full wrist magic with a *hint* of throat spectrum. He was only the second of his kind, in history. The first was his grandfather, Spry Scintillate, a leg mage with a few hair photons. I had no idea why, but the System had no special love for Spry. He was the reason Scarlet's family, once wealthy and powerful, lost its prestige. I never knew Spry because he passed away when I was four—the week Scarlet was born. Everyone said he 'died of a broken heart,' whatever that meant. The details of Spry's apparently-tragic life story weren't public knowledge.

"Hello, Fair," Caitiff greeted her melodically. "Scarlet was beginning to worry. Come on in."

Although Amytal could blow my cover anytime anyway, I stayed in the bushes, hoping to avoid getting mixed up in whatever fiasco I sensed was about to unfold.

"Why doesn't Scarlet come out and say hey?" Ambrek intruded, boldly. "We could fly kites or race scabrouses. Or, maybe, we can go swimming. Scarlet really likes swimming, doesn't she?"

Caitiff's face hardened as he regarded Ambrek. "Coppertus," he said, voice adopting a staccato edge. "Can I help you?"

"Fair was going to introduce me to Scarlet."

Caitiff seemed to know what was *really* going on, here. Advancing several paces, he harshly declared, "I don't think she's ready to know you, yet."

Fair, nonplused, cocked a white brow.

Ambrek spread his bulky arms. "I just want to make a friend. What's wrong with that?"

"Leave," Caitiff ordered, dissonantly.

Ambrek smirked. "Scarlet needs friends pretty bad, Carpus. She's really in no condition to turn them down."

"I said, leave."

Ambrek rubbed his huge hands together. "You gonna make me, choirboy?"

Immediately, Caitiff lunged, knocking Ambrek clean off his feet with a single swing of his mighty wrist. A high gasp sounded from the doorway.

There stood a girl so tiny, her waist couldn't have been thicker than Ambrek's upper arm. She wore a blood-red robe overtop a brown vest and a pleaded nearly-knee-length skirt. Her eyes were abnormally large and vividly green, and her hair was chaotically wiry and flamboyantly red. And, Ambrek was right: she certainly had an aura. A tremendously bright one. It was the most powerful aura I'd ever seen. It was alarming that one so small and young could have such an overwhelming spectral presence.

"Caitiff, what are you doing?" Scarlet chirped, taking a single step outside. "Who's that?" She peered curiously at Ambrek, who tried to smile at her despite his humiliation; the first time his betrothed saw him, he was on his butt! Sheepishly, he got to his feet, brushing sand and dirt from his copper-green robe.

"It's no one you need to know, anytime soon," Caitiff answered, casting Ambrek a distasteful glower. He put one hand on Fair's shoulder and the other on Scarlet's. "Come on." Steering the girls inside, he slammed the door in Ambrek's face.

I crawled out of the bushes, laughing. "That was smooth, Ambrek. Smooth as dragon scales." I held out my hand to take back my torch.

"Shut up," he spat, meaty palm snuffing out the flames.

An age passed, and he didn't speak to Scarlet once. He'd resigned to waiting until her thirteenth birthday.

"July seventh of the ninetieth age, Scarlet's going to get the best birthday gift of her life," he'd often say. "She'll get to know *me*." That day never came. By July of the eighty-seventh age, Scarlet was banished.

Ambrek didn't cope well with her sudden disappearance. He was broody and reclusive for a while, then he started hanging out with an unsightly gang of gypsy outcasts who'd recently migrated from the Dunes. That motley crew had no intention to stay in Ardor—or, any one village, for that matter—for more than a couple months at a time. Ambrek estranged himself from them right before they left town, claiming that his foray into their world was 'just a phase.' I told him that his little 'phase' probably blew any chance he had at becoming a warrior, because everyone knew the Dune Gypsies were the dregs of society—hardly worth the flame they were rationed—and the System was unlikely to forget his dalliances with them anytime soon. After those words escaped my lips, Ambrek didn't walk home with me for weeks.

Grandpa Ivy never liked Ambrek, even after he became a faux Red. He always warned me about 'that rusty one,' saying in his eerie voice, 'I don't like the look of him.' During the first round of the Red Revolution, Grandpa Ivy always grilled him whenever he stopped by Seventh Cabin. One such occasion was early in the morning on January seventh of the ninety-fourth age, when the bastard came to pick up the incendiary. Grandpa Ivy gave Ambrek a lot of grief before letting me hand it over. And, when Fair showed up that evening with the unconscious forms of Rusty Pypes and Cu Twentnine, Grandpa Ivy told Fair to go against Ambrek's orders. Fair didn't listen to him—at the time, most folks tended to ignore 'Leaf, that ancient mystic'— but, he turned out to be correct, in the end: Ambrek was bad news. The worst news Conflagria had seen since Tiki

Tincture. So, these days, we all paid attention to old man Ivy. We'd learned to, the hard way.

Which was why, when he began shouting now from the rooftops, "The Red One is coming!" I didn't dismiss his words, no matter how bizarre they sounded. I squinted at the orange horizon and, sure enough, saw a grey Nordic plane heading our way. How he knew Scarlet was the one in the cockpit, I hadn't a clue. But, I trusted his instincts.

My voice accompanied his and, soon, the shore was packed. When the plane landed on the beach, we all ran to greet her.

FAIR GABARDINE

Scarlet clambered out of the cockpit with a surprised smile on her flushed face. It was wonderful to see her again. "I wasn't expecting such a reception," she breathed faintly, throwing her thin arms around me. I could instantly tell there was something different about her, but I couldn't quite put my finger on it.

"Blame *them*." I jerked my thumb at Ivy Leaf and Prunus Persica. "They spent the last several minutes hollering from the roof of Headquarters like a pair of loony throat mages."

Blushing, Prunus chuckled and looked at his sandals. His grandfather raised his salt-and-pepper brows, intently studying Scarlet's frame. His astute gaze traveled up and down her tiny body before resting on her swathe. Then, he reached for her hand like a Nordic... but, didn't shake it. Instead, he squeezed her palm firmly, spindly thumb stroking her knuckles.

"Your aura," he whispered.

Eyes widening, Scarlet nodded. With that, Ivy released her and backed away, bowing deeply. I stared, baffled by their exchange.

"You and your grandson are free to go home, today," she told him, breezing on. Their home was Seventh Cabin, all the way in Ardor Village. Too bad—I liked having Prunus around, here at the northern shore. "Thank you for holding down the fort, in my absence."

Ivy smiled his missing-tooth smile and said in his south-eastern-Conflagrian accent, "Not a problem, July."

Scarlet didn't waste any more time, basking in our adoration. She was never the type to enjoy being fussed over… which explained how on earth she could manage a romantic relationship with someone as frosty as Cease Lechatelierite. (I couldn't imagine Cease offering the kind of affection or attention most girls would want.) She ushered us inside and got right down to business.

"This revolution is going to be a lot different than the last," she began. "Before, we had free thought, but no auras. Now, we have both mind and magic. So, what does that mean? For one, it means fiercer battles, with spectrum as the weapon-of-choice rather than swords or bows and arrows. It means that the System has full use of its original fleet, which puts us at a significant disadvantage, unless we get help from the Nordics." Which I wouldn't count on, not in a million eras. "It means that military might is no longer measured in scrap metal. It means that our bodies are stronger—but, so are theirs." She began pacing rapidly—a mannerism she never exhibited before. "I can tell by surveying this room that we have more support, this time around; I don't know several of you. I suppose that's because the biggest reason to support the System in the past—the desire to somehow restore the spectral web—is null." A long, strained silence ensued as she made deliberate eye-contact with each and every new Red, one at a time.

Oh, Tincture, I saw what she was doing here. She was essentially calling out all the 'summer soldiers and sunshine patriots,' as the First Earth saying went. She recognized there were some here whose motives were less than noble. She recognized she was standing amongst a few opportunists who took sides not according to what was actually right or wrong, but according to what would yield a greater and faster personal reward.

"I want all of you to ask yourselves why you're here," she demanded harshly, "because if you're not fully committed to the Red cause, ever willing to sacrifice your mind, body and soul for it—if you're only here because you're looking for a winning dragon to hitch your wagon—your 'support' isn't wanted."

The entire cabin seemed to hold its breath.

"I refuse to deal with the spineless and weak-hearted," she barked, sounding rather cold and Lechatelierite-like. "So, if you match that description, get your sorry ass off my saddle and out of my stronghold. Now."

No one moved.

"I learned my lesson the hard way, last time. I trusted Ambrek Coppertus," she went on, and everyone seemed to cringe at the sound of his name. "But, I won't be fooled again. I know that everyone here can't possibly be a real Red. Tell me one little lie, give me *one* reason to doubt you, even for a moment," her tone was low and menacing, "and you're finished. No second chances, no benefit of the doubt. Got it?"

"Ma'am, yes, ma'am!" the crowd cried, anxiety evident in every voice.

Scarlet continued to pace and speak for an hour, hair swinging and eyes flashing as though to remind us of her extraordinary and unusual spectrum. Urgency radiated from her aura. She spoke with fervor, planning umpteen major goals and immediate deadlines. And, in all her urgent promptings, she used fear as a motivator—making threats of imprisonment and execution—rather than the slower, harder method of making us *want* to serve her out of love. She was banking on the fact that we already loved her. Well, most people here did, but after such a long absence, reminding us of why couldn't hurt. As for the newbies, she was giving them a rather unpleasant first impression. Showing them a side that wasn't really her. A side so out-of-character, it strongly resembled the man who once tortured and tormented me until I literally begged for death at his feet.

After she dismissed everyone, I marched right up to her and blurted, "Magekind is *just* starting to relearn what it's like to think for itself. So, as a leader, you need to make your supporters feel safe and welcome, as to reassure us that we've used our newfound mental freedom to choose the right side—the side of truth and justice. You're not exactly doing that by acting like," well, I certainly didn't want to provoke her by saying anything negative about Lechatelierite quite yet, not when the man was barely a month in his grave, "like Principal Tincture."

"You want me to make everybody feel *safe?*" she echoed. "We aren't safe, Fair. This is war."

My hair twitched. "The new Reds—the ones who didn't join us for the First Revolution—have never served under a fair or benevolent leader. They don't know what one looks like. Teach them. Show them by acting like your *real* self. Like the Scarlet the rest of us already know and love. *That* woman is a role model who commands with charisma and compassion, not a tyrant who governs by fear. Fear isn't what the Reds stand for, nor is it *your* leadership style. It doesn't suit you."

"Fear?" she breathed, glancing down at her deceptively-delicate body. "Fear *me?*"

I chortled. "No one's fooled by your appearance, Scarlet. Not anymore. No one looks at you and only sees a petite sixteen-age-old girl. They see a powerful mind and unparalleled spectral prowess. They see the Multi-Source Enchant. By now, you're well aware of the terror that title can evoke. I can tell that's what you're trying to use on everyone now, to make us hurry. What I'd like to know is *why* you're in such a hurry. Rebuilding a nation isn't supposed to be an overnight task, you know."

She stared at her feet, frowning. In that moment, she really did look like a lost little child. "I'm not trying to scare anyone," she whimpered.

I folded my arms. "Then, what *are* you trying to accomplish by stomping around and issuing ridiculous ultimatums?"

"I'm trying to be more efficient. The last Red Revolution lasted five months and accomplished nothing. It cost a lot of lives and caused a ton of grief, only to come full circle. I don't want that to happen again. Because, this time, I really can't afford to waste a second."

She was kidding, right? "Scarlet, look at all the successful rebellions in First Earth history. None accomplished a damn thing in under five months. Historically, the shortest took seven 'years'!"

She pursed her lips.

"And, what do you mean, you can't afford to waste a second? You're sixteen, for Tincture's sake—you have all the time in the world, to rebuild Conflagria. Make it your life's work."

She gestured helplessly. "I... I can't."

"Why not?"

She threw her hands up. "Just look at this messed-up planet, Fair. I can't be selfish or nearsighted. This isn't the only country on the map that needs help."

I exhaled through my nostrils. "Scarlet, there's hardly an Ichthyo-Conflagrian War anymore; the System's too concerned with *us*, with the Magic Wars, to give the alliance the time of day. And, Cease isn't... around... anymore, so there's no reason—political or personal—for you to concern yourself with the Nordic world, ever again."

"The Ichthyo-Conflagrian War isn't *over*, Fair. Ending the Crystal doesn't end the war. We already learned that, the hard way."

My scalp prickled. "Let the Nurro-Ichthyothian military deal with the lingering skirmishes and let the Alliance Committee deal with forging treaties. None of that is your problem. For once, you just need to worry about your own backyard. That's it."

"You can't possibly know that," she retorted, icily. "I'm the Multi-Source Enchant, Fair, and that means I'm supposed to fulfill the prophecy. The prophecy doesn't say, 'tend to your own backyard, to the hell with the rest of humanity.' So, *no*, being the Red Leader *isn't* my life's work. I'm meant to do something else—something greater—before I die."

"And, what's that?" I growled. "All the theologians and philosophers in the world haven't figured out what the prophecy means."

"All the theologians and philosophers in the world aren't whom the prophecy addresses," she shot. "Which means I'd know better than them."

I was taken a thousand steps aback. "What's gotten into you? I've never seen your head so far up your own—"

"The prophecy is *my* responsibility, Fair," she cut across me. I swore I could see steam issue from her ears. For a moment, I really was scared of her. I'd never felt that way around my best friend before. "Mine. Got it? Ignoring it won't make it go away. I'd expect you, of all people, to understand the onus of duty."

I could sense her extreme stress undulating through the spectrum. That's when I noticed that her red aura was stained. Tinted. Her wavelength interval was too short for her. It was as though she had someone else's color inside of her. I couldn't believe my best friend changed so much in the past five months, her frequency was no longer familiar to me. What happened to her in Ichthyosis that made her come back like *this*?

Despite my anxiety, I stood my ground: "Scarlet, I do understand, believe me. But, may I remind you," I looked her square in the eye, "you left Ichthyosis. You made the choice to take off your Diving Fleet uniform, put on your mage robe, and come here. For us. For Conflagria. For the Red Revolution. Not the international war. Not the Nordic alliance. If *they* are still your priority, you shouldn't have come home."

"I'm finished with the international war, Fair," she muttered, tiredly.

"Really?"

She nodded. "Yes. I did all I could for the alliance. They don't need me, anymore."

I dared to exhale. "I'm glad we can agree on something. It's the Reds who need you, now."

"Yes," she chuckled dryly, "now."

Pieces finally fell into place. "Wait... you think the prophecy has to do with isolationism. You want to overthrow the Second Earth Order," I breathed, feeling sick inside, "don't you?"

She didn't answer. But, I could tell from the fire in her eyes that I was right.

She was crazy.

I took her blue-white hands in mine and they weren't just cold, they were downright freezing. "Scarlet?"

She wrenched herself from my grasp and stalked out of the cabin.

FAIR GABARDINE

I awoke before dawn to the sound of hurling, just outside my window.

I padded outside, barefoot, to the sight of Scarlet hunched over a bush. Dribbling down her chin was a thin stream of vomit that looked almost entirely composed of mucus and gastric acid. From behind, I pulled her hair back—a strange thing to have to do for a hair mage.

"I'm fine," she moaned. "I'm not sick."

"Really? Then, what exactly is *this*?"

"It's... nothing. I'm ok."

Clearly, she wasn't. "Maybe, you're reacting to the sudden change in diet?" I wondered aloud. After all, it'd be a rough transition for anyone—let alone Scarlet, who never had a robust digestive system to begin with—to go from salmon paste, crackers and ice-water to fired dragon meat, taro root and berry-wine. Then again, I didn't think she actually touched her wine goblet, last night...

"Yeah, that must be it." She wiped her mouth in her sleeve, face glacier-white. "Come on, let's get to work. Take advantage of our... early rising."

"Scarlet, you're so pale," I breathed. I'd never seen her cheeks so flaxen, not even when the spectrum diffused. "There's still about an hour before the sun comes up; I think you should get more rest—"

"No, no, I said I'm alright. Come on."

I caught her shoulder. "Does this have anything to do with Cease?"

She looked stricken. "Um," she squeaked, eyes tracking. "You miss him. Maybe, grief is making your tummy turn?" She didn't answer, face drooping as she fingered her collar. I put an arm around her. "I'm sorry about what happened." "No, you're not," she hissed, pulling away. "You hate him." I sure did, but that didn't mean I wanted him dead. Not when my best friend was madly in love with him. What kind of monster did she think I was? "Well, Scarlet, you know I'm not his biggest fan, but I'd honestly prefer if he were alive and well, just for your sake. It's you I care about."

She turned her back on me and stormed inside.

A week passed during which she kept throwing up. Every. Single. Morning.

"Alright, something's seriously wrong with your stomach," I now told her. She'd just returned from yet another hearty puking session.

She ignored me, snatching up her water pail and shuffling back outside.

"I'm going to get you a medicine man," I insisted, following her to the well.

"Don't bother." She busied herself with hitching and lowering her bucket. "I probably just need to drink more water. It's a lot easier to dehydrate here than in Ichthyosis. I'm still adjusting."

"You consume more water than a herd of hobnails." Though, curiously, she was still yet to drink a sip of berry-wine since coming home. Which was weird because she used to love the stuff. "It's been seven days; I'm going to fetch you a healer."

"I said no, Fair!" she snapped, dropping the rope. Falling, the pail clanged loudly against the well walls.

I'd had enough. "For Tincture's sake, what's gotten into you? I'm only trying to help. Comrades *have* to look after each other, you know; it's the only way to make it out of a war alive. You're my responsibility, and vice versa. That's how it works, when living under the gun."

She took a deep breath. "I know."

My arms folded. "So, quit biting my head off, all the time. I shouldn't have to walk on dragon-eggshells around you, not when all I'm trying to do is get us through this war in one piece."

"I'm sorry, I didn't mean to—"

"Red One! Gabardine!"

We turned. Prunus Persica, looking rather harried and handsome on scabrousback, skidded to a stop before us, kicking up clouds of dust.

"Second Cabin is under attack!" he cried. "Red One, we need your Nordic plane."

Holy Tincture, what exactly was going on, over there?

Scarlet blinked. "It's out of gas."

"What?"

"I flew three-thousand miles to get here, Prunus. I was literally gliding, by the time I reached the Fervor Sea." And, it wasn't like Conflagria had the resources to refuel. We'd need the alliance for that. I wasn't holding my breath.

"Fine. Do you have dragons?"

"We have scabrouses," I answered.

"Not scabrouses. Pine dragons or hobnails. Flying species."

"I know Fifth and Eighth have some."

The Reds, as a whole, had very few flying dragons since they were rare and high-maintenance. Any we did own, we stole from the System, usually at a cost of several human lives each.

"Alright, we'll reach out to them. But, regardless, we still need your manpower on the field. Both of you. Now." Prunus turned.

"Wait," Scarlet called, before he could gallop away. "Where's Kylarks; why are you doing his job?" Gel Kylarks was the quickest leg mage in the Red ranks. He often served as a 'messenger' because he could run faster than even the nimblest of beasts.

"His feet got torn off, last night," Prunus gravely replied, "by an enemy hand mage." And, with that, he took off.

Scarlet ran inside. She came back out a moment later, sporting a quiver... and a dragon-hide vest. I stared. During the First Red Revolution, she never wore armor. Her fighting style relied too heavily on speed and maneuverability. And, considering the diffusion was over, why would she bother with her old bow and arrow?

Well, there was no time for questions, now. I pulled on my own gear then shouted, "Let's go!"

We mounted our scabrouses and headed west to meet up with the rest of the hastily-assembling battalion. The threat in question was a System craft, sitting in the water, only a couple hundred feet from the shore.

I swore under my breath. Second Cabin's ridiculously-close proximity to the sea made it far too vulnerable. Headquarters was also a beachfront property, but at least it wasn't in the splash-zone. Yes, I knew we Reds couldn't be too picky about the locations of our strongholds since we didn't actually build any of them ourselves—we simply acquired them by either seizing System facilities or fixing up abandoned homes—but, in my opinion, maintaining Second was far more trouble than it was worth.

Where were the Nordics when we needed them? Water battles were for the alliance to handle. How could the Reds possibly stand against a seacraft?

I looked to Scarlet for the answer.

"You're our commander today, Fair," she declared.

What? "Why?"

"Because I said so," she answered, coldly.

All eyes turned to me.

"Uh, alright," I numbly said, taking my dragon to the front of the pack. To my surprise, Scarlet didn't follow. In fact, she rode to the very back.

I inhaled, mind racing. No one had a clue when the reinforcements from Eighth and Fifth would arrive; we couldn't count on them to save the day. So, I needed to devise another plan of attack. Now. Well, what did we have to work with? Scabrouses and our individual powersources. But, scabrouses could neither swim nor fly, and body-magic was useless in long-distance combat. Okay, so, we had to find a way to get closer to the ship. How? By swimming? That could be problematic; for all we knew, the ship was armed with Underwater Fire technology.

Wait. That was it!

I caught Scarlet's gaze, motioning for her to come forward. And, for the first time in the history of Second Earth warfare, Scarlet Carmine July refused to storm the frontlines. Shaking her head, she stayed put. What the hell?

"Scarlet, now!" I shouted. For Tincture's sake, *I* was the one in charge today; no one had the right to resist my orders. If Scarlet wanted control, she shouldn't have willingly forfeited it.

Reluctantly, she trotted over. "Yes, Fair?"

"I figured a way for you to attack the ship," I spoke quickly. "Me?"

"Yes, you. You're going to take it out with UF."

I couldn't help but grin; it was a brilliant plan. Scarlet was the only person in the world who could organically generate UF. And, if she dove in alone, she'd be safe from the ship's own UF, since it could only catch onto larger masses or clusters of divers. (Thank Tincture I couldn't remedy that design flaw, back when I was engineering the weapon…) Plus, Scarlet was an excellent swimmer. If anyone could handle the choppy waves without a scuba suit, it was her.

"But, Fair," she breathed, chest quivering, "m-most of the ship isn't submerged. UF wouldn't do a damn thing."

Was she playing dumb? "Burning its soggy bottom would still sink the whole boat, you know. Now, come on, no time to waste!"

Her lips parted.

"Go!" I urged.

At last, she slid off her scabrous, shedding her armor and robe so that she only wore her brown top and skirt. She ran across the beach and plunged into the tide, headfirst.

The System chose that moment to open fire on the rest of us. Total chaos ensued. Several Reds, myself included, managed to successfully dive for shelter in the rubble of the half-demolished cabin. Several *more* Reds, however, weren't quite quick enough. From my place in the wreckage, I saw a woman named Etoile Ilel get gunned, a split-second before she would've made it to relative safety. Her blood stained the sand.

Where was Scarlet? What was taking her so long? Did she drown? I peered at the sea, squinting between splintered wooden planks, and saw her head break the surface, mouth gaping. Her tiny figure bobbed in the current. What was the matter? Why hadn't she set the ship ablaze, yet?

She went back under. After a couple more excruciatingly-suspenseful minutes, her ghostly face popped up, once more. She swam to the shore and scurried across the beach, clothes clinging to her emaciated body. Her hair remained plastered to her skull, soaked.

Noticing Scarlet, the System ship abruptly turned its turrets. With a burst of light, she dropped to the sand. My breath caught in my throat. The world moved in slow motion. I was about to abandon reason and emerge from my hiding place… when Scarlet miraculously leapt to her feet and bounded into the ruins, beside me. I exhaled; so, she was only playing dead a moment ago, to dupe the enemy into leaving her alone.

"Scarlet, what the hell happened, out there?" I hissed, relief rapidly giving way to anger. "Why didn't you do it?"

She shook her head, panting and moaning.

I grabbed a fistful of her sopping hair. "Why's your hair still wet?" Hair spectrum typically eradicated moisture, instantly and effortlessly.

She coughed and shivered.

Something was definitely fishy. "My strategy fell apart and I need to know why!"

Her green gaze grew venomous. "You put the entire burden of the battle on one person. Some strategy."

"Like I had a choice? With neither ships nor dragons, we're stuck on land. You're the only one here I *thought* could reach the ship."

"I'm not, Fair." She was indignant. "You could've used the wing mages. They can fly above water, you know. They could carry others across."

I blinked. How come I didn't think of that?

"That," she snarled, "was obvious."

At last, the reinforcements from Fifth and Eighth arrived. They brought three hobnails and four pine dragons. Which meant fourteen mages could safely saddle up and deploy, alongside the wing mages. It was a no-brainer that Scarlet should be a part of the strike team. Sending her out would be like having another dragon on hand; her eyes could easily out-produce a hobnail's throat. Maybe, she was having difficulty producing UF at the moment, but 'dry fire' was her everyday specialty. And, as she'd pointed out, most of the target wasn't submerged anyway.

I straddled a hobnail, settling behind Pha Rynx, a throat mage. I chose Pha as my riding partner because it wasn't like I had an intercom to broadcast orders otherwise.

And, now, flanked by six wing mages, we were all mounted on dragonback and ready to roll. Everyone except—

"Red One!" called Culatio Carpea, a wrist mage. He sat solo on his beast, awaiting Scarlet's accompaniment.

She ignored him. "Brun," she addressed a young girl named for her long brown hair. "Take the last spot, go on."

Ette Brun immediately obeyed, even as shock struck her face.

I was seeing red. Scarlet's spectrum was needed on this mission. Why was she being such a coward? Since when did she shy away from a fight? Ette was no substitute for the Multi-Source Enchant. Not even close. I was pretty sure this was Ette's first real battle.

But, there was no time to argue. We took off.

…And, it turned out, the System ship was fireproof. Ette and Culatio's hobnail heaved and breathed, to no avail. Apparently, destroying the enemy vessel would require something more corrosive than dragon flame. I fumed. Scarlet could've easily provided that. Her eye-fire was far more potent than that of an animal or even Nordic weaponry.

Ette and Culatio's hobnail now dropped from the sky— the System made a clean hit to the beast's throat. Pha and I swooped down to catch Culatio, while a wing-mage named Ciel Kiite caught Ette.

The six remaining dragons circled.

"Now!" Pha boomed, at my prompting.

In turn, the dragons dove, depositing Reds onto the enemy hull where they started kicking and punching the structure apart with all manner of magical limbs. Before Pha and I could jump aboard, too—our steed was the last in the succession—a fantastic rumble sounded from overhead. I looked to the sky and saw an enormous Ichthyothian vitreous silica swoop in, emitting white light.

At once, the System craft detonated. Giant waves swallowed us whole. Wrestling off my armor, I fought my way to the surface.

Pha, Ette, Ciel and I eventually made it to shore, along with a single hobnail. The rest weren't so lucky. The Ichthyothians eliminated the threat but, in the process, killed sixteen Reds and five dragons.

Ciel had a broken wing and Ette, a twisted ankle. Pha and I were alright, albeit coughing up saltwater. We reunited with the others on the beach, by the ruins of Second Cabin. Scarlet didn't look at me. The vitreous silica disappeared into the horizon. The battle was technically a victory, but it didn't really feel like one.

SCARLET JULY

It was evening and Fair and I were arguing. Again.

"If you continue to deny the importance of the prophecy and my role in its fulfillment, I don't want your help with it," I retorted after hearing for the umpteenth time how she disagreed with my agenda and had no intention to co-operate. "All you do is drag me down."

Her white brows constricted. "What, you want to be surrounded by yes-men?" Her hair autonomously leapt over her shoulders, flashing silver in the moonlight. "When I call you out like this, it's not to undermine you, but to wake you up. When I say you're putting too much on your plate—and on our warriors' plates—I'm being realistic and pragmatic, not nasty or negative. Dividing our attention between a million goals won't accomplish squat, in the end; we need to focus exclusively on the Red Revolution!"

"I can't 'focus exclusively' on *anything* when I've been tasked with rescuing the *whole damn planet!*" I cried, throwing my hands up. She opened her mouth to protest, but I steamrollered her with: "Cease promised to stand by me through fire and ice; he vowed to help me tackle every possible interpretation of the prophecy. Why can't you?"

"Because I'm not Cease, Scarlet." Her voice went grave. "He and I are very different people who believe in different things. It isn't fair of you to ask me to live up to someone else's word." Her temples pulsed. "Not to mention," she added, slyly, "he probably wasn't in his right mind when he made that desperate promise. He wasn't thinking with his head."

I smirked. "Ah, so after all this time, you finally admit he has a heart."

"Oh, I didn't say he was thinking with *that*, either," she chortled, dryly.

Blood churned in my ears. "What?"

"You know what," she snorted. "I bet he said all that ridiculous gooey stuff just to get you in bed."

Red hot rage instantly flooded my veins. "How dare you!"

"Come on, Scarlet," she sneered, "what *were* the two of you up to, the night he uttered all those irresistible things you've always wanted to hear?"

My heart hammered. "None of your damn business."

She closely examined my burning face. She was my co-leader. My best friend. Shouldn't she be privy to the truth?

No, not all of it. Not until it was literally protruding from my body, for all to see.

"Fine," I finally blurted. "Cease and I… that night… we… um… he proposed."

"What?" Her oil-black eyes widened. "Well, *that* certainly wasn't what I expected you to say, but it does prove my point nonetheless. Cease wasn't thinking rationally when he swore he'd follow you to the ends of the earth. He was charged up with emotions and hormones and lust, and he definitely wanted something from you in return—a 'yes' to his proposal."

I remembered the spring day Cease and I faced-off the Trilateral Committee. 'If you don't understand the prophecy, maybe it wasn't meant for you,' he had said. Oh, Fair was right, wasn't she? Not about Cease lacking a heart or manipulating me for sex, but about the fact he'd only changed his mind about the prophecy in the heat of the moment, right as we were about to faux-marry. Literally, mere minutes before we started making love.

Yet, I still disagreed with Fair's bottom line: I knew I had to fulfill the prophecy, no matter what. And, if I came up with a dozen possible interpretations, it was my job to cover all dozen bases. 'To whom much is given, much is required,' the old saying went. And, I was given a lot. More than any mage in history.

"I think we should give the Red Revolution all the time it needs," Fair went on, "*then*, see if there's anything we could do to save the world. But, not bloody well until then."

"No," I replied, simply. "I'm sorry, Fair, I can't do that. I can't let my life—Second Earth's last chance—slip away, like that. I don't have the luxury of picking my battles or taking things slow. I have to use my time and resources wisely. And, I won't let you stand in my way. The Reds *will* do what I say."

"Do you hear yourself?" she gasped. "Is this a dictatorship? What has Cease done to you? You're not yourself, anymore!"

"Hey," I shot, "keep Cease out of this! He has nothing to do with any of this!"

"Yes, he does. The Scarlet *I* grew up with was patient, humble and compassionate. The Scarlet who just came back from Ichthyosis is an angry, hasty, self-righteous tyrant! Like him!"

Spectrum swelled in my scalp. "Cease wasn't any of those things," I roared, "and I'd be lucky to be *half* the leader he was!"

"That's dragon bull and you know it. You're twice the leader he was. Well, you *were*, until you *became* him!"

My stomach knotted up, in the instant. I knew why the accusation bothered me so much. Not because I was actually similar to Cease—we were as different as fire and ice. Fair's words weren't frightening because of *me* at all, but because of Commence. 'Like father, like son,' people always said. And, I didn't want to believe that could be a bad thing. Because, it sure as hell wasn't.

Was it?

Of course not. Cease was the most incredible man I'd ever met. He was strong, brilliant, selfless, brave, loyal, trustworthy, I could go on. I loved him, everything about him.

Well, no, not everything. He was human, after all. Human beings had flaws. Cease's were nothing outrageous. Right? So, he had a short fuse, sometimes. Who *wouldn't*, in his shoes? He lived under insane, nonstop pressure. So, he was cold and curt, sometimes. Whose heart *wouldn't* have some scars and callouses, after growing up in such a harsh environment?

"You barely knew him," was all I said to Fair. "He didn't treat his soldiers like his POWs. You never saw his good parts. Cease was a great person and all his men loved him."

"Really? If he was such a wonderful person, why were you always trying to change him?"

Oh, Tincture. I *was* always trying to change him, wasn't I? With sickening dread, I wondered: did I ever fall in love with the Cease who actually existed, or the softer Cease I imagined and tried to force on him?

What if our son inherited his dark side?

It wouldn't matter. Even if Commence was born with some wicked tendencies, they wouldn't get the chance to cultivate because *I'd* be the one raising him, not the military. And, I'd teach him compassion. As long as he stayed far, far away from the Ichthyothian military world, he wouldn't get corrupted. It was as simple as that.

My hands rested on my stomach. Yes, Commence was a child born from war. But, on my dead body, he wouldn't become a child *of* war.

SCARLET JULY

The Second Red Revolution was barely underway and I was already exhausted out of my mind. Because, this time, the fight entailed a lot more than just bows, arrows and swords. Spectrum took the fight to a whole new level. These were the days of the Magic Wars.

On July first, we reached out to the Nurro-Ichthyothian Alliance for aid. We didn't ask for much—just some plastics and metals, since Conflagria had none, and a couple crafts and arrhythmic suits, in case the Second Cabin fiasco ever repeated.

Late on July seventh, we received their answer.

No.

"Those arrogant Nordic bastards," Fair spat. "Some birthday gift, huh?"

I cocked my head. It *was* my birthday, wasn't it? I didn't even notice. I was seventeen, today. Though, honestly, it felt more like seventy.

Along with the formal letter from the Trilateral Committee, we got a poorly-written note from the Leader of the Ichthyothian Resistance, Commander Inexor Buird, and his Second, Krustallos Finire VII, angrily ranting about how the Diving Fleet would've provided everything the Reds needed, if their hands weren't tied. The bottom line was: the TC didn't give a slimy dragon turd for the Red Revolution, and foot soldiers like Inexor and Seven had no choice but to suppress their personal convictions and obey their governing authorities.

"Either that or have a coup," Fair suggested.

I shook my head. "I can't picture Inexor doing that. Seven, possibly. He's the type, believe me. But, Inexor? No way." I exhaled. "You know, I wonder how Seven got to be Second Commander, in the first place. Cease demoted him to the pit of hell, back in the spring—for good reason. How on Tincture's island did he manage to bounce back, so fast? Why's anyone *willing* to serve under him, after what he did?"

Fair shrugged, a small smile tugging the corners of her lips. "I guess some people are just born to lead, no matter their flaws. Some people just have the gift of inspiring undying devotion, stirring a following even as they march straight into the flames. Right?"

I didn't answer.

SCARLET JULY

July twentieth. Roughly two months since the Second Red Revolution began.

Began. I smiled to myself as I remembered the Fire-Pit riddle that Cease and I faced during the First Infiltration. 'Speak the name, or the meaning of the name, of the Son of Nations,' the stone read. The words 'begin Lechatelierite' wound up working. I understood it, now: the 'Son of Nations' was the son of Conflagria and Ichthyosis. *Our* future son. I said 'begin' instead of 'Commence,' but it still worked. The meaning of the name.

It was bedtime. Hiding in my closet, I threw off my robe, vest and skirt. I didn't change in front of Fair anymore, fearful she'd see the beginnings of my belly's bulge. Mages who got proper aura-coagulation therapy didn't show much until at least five or six months along, like Infrareds. But, I couldn't seek treatment because it'd entail heavy spectral irradiation, which could poison my half-Nordic child. So, the aura-clots in my womb caused a painful premature protrusion.

Fair and I now lay in our straw tarps, counting ceiling beams and trying to fall asleep. At times like these, I got strongly reminded of my nights in the Nurian Diving Academy barracks, where I spent endless hours staring at the underside of Nurtic Leavesleft's bunk, aimlessly examining the stitches in the white fabric. Our first evening at the academy, Nurtic brought his utility-belt flashlight and illegal bible to bed with him, like a little kid who'd secretly stay up late to read comic books under the covers. When I tossed and turned, mattress creaking noisily, he leaned over to look at me, sandy hair hanging.

"I'm sorry," he whispered, frowning. "Did I wake you up?"

"No, you're fine," I replied, dryly. "That would require falling asleep, in the first place."

"Yeah, I'm with you on that."

I rolled over, irritably wishing he'd just go away already but, of course, he didn't. At the time, I was dead-set on keeping my heart unattached to anyone or anything. But, what did I wind up doing within thirty-six hours of enlisting? I got stuck in a bunking arrangement with a nice guy who was determined to go out of his way to befriend me.

I could feel Nurtic's eyes on the back of my head.

"What do you want, Leavesleft?" I hissed, turning.

"Um, could you put this under the bed for me?" He held out his bible.

"Okay."

But, before I could reach for it, it slipped from his fingers. I snatched it from midair, a split-second before it would've hit the metal floor and woken the entire barrack.

"Whoa," he breathed, "great reflexes!"

"Thanks."

I'd caught it open-faced, where his ribbon was. The Book of Judges. I hummed in recognition.

"Familiar?" he asked, excitedly.

I snapped the book shut. "Uh huh, I've read Judges." Along with the rest of the bible, in a single day, when I was ten ages old and studying at the Nurian National Library.

"Cool! I'm at the part about Ehud, now."

"Of course, *you'd* like Ehud—a lefty warrior."

He grinned. "We share a middle name, too."

Despite myself, I smiled. It was a true challenge to stay frosty toward someone like Nurtic. Nurtic Ehud Leavesleft. Tincture, that was a mouthful. Though, nowhere near as bad as Cease Terminus Lechatelierite.

As I tucked the book away, I thought about Ehud and the circularity of human behavior. Throughout the bible story, Israel followed a consistent pattern: the masses would succumb to evil, a leader would come along to guide them, things would get better until the good leader died, then everyone would start to screw up again. When Israel's continued debauchery opened the door to invasion by bad guys, a valiant warrior named Ehud saved the day by slaying the corrupt king. It figured Nurtic would like that story.

"Goodnight, Scarlet."

"Same to you, Leavesleft," I murmured, drawing my blanket.

"You don't have to keep calling me that, you know. It's not like I'm your officer or anything. Yet."

At that moment, Nurtic's playful teasing reminded me of my late brother, Caitiff. My heart ached. How I missed Caitiff and Amytal.

"Yet? I wouldn't count on it," I chortled.

He grimaced. "To be honest, I'm not counting on anything. Not even on getting out of this academy alive. And, to think, I turned down the University of Vita to come here—the school of my dreams."

UVA was the top public college in all of Nuria. "Wow."

"Yeah. That's why I better not be here for nothing."

"You're not." I meant to sound reassuring, but my voice came out flat... maybe, because I'd also already found a few reasons to feel discouraged that day.

"I bet even UVA would be a cakewalk compared to *this* place," he mumbled. "We've been here for about thirty-six hours and I'm already running on empty."

I rolled my eyes. "We all are. Come on, this is the military; what did you expect?"

"I expected to understand at least *one* word in my classes today," he moaned. "I'm in over my head. I doubt I'll make it a week before getting sent home. In a body bag."

"Don't talk like that," I protested. "You were great at piloting." 'Great' was too mild a word. He was positively brilliant.

"Yeah, *piloting*. Maneuvering ships and planes is just about all I can do."

As if that were a small feat! It seemed like most of our comrades couldn't fly their simulators for more than ten seconds before spinning out, crashing or squishing their virtual surface-riders. I had a strong hunch that 'maneuvering ships and planes' would be a pretty important part of fleet life.

"No, you were also a lot farther along than everybody else in Ichthyothian." I wondered why that was? Nurtic once mentioned that he flew little prop planes back home, so it made sense he'd know a thing or two about pilotry already, but where did his mad language skills come from?

"That's not true, Scarlet—*you* were the best in that class. Your accent was as good as the teacher's. Are you already fluent or something?"

"No." I hoped, in the darkness, he wouldn't see the lie on my face. I thought I did a decent job feigning some measure of ignorance in that class. Guess not.

"Really? You didn't study it at *all*, beforehand?"

"Come on, I'm from Alcove City, like you. Where would I find Ichthyothian material, out there?"

He gave me a sideways grin. "The Order Chairman's private library."

For a moment, I was stricken. Was he aware that I once snuck into the Link mansion?

No, of course not. There was no way. He was just bragging about himself, here. In high school, *he* had special access to the Link library because of his friendship with Arrhyth and Linkeree.

Against my will, I found myself laughing. "I see. Fancy yourself an Ehud, huh?"

His face burned—whether from embarrassment or prolonged inversion, I couldn't be sure. "Maybe, I do." And, with that, he hoisted himself back up and went to sleep.

From then on, the two of us had a lot of nighttime conversations. They were hard to avoid. We talked about everything—books, music, diving, schoolwork, bible stories, hobbies, Alcove City, the list went on. I generally tried to ignore Nurtic during the day though, so he wouldn't think I was interested in being a real fulltime friend. Not that my bipolar attitude ever discouraged his hot pursuit.

Anyway, until I met Nurtic, it'd been six ages since I had a lighthearted talk with anyone. Before I got deported, Fair and I used to hang out every Sunday afternoon. We'd gossip about the cool kids in town, speculate about our future spouses, and giggle at Fair's funny school adventures.

And, now, as she and I lay in our tarps, battle-worn and weary, I longed for some fun chatter to take my mind off things. These days, it seemed as though I only ever opened my mouth to discuss strategy, tactics and politics. Well, tonight, I didn't want to think about war or government. I wanted to pretend that Fair and I were little kids again, without a care in the world. (Not that my childhood was *really* carefree, even before my deportation—my Useless designation assured that. But, that was beside the point).

So, I propped my head on my palm and randomly spouted, "Fair, have you ever loved anybody?"

She stretched her long legs. "I love you and all our comrades."

"No, I mean, have you ever loved someone the way I love Cease? Like, been *in* love, or anything like that?" I babbled clumsily. Tincture, it was like I'd forgotten how to girl-talk.

She shook her head.

"Not ever?"

"Nope. How about you? Besides Cease, I mean."

It was my turn to shake my head. "Cease has pretty much been it, for me."

"Huh," she chewed her lip, "well, I always picked up an amorous vibe from you and Ambrek—back before we had a clue he was actually a flaming puddle of scabrous vomit, that is."

I shuddered, remembering the December day Ambrek tearfully professed his undying love for me on the sea-shore. He seemed so earnest, so sincere. I imagined it'd be hard enough just to feign casual friendship with a person you sort-of tolerated. But, to pretend to be madly in *love* with someone you *hated?* Impossible. Ambrek embraced me, kissed me, pleaded for me to reciprocate, wept when I rejected him. Sometimes, I seriously wondered if the man were a sociopath.

"He definitely tried to take things to the next level between us," I admitted, "but, I refused."

"After you let him stick his tongue down your throat, you mean," she added with a smirk.

She saw that? For Tincture's sake, first Cease and now her! Was *everyone* on Second Earth privy to what Ambrek pulled on me, that night?

"I didn't *let* him do a damn thing; he forced himself on me."

"So did Amok, whom you whooped afterward."

"I-I couldn't react to Ambrek the way I did Amok. I genuinely cared about Ambrek and didn't want to hurt him. I had to let him down easy."

Fair's hair crinkled. "Ugh, I don't know how you can discuss any of this so calmly. I want to break that bastard's face. Both of them."

I exhaled through my nostrils. I'd already forgiven Ambrek for tricking me into thinking he was my comrade-slash-friend-slash-quasi-boyfriend during the First Red Revolution, but I was having a harder time getting past the fact he'd killed the one person I loved most in the world.

"He's one hell of actor, that's for sure," I murmured. "He'd probably make it big in Hollitown."

"What's a holly town?"

"It's a glamorous city in western Nuria, where lots of Nordic movies are made."

"Oh." She rolled over. "Well, what about now? Anybody caught your eye since you've come back home?"

What? "Are you kidding?" Cease was barely two months in his coffin!

She yawned. "You have to move on sometime, you know."

"Not now, I sure as hell don't."

She shrugged.

"What about Prunus Persica?" I shifted the focus away from me. "Isn't there something going on between you two?"

She hummed. "Sort of. We've been in limbo, for a while. I'd like to date him, but I recognize that the circumstances are far from ideal—Seventh Cabin isn't exactly around the corner, and the Red Revolution doesn't exactly leave us with ample opportunity for torchlit dinners or moonlit strolls." She rolled her eyes. "I think, the last time I saw him, I was covered in dirt and blood, having just emerged from a grisly battle. Real attractive, I'm sure," she chuckled. "So, to answer your question: yes, I do like him a lot, but no, I'm not pushing for anything more, at the moment. I'm sure that if it's meant to be, it'll be, eventually. Meanwhile,

I'm just kicking back and enjoying the ride, seeing where our casual flirtation goes. We're young; we've got time."

Time. A privilege Cease and I never had. We never had the freedom to let our relationship progress slowly and organically. Not when we always had to run and hide. Not when we always had to race against the clock as it ticked down to our imminent separation. We faux-married in a whirlwind, desperate to solidify our status before I had to leave. I wondered how our story would've played out if we didn't have to deal with deadlines or secrets. If we were afforded the same luxuries as Fair and Prunus, who could openly 'enjoy the ride' and anticipate the future.

"Maybe, someday, life will calm down," Fair went on, "giving me and Prunus a real shot. Until then, I'm in no hurry to further complicate my life. I mean, I don't know how you and Cease pulled off an epic romance in the middle of giant international disaster."

I wasn't sure what the hell we actually 'pulled off' aside from a Shakespearean tragedy worthy of Hollitown. "I don't know if 'epic' is really the right word. Honestly, I don't know if 'romance' is either. It wasn't a particularly romantic romance, if you know what I mean…"

"What, Cease wasn't the gushy type?" she joked, batting her lashes.

"Heh, you could say that. But, the real damper was the fact that we had to keep everything under lock and key. So, like you and Prunus, we never got the chance to really 'date.'"

"Well, if your relationship made it all the way to engagement in less than an age, you apparently still managed to cover a whole lot of romantic ground in a short span."

I shrugged. "If we gained traction fast, it was because we spent nearly every waking minute together for five straight months. But, most of that time was spent working, not hanging out. Working and trying *not* to break the Laws of Emotional Protection… until we just couldn't hold out, any longer. Not exactly a fairytale." For Tincture's sake, was Fair actually *jealous* of mine and Cease's catastrophic 'romance'? I found nothing enviable about our terrible tale. "So, what about Inexor?" I shifted the conversation focus, yet again. "Any sparks fly between you two, while he was here?"

"Inexor? No way."

"Why not?"

"He's Ichthyothian, Scarlet," she said incredulously, as though that explained everything. It took her a moment to realize who she was talking to. "No offense," she quickly croaked. "I mean, it'd be pretty messed up for a captor to pursue her prisoner. That'd be rather creepy and predatory. There are certain ethical lines a soldier just shouldn't cross, you know?"

"Ethical lines, right, I'm sure that was it," I retorted, tone far harsher than I intended.

"Come on, Scarlet, I just didn't see him in a romantic light, okay?" A lock of white hair spontaneously jumped across her tarp, spilling over the edge and onto the floor.

"Because he's Ichthyothian," I pressed.

"Yeah, so what? Why must you turn everything into a confrontation?"

I was silent.

"Alright, you want to prove I'm racist?" she reeled. "Fine, I'll own up to it. I'm on the alliance's side in the international war because I think imperialism is wrong and because the System is *our* enemy, too. But, otherwise, I have no special love for Nordics. They're arrogant overlords who believe, just because our society is magical instead of technological, we're third-world barbarians. All they care about is winning the war for *their* sake—they don't give a dragon turd what happens to us along the way. The 'Cobalt-60

Project' spearheaded by your dear beloved's father is proof enough of that."

Heat flared to my scalp. "That project was a scandal. All of Nordic society was in uproar when word got out. And, Inexor publicly denounced it on behalf of the entire Ichthyothian Resistance."

"Yeah, the Nordics went nuts because the bomb wound up going off on *their* turf. If it landed here, like it was intended, they wouldn't give a damn. It wouldn't be a scandal *then;* it'd be a 'necessary evil for international security.'

"Fair—"

"And, you saw what unfolded after the first Crystal ended; the Nordics just swooped in, turned our lives upside-down, then skipped along home. Since then, whenever we've asked them to throw us a scabrous bone, they've spat on us. And, the funny thing is, the only reason they were able to make a dent in the Crystal in the first place is because of *you*—a Conflagrian! The Diving Fleet wouldn't have gotten anywhere in their war if they didn't have one of us 'fire-savages' on their side."

I hated how much sense Fair was making, despite her obnoxious diction. I knew so many Ichthyothians personally, I couldn't help but love them, by now. But, I didn't always. When I first arrived at Icicle, I'd heard enough about 'fire-savagery' from their lips to ignite my every photon. And, by refusing to assist us now, the Nordic world was indeed being ungrateful and haughty. If the blacklisted nations wanted to survive this horrendous chapter in history, they needed to work together. Neither Ichthyosis, Nuria nor Conflagria were Order members; nothing prevented the alliance from collaborating with magekind. So, why were we self-isolating? Because of stupid racist ideologies?

"Scarlet, you can hate me for saying this, but I'd never let myself get too close to an Ichthyothian, Inexor included. Not to mention, he's a soldier."

"So, what? *You're* a soldier."

"No, I mean, he's a soldier trained by the *Childhood Program*. The Ichthyothians dare call us barbaric while they have the most uncivilized, inhumane military training method known to Second Earth. They're no better than the System."

"That program no longer exists," I pointed out. "Cease and I tore it down. And, so what if Inexor grew up in it? That doesn't automatically make him a bad guy. I know Inexor—he's a good man, and he loved you dearly."

She snorted. "No, he didn't love me. He was attracted to me, being as he'd never seen an age-appropriate female before in his life. But, no spawn of the Childhood Program could possibly fall in love. Inexor told me all about his upbringing," she shuddered, "and his stories scared the living photons out of me. At least, the System lets you learn to walk and talk and wipe yourself before teaching you to shoot. But, the Ichthyothians? They beat out your individuality, force you to ignore all your physical and emotional needs, and coerce you into conforming to their way-of-life until you're barely alive at all. Inexor was the first POW I ever held—the first 'base-raised' Nordic I ever really got to talk to. And, he was a machine. A machine who suddenly discovered something called sex—a more natural outlet for all that testosterone than killing people. What on Second Earth are those men supposed to do upon retirement? I can't imagine Inexor—or, any Ichthyothian soldier, for that matter—functioning in the civilian world."

"Retired veterans aren't just cut loose into civilian society, if they don't want to be," I explained. "Sure, they stop going to battle but, if they'd like, they can keep living on a base—

working as teachers, consultants or analysts—or, if they're high-ranking and well-decorated, they could get invited to serve on the Trilateral Committee. Most base-raised vets never really leave the military world. Not entirely."

"That's because they *can't!* They wouldn't know how to do a thing—hold a normal job, run a household, provide for their needs, cook meals, do laundry, maintain functional relationships, the list goes on. All they can do is make war, eat, sleep a little, and make more war. They're brilliant at warfare—tactics, combat, pilotry, swimming—but, stupid as a scabrous in all other areas. Did you know that they don't even have a clue what visual art is?"

"Yeah, I know," I sighed. "I've been over that with Cease."

"When I tried to explain it to Inexor, he said that it's pointless to draw something without any practical purpose behind it, like a battle diagram. He said, if you want a pretty image of a mountain or something, just take a photograph of it; why spend time and effort drawing it?"

"Cease once said something similar, when he looked at my sketches. He thought that imitating reality must be the only purpose to art. Which means, as long as you have a camera to get the job done otherwise, there's no need to sketch."

Fair chortled, "And, you expect me to fall in love with someone—no, some*thing*—like that?"

"It takes work, but they are repairable," I instinctively spouted. Tincture, I hated how dehumanizing my own words sounded. What was I implying, that Cease and Inexor were computers we could program? "It's worth it, to change someone's life like that," I hastily corrected.

"Why go through the trouble of fixing a broken machine when there are plenty of fully-functional flesh-and-blood human beings all around me, here in Conflagria?"

"*Fixing a broken machine?*"

"Come on, Scarlet, they don't have the cultural awareness of a two-age-old. Inexor didn't even know that his nation's Founding Father was the ancestor of his own best friend. For Tincture's sake, even the System Water Forces teaches its trainees the name of Founder Lechatelierite!"

What did cultural awareness have to do with love? In fact, as far as I was concerned, society tended to teach all the *wrong* ideas about love—that love was a crazy, fleeting Hollitown-style emotion that came and went like ocean waves, not a permanent choice to serve another in both good times and bad. "Just because Ichthyothian soldiers aren't explicitly shown how to love doesn't mean they don't have the desire or ability. You said it yourself—Inexor and Cease were *best friends*. That title implies some measure of attachment and commitment."

She grunted, "Uh huh. Inexor once gave me the scoop on their so-called friendship. Basically, as kids, Inexor used Cease to get to the top."

"What?"

"Need me to break it down further? Alright, then," she cleared her throat, "Inexor kissed Cease's ass because he knew the twerp was going places. So, Inexor was never Cease's friend, he was his parasite."

I realized, in that moment, how little I actually knew about Cease and Inexor's history. But, regardless, I refused to doubt the authenticity of their bond as adults. Perhaps, self-advancement was Inexor's initial motivation to get close to Cease when they were little, but it sure developed into something much greater than that, by the time they grew up.

"There was obviously so much more to it than that," I argued. "Why do you think Inexor even got imprisoned, in the first place? He put himself in harm's way to save Cease, his friend."

"He was just doing his job, Scarlet. Soldiers aren't supposed to leave each other behind in battle, if they can help it." She waved her hands. "Anyway, all that is beside the point. My point is: Inexor didn't love me... because his kind can't."

My eyes closed. "Then, what does that make of Cease and I?"

She shrugged at the ceiling. "I'm sure he tried to love you, as best he could. He probably felt *some*thing for you, like lust and intrigue. You were the first girl in his life, and likely the only person to ever give him real, personal attention, for something other than his military prowess. He also probably enjoyed being loved *by* you, even if he couldn't properly reciprocate."

And, now, I was starting to boil. I tossed in my tarp, fingers probing the Silver Triangle under my nightgown. I refused to believe that the living being in my womb was a product of anything but authentic mutual love.

"My relationship with Cease wasn't just infatuation or chemistry," I replied, hotly. "He loved me!"

"Really? How do you know?"

"Well, for one, he said so."

"Yeah, but did he know what he was saying?"

"Yes!" I roared. "He didn't take his decision lightly! He wrestled hard with himself before reaching that conclusion!"

"Are you *supposed* to logically contemplate love?"

"That's how his mind *works*, okay? He doesn't 'fall' or get swept away; he needs to think things through and rationalize every move he makes!"

"So, he *calculates* his *feelings* for you, and you want to call that genuine?"

I sat bolt upright, spectral static flickering through my hair. "YES!"

Her hands flew up. "Alright, alright, fine! Chill. Lie back down. Please."

Exhaling through gritted teeth, I obeyed. A long pause ensued.

"So, um… who did the System betroth you to, when you were thirteen?" I finally squeaked, trying to reset the conversation.

"I was drafted before I turned thirteen, so I never got my formal notice. Of course, my parents always knew, but I never cared to ask because it doesn't matter anymore. I don't suppose you ever got your assignment, either?"

"Nope, deported too young," I said, stomach twisting. "But, someone clued me in, several ages later. The problem is, I'm not sure that source is reliable."

"What?"

"He called me 'my betrothed,' when I saw him in May."

"May? You didn't come home until Summer Solstice Day." Fair propped herself up on bended elbow. "Wait, you spoke to him when you were here for the Second Infiltration?" She cocked a white brow. "Who is it, Scarlet?"

"Like you said: it doesn't matter, anymore."

"Come on, you can't tell me this much then stop!"

I curled into a ball, a grenade growing in my throat.

"Ambrek Coppertus."

AMBREK COPPERTUS

July was waning. What a tedious cycle my life had become. Since the end of May, I passed my days here in the Castle Clinic, bedridden. The damn Crystal detonated while I was still in the Fire Pit. On the brink of death, I got rescued by a special-ops team. And, now, I was condemned to a cot for who knew how long, enduring an array of agonizing spectral treatments. Thankfully, I was expected to make a full recovery.

Yes, I'd owed it to my sister, Crimson Cerise, to assassinate Cease Lechatelierite. Yes, I knew the world was better off without him. Yes, I was glad he was gone forever. Yet, the manner in which he died cost magekind far too much.

But, at long last, the System had figured out how to take care of all that. By now, Tincture's spectroscopers had already started executing the project, though it'd probably be a little while before the general public noticed anything.

When they did, it'd already be too late.

FAIR GABARDINE

July twenty-fifth of the ninety-fourth age.

We all stood in his room, watching as his life slowly ebbed, holding his hands, stroking his face, weeping into his hollow chest. Ivan 'Ivy' Leaf was expiring from old age during a season in Conflagrian history where hardly anyone had the privilege of passing from natural causes, anymore. At seventy-seven, Prunus Persica's only non-System-supporting relative was going in peace, surrounded by friends and comrades. It was sad, yet strikingly beautiful, to watch him fade way, serene and loved. It was a death one could only wish for, during these violent Magic Wars.

We all took turns hovering our ears over his lips so he could utter personal farewells. I was worried he wouldn't last long enough to get around to everyone.

Scarlet and I were the very last in line.

"Go ahead, Fair." She waved me on. I nodded and advanced; there was no time to argue.

"Gabardine," Ivy wheezed, "you're angry, but wise. Wiser than the Red One believes. She should give your words more gravity, save for those spat in rage."

I kissed his wrinkled forehead, told him how much I loved and appreciated him, then backed away.

When Scarlet came forward, the old man grabbed her robe with far more vigor than his feeble frame should've had left.

"Red One!" He placed a trembling hand on her swathe. "Protect him, at all costs."

Her emerald eyes went wide.

Ivy took a long, rattling breath. "Promise me!"

"I-I promise, Ivy," she whispered, upper lip quivering.

Apparently satisfied, his lids scrunched for the very last time, causing everyone's sobs to crescendo.

But, I didn't shed a tear. Instead, I stared at Scarlet, fury building in my chest. Of course. Everything made sense, now. Why she was no longer fearless in battle. Why she wore armor. Why she often puked in the morning. Why she no longer undressed in front of me. Why she was in such a rush to get the Red Revolution over with.

Prunus asked to be alone with his grandfather's body, essentially dismissing the crowd. We filtered out the door, scurrying off to our strongholds for the night. Back home, Scarlet shut herself in a closet, to change. So, I brazenly yanked open the door, without knocking. Gasping, she tried to cover up with a random burlap rag. I snatched it from her... revealing a distinct distention of her lower belly, just as I'd suspected.

"I don't believe this." My scalp grew hotter than a hobnail's throat. "How *could* you?"

"How could I, what?" She hastily pulled on her nightgown. "I don't answer to you!"

"You're a warrior, dammit!" I growled. "Soon, you won't have the strength to wiggle a single strand of hair, let alone fight!"

"That's already happening," she moaned, panic creeping across her flushed face. "I constantly feel cold and tired, and my eyes can hardly produce a flame anymore."

This was an absolute nightmare. "Scarlet, *what were you thinking?*"

"I-I wasn't." Tears dotted her crimson lashes. "You can't tell anyone, Fair," she pleaded. "Promise you won't say anything!"

"No matter what I do or don't say, everyone will see for themselves, soon enough!" I cried. "How far along are you?"

She swallowed. "Two months."

Only? She shouldn't have been showing yet, at all... unless, of course, she was neglecting to get proper anti-aura-coagulation therapy, jeopardizing both her life and the fetus's. Why on earth would she abstain from treatment? Unless...

"Who's the father?" I demanded.

"You know," she whimpered.

Of course. "That son of a—"

"Stop!" she cut across me. "You're not helping!"

"You're the first woman in history attempting covalence, and you don't expect me to freak out a little? You're carrying a half-blood!"

"*Half-blood?*"

"Scarlet, he's going to have health problems. Spectral deficiencies. Developmental issues. He'll be sick. Weak. All the time. His immune system could reject your frequency like a transplant-patient rejects an organ. Non-magical bodies have strict limits to how much spectrum they can handle, all at once!"

"I know, I know." She cupped her rosy cheeks in her palms. "Cease almost died from spectral poisoning last spring, after the whole 'sphere of fire' debacle. He went under for a week!"

She'd told me all about that battle. "If that happened to Cease from just *touching* a mass of spectrum, what do you think'll become of your half-Ichthyothian child? Your magic could kill him. But, abstaining from prenatal aura therapy could kill *you*."

"No," she breathed, clutching her stomach protectively. "No, no, no."

"Scarlet, you've got to do something about this."

"What could I possibly do, now? What's done is done!"

I looked her in the eye. "You know what I mean. You have to save yourself. Before it's too late."

Silence. I watched my words slowly travel from her ears to her brain.

"No. Absolutely not, Fair!" she wailed. "Ivy told me to protect him, at all costs!"

"Know what else Ivy said?" I reeled. "He said I'm wiser than you're willing to believe, so you should listen to me more often."

"Not when you're angry! Not when you're telling me to kill my son!"

"Let's make things abundantly clear, shall we?" I bellowed. "Covalence could be a death sentence for either of you, any minute. And, even if you two *do* make it out of this pregnancy alive, you're still a seventeen-age-old war leader who can't afford to burden herself for ages upon ages, raising a freak!"

Her eyes flashed. "That's the most selfish thing I've ever heard! Mothers put their children first; I can't just think about myself, anymore!"

"Alright, you really want to think about your son?" I raged. "Let's think about him, then. Let's think about what kind of life he'll have, if he isn't stillborn. The moment the System discovers his existence—and, they will—they'll drop an enormous bounty on his head. You can't keep his father's identity a secret forever, you know; once he's born, his covalence will be pretty damn obvious to the world. The child of the two most controversial figures on Second Earth will have more enemies than anyone on the planet!"

She wrung her hands. "I-I'll protect him."

I snorted. "You're the Red Leader—do you honestly think you could provide the twenty-four-hour guard he'd need? Moreover, what kind of life would that be for him? He'd have to stay under constant lockdown to evade kidnap or murder. Face it, Scarlet, you're just bringing another miserable, unwanted child of war into this world."

"How *dare* you!" she yelled. "How dare you assume I don't want my son! How dare you assume I wouldn't care for him or give him a good life! You're worse than that Icicle nurse who tried to make me have a medication abortion—"

"Well, you should've taken that pill when you had the chance because, with all that spectral swelling, a grisly surgical termination is the only option you've got left, now. Either that or give birth to a fatherless war-child with a giant bullseye on his back!"

"This is the only baby Cease could ever have!"

Unbelievable. "Do you hear yourself? Cease is *dead*, Scarlet—where is he now, to appreciate having a son?"

"This boy is the last of his bloodline! Otherwise, there won't be any more Lechatelierites!"

I threw my hands up. "And, that's a bad thing because…?"

Her jaw dropped. "I get it, now. Your concern has nothing to do with my safety or my kid's best interests, does it? This is because you hate Cease!"

I was the selfish one, here? "You just want to hold onto whatever scrap of Cease you've got left, paying no mind to the hell it'll cause the rest of us!"

"I'm not murdering my child!"

"You don't know that. For all we know, your spectrum is slaughtering him, as we speak!"

"Don't talk like that!" she shrieked.

"Mark my words, Scarlet," I growled. "On July twenty-fifth of the ninety-fourth age, your best friend warned you that covalence is a death sentence."

"*Shut up!*" she screamed, and I actually did. I was wasting my breath, anyway.

FAIR GABARDINE

If I hated Cease before, it was nothing compared to how I felt, now. I was seeing red. How dare he ruin Scarlet's life. How dare he bring another miserable child of war into this world. Already, there were far too many sickly, disfigured, battle-wounded orphans haunting the dusty paths of this dismal island. Out of desperation, most of these kids felt they had no choice but to become plunderers or prostitutes, to survive. Was that the future Scarlet wanted for her son?

In June, shortly after Scarlet came home, a random toddler snuck into a Red Headquarters storage closet and hid there for who knew how long, eating trash and going to the bathroom on himself. Stench pervading, we eventually opened up and found the poor boy crouched behind a bin of old archery equipment, emaciated and soiled. Limbs like vines and silver wings like crumpled tin-foil, starvation had rendered him too weak to walk or fly. We were so stricken by the sight of him, we didn't kick him out. Instead, the Reds collectively adopted him. From then on, he got passed from stronghold to stronghold, under the care of different Reds every few days. It wasn't the best way to raise a kid—no doubt, the instability of his upbringing would take some sort of toll on his mental health in the long run. But, for a child of war, he was lucky.

Once strong enough to curl his lips and move his cheek muscles, he told us that he was Ash Argent, the four-age-old son of a pair of recently-deceased System warriors. Expressing a notion far wiser than his ages, he conveyed in his childish pidgin that he no longer bore any allegiance to the System—our choice to love him made him 'as Red as the Red One!'

As busy as she was, Scarlet found time for Ash. The kid spent three days at Headquarters, during which Scarlet curiously insisted on being his fulltime caretaker. I thought it ridiculous that the Red Leader herself would spend so much time and energy playing mommy to a stranger when she could've easily gotten a subordinate to do it. A mere half-week of babysitting took a noticeable toll on her, too. She slept less, ate less, neglected her work and grew jumpy and irritable. I was relieved when the boy moved onto another cabin.

And, now, in only seven months, Scarlet would have a child of her own. A warrior's life was always on the line; soldiering entailed accepting that your body was an expendable resource. Scarlet's baby was already fatherless; he was only one step away from becoming an orphan.

I tried to imagine Scarlet's son lurking amongst the gangs of the paths, ransacking cabins for food and sleeping in the sand. How absurd. If Scarlet died, there was no way her progeny would become one of them. He wouldn't be ignored by the world, like that. His peculiar parentage assured that. He'd be sought after, weaponized in whoever's hands he landed.

I'd like to say that I'd take responsibility for him, should anything ever happen to Scarlet in the future. I'd like to say that I'd rise to the occasion, willing to sacrifice my own wellbeing for my best friend's legacy. But, I'd be lying. I wasn't ready for motherhood and, unlike Scarlet, I didn't want to be, at least not anytime soon. I was too young and too busy. Of course, I'd want Scarlet's son to stay strictly under Red supervision. But, I wouldn't personally become his adoptive mother.

Yet, I knew it'd be problematic, to try to raise Scarlet's kid the way we were raising Ash. To the rest of the island, Ash was a forgotten soul. No one was looking for him. He was invisible to the System. He could probably run around the Mage Castle without warranting a second glance. But, the covalent son of the Multi-Source Enchant and the Nordic Resistance Leader would be a different case, entirely. He'd be hunted for. Wanted. If he slipped out of sight for a second, it'd be all over.

Which brought me back to my initial conclusion: he should never be born. His existence was a huge risk, to countless people. A threat to national security. He was a danger to Scarlet and to the entire Red Revolution. I was convinced that Scarlet should abort him before she started really showing through her robe. It was the smart thing to do. Scarlet needed to listen to me for her own sake and for the good of all magekind.

* * *

"Fair?"

My insides abruptly turned to ice. Though I hadn't heard that voice in nearly twelve months, I instantly recognized it. The very sound filled me with terror, like it all happened yesterday. Where was he? Where was *I?* All I could see was blackness.

"Fair?" he repeated.

I opened my lids—a strange thing to do when I thought they were already peeled wide—and there he was. Commander Cease Lechatelierite stood before me, stare steely and stoic. I was so much larger and taller than him, it was almost comical. But, naturally, he wasn't intimidated in the least; he brazenly advanced on me. I tried to run away… but, there was no floor to move across. The darkness seemed to hold me in place, as though I were submerged in a tub of glue. I was trapped! I was his prisoner, again!

He was now within arm's reach—far too close for comfort. I trembled, violently. Tincture, how on Second Earth did Scarlet ever muster the courage to willingly touch him? To put her arms around him? To kiss him? To make love to him? Just being a couple feet away made me want to simultaneously scream, vomit, urinate and defecate.

Since my captivity, I had imagined our hypothetical confrontation at least a thousand times, always picturing myself bold and brave as I put him in his place. But, of course, it was far scarier to face the real thing than a fantasy.

But, was he the real thing? It was impossible; he was dead. *I'm ready to wake up*, I thought to myself. That usually worked whenever I found myself in a dream I wanted to cut short. *Wake up, Fair!* I silently ordered. But, the oppressive darkness didn't retreat.

"Fair Gabardine, I've been wanting to talk to you," Lechatelierite said, tone piercing my eardrums like that of a throat mage. How could an Infrared sound like that? I could swear there was spectrum in those soundwaves. "Don't be afraid."

Don't be afraid? Was he serious!?

"This isn't happening," I replied, voice embarrassingly soft and weak. "You aren't real. I'm going to wake up from this nightmare, right now."

He shook his head. "I'm sorry, but you aren't going anywhere until I'm done with you."

What? I looked at his pinched face in disbelief, anger abruptly overpowering all reason.

"How dare you!" I erupted, though well aware that provoking the likes of Lechatelierite—whether real or imaginary—couldn't be a good idea. "How dare you try to… to *control* me, again! Have you come to finish what you started?"

"Fair," he gently breathed, "I came to apologize for how I treated you, last summer. I've been wanting to say this since before you left Ichthyosis in August. The guilt has tormented me for nearly an age." He crouched. "Please forgive me," he bowed deeply, "and lift the burden of hatred from your own heart."

I was instantly derailed. Lechatelierite was a machine programmed by the Childhood Program; there was no way his conscience actually ached over what he did to me. The invaluable intel he extracted from me, then an enemy POW, turned the whole war on its head—there was no way he actually regretted the means to those ends. There was no way someone like him would sincerely plead with a former prisoner, a fire-savage. On his knees. It wasn't just awkward, it was downright humiliating. This wasn't real. He was acting. And, not well, either. Normal people didn't kneel while apologizing. It was heavy-handed. He was trying too hard. His voice was calculated; his gestures were overt.

He was manipulating me.

"Liar," I hissed. "Get up."

He didn't move.

My blood boiled. I couldn't take his passive insistence, any longer. I wanted him to stand, so I could fight him. Yes, he was already dead, but… I wanted to kill him. At least, I wanted to hurt him—to cause him a fraction of the pain he caused me.

A fraction of the pain he caused Scarlet. Venom coursed through my veins.

"Get up!" I screamed. "Quit patronizing me and get the hell up! If you really want to apologize, do it to Scarlet and to the entire Red Revolution!"

He finally raised his gaze then, and I couldn't believe what I saw in his silvery stare. Terror. Pure unadulterated terror.

"She's dead, isn't she?" he whispered, thin lips quivering. "Ambrek Coppertus killed her in the Fire Pit, d-didn't he?"

He covered his face, entire body shaking. He looked so very small and vulnerable as he doubled over, cheeks reddening between his fingers.

I froze. No one was *this* good of an actor. Not even Ambrek. Were Lechatelierite's emotions legit? Was it possible that he actually cared for Scarlet?

"Scarlet... isn't dead," I began.

He removed his hands, revealing a shocking mess of tears and mucus.

"But, she's facing a tremendous burden," I went on. "We all are, because of *you*."

He blinked. "Me?"

"How *dare* you sow a bastard on a war leader! Scarlet has more important things to do than raise your half-blood spawn!"

His jaw literally dropped. Then, he smiled. No, he *grinned*. With teeth.

Heat rippled through my hair. It was so wrong, so infuriating, to see him rejoice in the face of disaster. Disaster *he* caused.

"Scarlet's alive!" he called, joyfully. "Alive and carrying *my* child!" And, with that, he started cry-laughing uncontrollably, the sound overtaking me as though imbued with a vibrant photon rainbow.

I was suddenly aware that my sword's hilt was clenched in my fist. I wasn't sure how it got there; I didn't remember picking up anything. Screaming, I lunged at Lechatelierite, a loud crunch filling my ears.

I opened my eyes. Sure enough, I was standing, weapon in hand. And, at my feet, lay my tarp. Broken in two.

SCARLET JULY

A loud snapping noise jolted me awake. I sat up and saw Fair, panting and shaking as she stood amongst shreds of wicker, sword in hand. What on earth?

"Fair?"

She dropped her weapon with a clatter, backing away from her spliced tarp.

"I... I saw him," she breathed.

"Who?" I blinked. "Like, in here?"

She hesitated. "I had a... a vision of Cease. It was terrible."

In a flash, I sat upright. "What?"

"He wanted to apologize to me. But, I told him it was *your* forgiveness he should've been begging." Her eyes raked my stomach. "When I mentioned your pregnancy, he started laughing. He laughed until there were tears in his eyes. He laughed until I wanted to scream. Until I did scream. It was sickening." She shuddered. "And, then," she paused, looking down at her moonlit blade, "I tried to kill him. I tried to kill him though he's already dead. I wanted him to be alive for a moment, just so I could kill him and he could die, again."

I looked away, caustic anger coursing through my frame like spectrum of the wrong frequency.

"I can't believe you," I growled.

"I have plenty of valid reasons to hate him, Scarlet. You know that."

"He came to *apologize*," I seethed. "He tried to make things right. And, how did you react?"

"Scarlet, think about how he hurt me. How he hurt *you!*"

"You should be grateful to Cease for what he's done for Conflagria," I spat. "If it weren't for his sacrifice, the thoughts in your head right now wouldn't be your own! You owe him your freedom!"

"I don't care," she retorted. "I'm never going to forgive him. His memory makes me sick. He's still oppressing me, from beyond the grave. And, now, that nightmare-vision is going to haunt me for the rest of my life!"

Suddenly, I broke into noisy sobs.

Fair was thoroughly startled. "Scarlet?" She rushed over, dropping to her knees. "Tincture, Scarlet, I'm sorry, I didn't mean to—"

I held up my hand. She didn't know why I was so upset. It wasn't really because of her vitriol—that was old news—but, because her vision reawakened something in me. In the last couple weeks, I'd finally started to come to terms with the permanence of Cease's absence. I'd finally begun to progress past the denial phase, extinguishing the delusion I'd somehow see him again. But, now, Fair's incident gave me a painful glimmer of hope. Because, until this moment, I didn't know that it was possible to have visions of the dead. In all of Conflagrian history, there were no documented cases of postmortem apparitions. And, if Cease could visit Fair, why shouldn't he appear to me, too? After all, Cease was more spectrally twined to me than anybody. He loved me.

Fair seemed to sense my thought-process. "Scarlet, he's gone. Forever. What I saw… it wasn't actually him; it couldn't have been."

I swallowed. We were entering uncharted territory. Like covalence, nothing could be said with any certainty on the topic. But, Fair was a genius spectroscoper. Her guess was better than anybody's.

"So, don't torture yourself, waiting around for him to drop by," she continued, solemnly. "I'm sure the real Cease would want to see you again, but visions don't work that way. They don't come on demand. Okay?"

I nodded, sleeve-wiping my face.

"Chatting with his ghost wouldn't help you in the long run, anyway. All it'd do is stir more grief and stunt your recovery." She rummaged the messy room, unearthing a floormat from somewhere. "Let's stop talking about him now, alright?" She lay down. "Because, we'll never see eye-to-eye when it comes to him. I'll always hate him and you'll always love him and, well, I suppose that's that."

I didn't answer. I wondered what it'd be like to go through life bearing the weight of perpetual hatred. Ambrek took my world from me, yet I still couldn't make myself *hate* him. Hatred was a toxin that poisoned the hater far more than the hated. But, alas, there was no way I could *force* Fair to forgive Cease. I could fly a pine dragon to unfamiliar shores but I couldn't make it land.

SCARLET JULY

My aura tended to drain into Commence. All of it. If I didn't actively concentrate on redistributing my spectrum—consciously willing my photons to circulate my body—I became entirely powerless. Forget battle, it made sleeping nearly impossible. Several times a night, I'd wake with a start, muscles cold and achy from lack of spectrum while, in contrast, my womb throbbed and burned. Then, I'd waddle to the outhouse, vomit (or, at least, dry-heave), come back inside, revive the fireplace, huddle by it for a while, toddle to my tarp and (slowly, maybe) fall asleep. It was an exhausting cycle.

"There *are* treatments for this, you know," Fair now grumbled, irritated from the constant disruptions. "Treatments that'd allow you to hold onto more of your powers—and, your meals."

I curled up in bed, shivering violently. "You mean those crazy therapies where they bombard you with concentrated emissions of your complimentary color?"

She rolled over. "Yeah, those."

"Those could give a *mage* spectral poisoning."

She was silent.

My heart leapt into my throat. "You *want* my son to get poisoned, don't you?"

"No, I just hate seeing you suffer like this all the time, and for what? It's not worth it."

"Yes, it is. To me."

She sat up. "Your life is worth a hell of a lot more than some unborn half-blood's. I hate wondering, every single day, which will kill my best friend first—her aura clots or the fact that she's a *warrior* without proper control of her magic?"

I swallowed. "Fair, I just have to be careful for a few more months, then I'm in the clear."

Her oil-black eyes rolled. "Careful. Right. You can sit in Headquarters all day and *still* be unsafe, because you're you. A wanted woman. People don't lead major rebellions if they want to be careful," she snorted, lying back down. Then, she added, under her breath, "Sleeping with Cease on a whim wasn't very *careful*."

My face grew hot with rage and embarrassment. "Hey, that's none of your—"

"I mean, if you're going to do it, at least you could plan ahead and take some precautions."

For Tincture's sake! "Fair, what's done is done. I can't change the past, so quit harping me about it already, okay?"

She exhaled through her nostrils. "I'm just confused, Scarlet, because you're too smart to have been that negligent. I mean, when you and Cease hopped into bed together, you didn't think *at all* about the possibility of pregnancy?"

"Fair, it was the night before the Second Infiltration—the most dangerous mission of our lives. We were under a lot of pressure. We both felt like it was our last chance to be together. You know?"

She cocked a brow. "No, I really don't."

I gestured, helplessly. "Try to see things from my perspective. I was scared out of my mind, consumed by this intense... I don't know... *foreboding* feeling—this inexplicable, overwhelming sense that disaster was about to strike and we were running out of time. I wasn't thinking straight. And, I could tell he was also pretty shaken up. He remained agitated and tense, even when he kissed me and held me and reassured me that we'd be together forever."

Fair was unmoved. "So, on the spur of the moment, the two greatest military geniuses in Second Earth history decided *not* to get some rest before the biggest fight of their lives, choosing instead to fool around without taking any precautions… because they were scared."

She made us sound so stupid.

"Well, no matter what," she went on, hair twitching, "Cease had no business promising a future to anybody at a time like that because, if he were still alive right now, he'd still be leading the Ichthyothian Resistance. He wouldn't have any time for you or your kid. He wouldn't be there for either of you, at all. You'd be just as alone as you are now. A single mother."

"Cease vowed to move to Conflagria permanently, after the state-of-emergency lifted and he finished his prison sentence," I whimpered.

She shook her head. "The alliance would be lucky to call off the state-of-emergency in seventeen ages," she chuckled bitterly, "*after* which Cease would spend at least seven more months behind bars. So, by the time he'd come back for you, your son would be all grown up. What kind of family would the three of you be then, after nearly eighteen splintered ages?"

It was a good question. My heart hammered against my ribcage. In the hypothetical scenario Fair described, Commence and Cease would wind up complete strangers, in the end. Who knew, maybe Cease and I also would— after all, eighteen ages was plenty of time to learn to live without each other. Commence would probably struggle with forgiving Cease for his prolonged disappearance and Cease would probably torture himself over missing out on

Commence's upbringing. Once reunited, everyone would make a total mess of trying to love one another and atone for lost time. And, stuck in the middle of it all would be me. After living half my life hinged on an adolescent hope, I'd find myself physically surrounded by family but still horribly isolated.

"When you and Cease threw caution to the wind, that night," Fair plowed on, "you didn't realize that you were essentially committing to a bleak future. You now mourn because you think his death is what ruined your dreams. But, in truth, even if he never fell into the Fire Pit, there'd still be a ton of insurmountable obstacles standing in your way. I hate to say this but, practically, a one-night stand was the farthest your relationship could ever go."

Tears streamed down my face. Fair was right. Perhaps, things turned out for the better, after all. Now, Commence was free to grow up believing that only death was to blame for his father's absence. He was free to love the idea of his dad—the war hero who liberated his homeland.

I buried my face in my burlap blanket. Fair didn't come over to comfort me.

"I'm sorry, Scarlet," was all she said.

"Well, I still d-don't regret anything," I choked.

"If you say so," she sighed.

"I do say so." Inexplicable anger bubbled in my chest like Fire Pit lava, abruptly overwhelming my sorrow. "So, let's quit obsessing over my past choices and what I *should've* and *could've* done, and start focusing instead on what we *need to do* next, for Conflagria! Stop acting like my pregnancy is a tragedy!"

She rubbed her temples. "I'll keep saying this until my photons diffuse, Scarlet: without complementary-color therapy, childbearing could kill you. If that isn't a tragedy, I don't know what is."

"I'm not going to die, Fair," I insisted, even as fear prickled my scalp. "I've been through so much in my life, I can't count the number of times I shouldn't have made it. And, yet, here I am. I'm pretty good at cheating death."

"You're probably the first mage since the third era to carry a baby this long without the treatment."

"Exactly. The Conflagrian population managed to survive the first couple of eras, just fine."

"Yeah, but none of those historical women attempted covalence, on top of everything. I mean, I was just thinking about it, this afternoon: what if your half-Nordic child poisons *you?*"

Wait. "What?"

"All this time, we've been concerned about your magic harming *him*. Well, what if things work the other way, too? What if you have a sort of... I don't know... allergic reaction to him, or something?"

Huh? I knew aura-clotting was dangerous, but Commence's DNA itself certainly couldn't harm me. What on Tincture's island was Fair talking about?

"That's the most ridiculous hypothesis I've ever heard. Humans can't be *allergic* to one another. I mean, Cease and I were able to conceive, after all—it's not like we're different species."

"Yeah, but you're radically different races."

"So, what? *Races* can't be allergic to one another, either. For Tincture's sake, race doesn't even exist!" Not as a bounded biological phenomenon, anyway. As a social force, however, it was alive and kicking.

She blinked. "What do you mean, race doesn't exist? Of course, it does. We're physically different than the Nordics. How can you deny that?"

"The only difference we have is magic. But, the reason for that isn't purely nature, but nurture and environment.

Nordics and mages are geographically isolated from one another: Conflagrians live in close proximity to the Core Crystal—an environment that cultivates magic—while Nordics live far away and must resort to technology to survive. But, maybe, if covalence and spectral twining become commonplace and Crystal fragments get transplanted around the world, our gifts would spread. The only reason we think of race as a solidified biological entity is because that's what the theory of isolationism teaches."

"Isolationism? Conflagria hasn't given a slimy scabrous turd for isolationism in four eras."

I shook my head. "Just because a nation is blacklisted doesn't mean it isn't still influenced by Order ideologies. We all are. We think of race as an organic reality while, in truth, it's nothing but a stupid societal construction. A product of Order politics."

Her lily brows scrunched. "Scarlet, there are definitive genetic differences between races. You know that."

"Sure, but did you know that there's a greater genetic difference between a tall and short Nordic than there is between a Nordic and a mage of the same height? So, if we want to discriminate according to actual *genetic differences*, why don't we do so according to height?"

She blinked, again. "That's dumb."

"Bingo."

There was a pause.

"But, Scarlet, wouldn't all this mean that Nordics can just," she gestured wildly, "*learn* magic?"

"Yes."

"That's crazy. You have to be born with it."

"Cease wasn't born with it. Didn't stop him, did it? He used magic, several times. He communicated telepathically with each of us via the web, he diffused the sphere of fire, he destroyed the Core Crystal, he appeared to you in a vision… shall I go on?"

"He was only able to do all those things through *your* aura. Because you two were twined."

"The very fact that a Nordic can spectrally twine to a mage just proves my point further." I got up, padded over to Fair and grasped her hand. "Feel my wavelength. Notice anything?"

"I have since you came home—your aura is no longer just red. It has a black tint to it."

"Do you know what that is?"

"No…"

"It's Cease's aura. It lives in me."

She pulled away, repulsed. "Cease doesn't—didn't—whatever—have an aura. He used *yours* to do magic, Tincture only knows how. But, he never had a visible wavelength of his own."

"Cease's aura may've originated from mine but, by the time he died, it was no longer mine. It was distinct. Like a cell in mitosis, it had two defined forms by telophase, though still encased in a single membrane. Then, it broke apart into independent cells."

"What language did you suddenly switch to? You totally lost me."

"By the time he died, Cease had developed an aura. His *own* aura, that I had no control over. He had a unique wavelength, a different color. He was a throat mage. Untrained, yes. But, a throat mage, nonetheless."

"No."

"Yes."

Her nose twitched. "Well, if we're all one big happy family, how come Conflagrian bodies are so spectrally-dependent while Nordic bodies aren't? How come we slowly waste away without the Crystal and they don't?"

"Like I said before—there are environmental factors at work. One can *become* dependent on the Crystal. If Cease got proper training, developing his aura to capacity, he'd suffer when cut off from the web, too."

She chewed her cheek. "So, if the non-magical can become magical, how come there's such a thing as spectral poisoning?"

"If Nordics come in contact with too *much* magic all at once, they can go into shock. They have to be eased into it. Learning and adapting is a process, not an incident. I mean, you wouldn't just throw a civilian on the frontlines and expect him to make it back from battle in one piece, would you? Of course not—he'd need some toughening up, first. Likewise, Cease's aura was developing, but it wasn't as strong as yours or mine yet, so it couldn't handle much. The same goes for my son, I guess. I can't just get wave-therapy and bombard him with photons when his frequency is barely budding."

Fair was incredulous. "Did you and Cease know all along what was happening to him? I'd expect the idea of becoming a mage to scare the dung out of any Nordic."

"No, we didn't know, not all along. At first, I just sensed an odd haze around him. But, somewhere along the way, I figured out that it was his aura, turning from infrared to black."

"I can't believe this. This is nuts."

Of course, she was stunned; I'd just told her that ice could learn to become fire. Sure, she believed she was anti-isolationistic, but she—like most everyone on Second Earth—didn't realize just how much the theory of isolationism permeated her thinking. She disliked the political and economic *results* of the global system, but never considered the complex racial ideology behind it. No one did. Most anti-isolationists didn't truly understand why isolationism was bad. They only knew that it was doing terrible things to the world. They were ignorant of the roots, while opposing the results. Isolationism needed to be struck at its core.

Sooner or later—hopefully, sooner—I wanted to spark a worldwide revolt against the Order. But, for that to happen, my fellow protestors needed to be made aware that, even though they objected to the political and economic effects of isolationism, they still often *thought* the same way as isolationists when it came to their day-to-day ponderings and dealings. My fellow revolutionaries would have to purge this toxic ideology from their own minds before asking the world to break free of it in economic and political practice.

Surprise: fire and ice weren't so different, after all.

LINKEREE LINK

My brother's good friend, Nurtic Leavesleft, came home at the end of June, surprised to find himself hailed a national hero. He was quickly reaccepted into the University of Vita, the top public college in Nuria, and was set to begin his freshman age this fall, at twenty. I was eighteen and a fellow member of the UVA class of ninety-eight.

He and Arrhyth knew each other since elementary school, but their friendship didn't really take off until they became swim-teammates during the first semester of their senior age at Bay River Secondary. Back then, Nurtic often came home with Arrhyth after practice to hole up in father's library, reading books about the Ichthyo-Conflagrian Wars.

When not at the Link Library or the school pool, Nurtic could be found at the Alcove City Flight School. Within months of starting pilotry lessons, he became the institution's star pupil. My family attended some of his student airshows. One day, after a particularly incredible spectacle, I mentioned offhand to Nurtic how cool I thought it'd be to ride in a little prop plane. Immediately, he offered to take me up sometime. I was surprised because I wasn't actually asking; I was merely dreaming aloud, with the expectation of being ignored. But, Nurtic was the one friend of Arrhyth's who never cast me off. He was always very nice to me, instead of treating me like 'Link-Link, Arrhyth's pestering little sis,' as Dither Maine—the third musketeer of their trio—often did. Nurtic never made fun of my redundant name and was typically willing to include me in his friends' activities, games and discussions. My silly adolescent crush on him had just begun budding when he, Arrhyth and Dither ran off to northern Nuria to begin their military careers.

This past June, Nurtic came home from the war. But, Arrhyth didn't. Arrhyth was still serving in the fleet to this day, and to say that I missed him would be the understatement of the era. I cried hard when I learned that I may not see him for seventeen more ages.

Today, August seventh, as I biked home from the community pool where I worked as an after-school lifeguard, I spontaneously decided to visit Nurtic since he was literally the only person in the country who interacted with my brother relatively recently. Leaving my bicycle in the driveway of the Leavesleft home, I rang the bell and waited, curly hair dripping chlorinated water all over the baggy t-shirt covering my one-piece.

I heard the sound of stairs creaking inside. That's when I remembered that I hadn't actually seen Nurtic face-to-face in nearly two ages. Immediately, I felt the urge to put as much distance as possible between myself and this porch. If only my feet weren't rooted to the spot…

The door swung open, revealing a hollow-cheeked, leather-skinned, emaciated corpse.

"Nurtic?" I breathed.

He stared at me with those big hazel eyes of his—those eyes that seemed all the more enormous now that he was half his own weight. There was something peculiar about his gaze. It took me a moment to decipher what it was. Of course. It was the look of someone who'd seen death. The look of someone whose soul got torn apart and put back together, all jumbled up, with pieces missing. Clearly, he would never be the same, again. The joyful boy I once knew was gone forever, replaced by this tortured veteran.

"Hey, Ree," he greeted me without expression, "you're a lot taller than when I saw you last."

"Um, yeah, you too," I responded clumsily, shifting in my sandals. "You're like, what, seven feet, now?" My heart pounded so loudly, I wondered if he could hear it.

"Just six-foot-seven, but I understand why you'd think otherwise."

I winced, internally. I didn't mean to call attention to his unhealthy weight loss, stretching him out like a beanstalk.

"Would you like to come in?" he asked, watching me cautiously. Why, oh why did I think this was a good idea?

"Sure," I replied, grinning like a total moron. He didn't smile back.

I stepped inside. The air-conditioning was on, full-blast. Either Nurtic had grown accustomed to freezing in Ichthyosis or he was trying to compensate for having roasted in Conflagria. Following him to the living-room, I caught a glimpse of my reflection in a mirror across the hall. Ugh. It was my first time hanging with Nurtic since I was sixteen… and I was wearing a baggy shirt, boy-shorts and no makeup! Embarrassment heated my cheeks.

Nurtic busied himself in the kitchen for a couple minutes, undoubtedly fetching a snack or drink I didn't ask for.

He returned and, sure enough, handed me a mug… of hot chocolate. What a strange beverage choice for August. Then again, it was as cold as January in here.

"So, let me guess, you came to ask about Arrhyth," he said, rather brusquely. He sat rigidly, at the opposite end of the couch.

I nodded. It figured that Nurtic wouldn't beat around the bush. No small talk, no pleasantries, aside from the brief height thing. No asking how I'd been, all this time. He was a soldier now, and soldiers meant business.

"Seventeen ages," I swallowed, "that's the modest pre-diction—the alliance's goal—for ending the war. I'll be at least thirty-five by the time Arrhyth's back…"

And, to my profound horror, I felt my eyes burn. Oh, no. I looked away, desperately hoping Nurtic wouldn't notice my distress.

But, of course, he did. Wordlessly, he got up and retrieved a tissue-box from the bathroom. When he returned to the couch, he didn't do what his high-school self would've done—hug me while chirping, 'everything's going to be okay.' Instead, he just sat there and observed me, blinks few and far between.

When I was done blowing my nose and wiping my face, I croaked, "How's Arrhyth's health?"

"Just fine," Nurtic answered, mechanically. "No injuries or illnesses that I know of."

"What about his mood? How's he holding up, knowing how long he's in for?"

Nurtic shrugged. "Not too bad, I guess. He's willing to believe that the war could wrap up before the economy totally tanks. But, he's not particularly optimistic about the possibility of Nuria or Ichthyosis getting reaccepted into the Second Earth Order—especially after what happened to our commanders at the Trigon Center, last spring. He called me 'borderline delusional,' just for suggesting it." And, with that, Nurtic laughed. He actually *laughed*. My heart soared—the beaming boy I once knew was back, if only for a moment. But, after his chuckle ended with a strained choke, it occurred to me that he wasn't cracking up because he honestly thought his words were funny, but because the only other alternative was to cry.

For the next couple of hours, Nurtic entertained any questions I had—about Arrhyth, Dither, himself, the late Resistance Leader and military life in general. He told me about his brief fling as Fleet Commander—leading men into battle and busting Lechatelierite himself out of court—and about the long months he spent marooned in Conflagria, hiding out with a teenage hair mage named Fair Gabardine.

And, then, he spoke about Scarlet July. It was like he'd been anticipating the topic, all afternoon. Once he got started, he couldn't stop. She was the Red Leader, the legendary warrior, the most powerful mage in history, the possible fulfillment of the ancient prophecy. She was an amazing soldier, artist, linguist, friend—you named it, Scarlet was incredible at it. It was obvious that Nurtic didn't just respect her as a comrade or like her as a friend. He was head-over-boots in love with her. And, when I realized that, a small part of me died. Because, it was then that I also discovered that my old feelings for him hadn't totally vanished, even after all this time.

Two cups of hot chocolate later, I decided to get going. I had just one more question: "How come you didn't have any coco?" He'd been drinking ice-water, instead.

"I haven't consumed anything sweet in two ages. At Icicle, everything is salty, sour, or—most commonly—bland. Base-raised soldiers have never even tasted sugar."

"Wow," I breathed. "What about when you were in Conflagria?"

"We lived off taro skins and dragon giblets, from the trash."

"But, you're back home, now," I pointed out. "Why don't you eat what you want?"

He shrugged. "I do. I just don't really want junk, anymore. I suppose I sort of lost my taste for it. Not to mention, it'd probably be a shock to my system."

We stood.

"Well, I really enjoyed this conversation, Ree," he solemnly declared, shaking my hand like we were business associates at a conference rather than two kids chatting on a lazy summer evening.

"Me, too."

I expected him to offer to hang out again sometime but, instead, he said, "So, I guess I'll see you in October, at UVA."

"Guess so." My heart nearly sank through the floor. But, then—

"How about a lift there? Some company on the way sounds good to me. And, I'd be happy to haul your things and help you move into your dorm, in exchange for some of your mad organization skills in mine."

"Oh, no, that's okay; I wouldn't want to put you out, or anything." I also didn't think his parents' flivver could fit both his stuff and mine. We'd have to drive separately, no matter what.

"Are you sure? Because I remember promising a planeride, a couple ages ago."

I stared.

"I got a part-time job at Frost's Delivery Service," he went on. "My boss said I could use the company plane for personal matters as long as I pay for the extra gas myself and stay modest with the mileage. They're being especially accommodating so I can keep my job while in school."

A few weeks ago, my dad talked with Nurtic's and learned that the Leavesleft family was in dire financial straits. John-Paul and Mary-Esther always worked in ministry, which paid next to nothing, so what their livelihood really depended on was the stock market. Unfortunately for them, however, they had invested heavily in the Nurro-Ichthyothian Underwater Vessel Manufacturing Company... whose primary facilities and factories literally went up in flames on January seventh. Nurtic's parents were now barely able to keep up with their bills, let alone shell out thousands for UVA tuition. And, Nurtic's military pension couldn't exactly compensate since Ichthyosis didn't have the resources to pay their veterans properly. So, though scholarships helped, Nurtic still had to work through college. (In this dismal economic climate, no student got offered a full ride anymore, apparently not even war heroes).

Not that it'd be too hard for someone like Nurtic to get a job, even in this rough market. Nurtic was a celebrity, often featured in magazines, newspapers, tabloids and TV broadcasts… though, ironically, he never actually volunteered for an interview or photoshoot. The media mostly relied on stolen snapshots of him going about his usual business, oblivious to the cameras.

To me, Nurtic was a childhood friend, not a rock-star. Sure, I thought he was handsome, but not because some magazine told me he was 'eligible.' It was ages ago that I noticed his dimpled smile, sandy hair, tan complexion, hazel-green eyes and, above all, incredible character. He was generous, kind, charismatic, optimistic, brave, humble, I could go on. It was his humility that attracted me the most. He acted like he didn't have a clue how amazing he was.

"Th-the ride would be great," I sputtered.

He beamed.

I didn't see him again until college move-in day, the first week of October. But, all the while, I didn't forget that cute grin for a single second.

SCARLET JULY

August twenty-fifth.

These days, it wasn't uncommon for mothers to get raped en route to the Fire Pit, or for fathers to vanish from their work commutes, or for kids' bodies to wash up in the Fervor River. It was nothing special to see mobs of orphans prowling the paths with distended bellies and protruding ribs.

For all its good intentions, the Red Revolution was yet to accomplish a damn thing. While many morally agreed with our goal, most saw it as futile to pursue. They considered it as idealistic as it was beautiful. And, above all, they saw it as unworthy of all the violence it appeared to spurn.

"If you just quit picking fights," an old widow told me, a couple days ago, "the System would stop hitting back. Life would return to normal. You're the offenders, Reds. You alone have the power to end this war and stop innocents from dying."

Oh, how black-and-white she made everything sound. How simple and clear-cut. The Reds were the match-strikers. We could simply retreat and the violence would cease. If we just lay down our swords, all of Conflagria would live happily ever after.

But, it wasn't that easy. It wasn't easy to resign your people to total oppression. It wasn't easy to give up everything you believed in, for the sake of a temporary peaceful façade. If the Reds stood down today, what would prevent another revolution from popping up in a few months or ages? The typical pattern of a failing state was that of recovery and relapse, recovery and relapse, over and over and over until everybody was either dead or a slave. Conflagria would be condemned to this wretched cycle until disrupted by an extraordinary effort. To stand still today would be to selfishly and inevitably place that tremendous burden on others in the future. My son's generation, perhaps. Or, his children or grandchildren. So, in truth, my warriors' hands were far cleaner than that of the apathetic finger-pointers.

I hoped the Red Revolution would author the beginning of a new chapter, not only for Conflagria, but the planet as a whole. There were only six ages left of the seventh era, and I wondered each and every day what those ages had in store. I sure knew what I wanted.

I wanted the whole world in revolt. I wanted to scream so loud, even the farthest reaches of the southeastern hemisphere would hear. I wanted to help give sight to the billions of blind people who followed the Order like leashed scabrouses. I wanted humanity to taste true freedom and realize that poison was the only thing they'd ever swallowed thus far. I wanted to see mankind redeemed. I wanted to watch Second Earth become a worthy home for Commence July Lechatelierite.

* * *

Battle.

From across the field, a helmeted warrior rubbed his hands together until they literally ignited. Then, he rolled the flames into a ball that he hurled my way. Inhaling with an open mouth, I threw my hair forward to snatch it from midair. It took everything in me to do it. My powers were so frail and flighty, these days. My hair-movement was limited, my eye-fire was liable to extinguish without warning, my sight unpredictably oscillated between sharp and dim, and I could barely heal a papercut. Eidetic memory was the only reliable magic I had left. Behold the mighty Multi-Source Enchant. Sooner or later, my comrades would notice my inadequacy… and the cause for it. Thanks to my coagulating aura, I was already beginning to show a little, through my robe. I knew, it'd be a matter of weeks, if not days, before my Reds would discover the truth. Weeks, if not days, before they'd lose all confidence in their war leader.

That flame-throwing hand mage was doing too much damage—he needed to be eliminated, ASAP. I charged at him, hair swinging with my every last photon, aiming to decapitate. But, he ducked right in the nick of time, causing me to merely swipe off his helmet. And, so, I met the gold gaze of the very man who'd kissed me on the seashore, eight months ago. The very man who, less than half an age later, killed the father of my child, before my very eyes.

Grunting like a gelid, Ambrek Coppertus now caught a tuft of my hair. Immediately, inexplicable pain struck my collarbone and belly. Apparently, he must've felt something too, because he quickly dropped my lock like a poisonous snake, turned on his heel and bolted away, leaving his helmet in the dust. Terrified and baffled, I didn't pursue him.

I could hear Prunus Persica hollering my name from somewhere. Wheeling around, I spotted him from several yards away, wrenching his sword from an enemy's gut. As a skin mage, he was one of very few unfortunates who had no choice but to rely on inorganic weapons in combat, like swords, torches and arrows. (On the flipside, his source meant he didn't need armor. Armor was heavy and cumbersome. Though I hated wearing it, I did so for Commence's sake.)

Aside from my name, I didn't have a clue what Prunus said. Sometimes, my comrades expected too much of my senses. Just because I was supposed to see well didn't mean my hearing was also heightened.

I ran to him. "Persica, what's the matter?"

"The lung mages who were here, a moment ago," he panted, squinting at the sunset, "do you have any idea where they ran off to? Are they circling back from somewhere? Can you scan the horizon for us?"

Oh, Tincture. "Um," I squawked, blinking helplessly at the skyline. "I-I don't see anything."

He grumbled, "They can't have just vanished!"

"Wait a minute... yes... they're approaching from the northwest!"

But, by then, it was too late. By then, they were close enough for anyone to see, and they were taking us by storm. Literally.

As the lung mages blew and blew, it seemed as though the sand beneath our feet turned to arrhythmic fabric, rippling and twisting and tossing our bodies like burlap rags. Consumed by the orange oblivion, we coughed, choked and flailed. Sand pierced our flesh, burned our skin, clogged our throats, filled our bellies.

It would've been ideal to attack the source of the tempest, the lung mages themselves. But, they were far away and we couldn't safely launch fireballs or arrows in a sandstorm—there'd be no way to control their trajectory. Perhaps, we could attack the living wind itself? But, how? I fingered the spool of deadline, under my swathe. Maybe, we could... lasso and throttle the magical wind, like drapery? It seemed a bit unorthodox and far-fetched, but I didn't have any better ideas.

Pha Rynx let out a sonic scream as he flew past me. Empowered—by adrenaline, not spectrum—I caught him with a coil of cord, pawed his shoulder and bellowed directly in his ear, "Rynx, broadcast my orders!"

Pha let out a thunderous sneeze; a muddy wad landed on my cheek. Then, he bellowed, "Ma'am, yes, ma'am!"

"Tell the hair mages to use half their hair to weave a web, binding everyone together. Then, once we're all anchored, the rest of their hair can gather and stifle the sheets of sand."

Pha promptly delivered my instructions. For the next several minutes, I watched stage one of my plan unfold, my own locks blowing uselessly in the wind. Then, I felt the brown hair of a young woman named Ette Brun encircle my midsection.

"Red One, loop back to me for reinforcement," she called.

I obeyed—with deadline, not hair. Then, I swallowed and said, "Lead the compression effort, Brun."

There was a dumbfounded silence, followed by, "What?"

"You heard me."

"But, a-aren't you going to do it?"

"We don't have time to argue. I believe I gave you an order."

And, before she could object again, I asked Pha to tell everyone to follow her lead. She was trapped.

The battle was out of my hands, now. All I could do was watch and wait.

Slowly, Ette's hair became the primary lever around which the rest twined, forming what looked like an immense, scintillating, multi-colored anaconda. The sheets of sand thrashed like netted fish as the hair mages, screaming and crying under duress, squeezed tighter and tighter.

And, at the center of it all was Ette, a teenage girl who barely had time to graduate from the Mage Castle before the Red Revolution took over her life. She shook and wept and clawed her scalp, eyes boggling.

"Help me, Red One," she whimpered, face resting on my collarbone. Radiating a myriad of colors, her body felt stove-hot against mine. I knew it was dangerous for Commence to be so close to so much spectrum, but I couldn't exactly back away. "Please, Multi-Source Enchant, take this burden from me!"

Looking down at her trembling figure, I solemnly said, "I can't, Brun. I'm sorry."

After ten more agonizing minutes, the wind finally died and we all came tumbling to the ground.

Ette's sobs echoed in my ears, all the way home.

SCARLET JULY

The entire battalion migrated to Headquarters, feet dragging. I nearly fell through the doorway, the last straggler to arrive. Dozens of dreary Reds sprawled on the floor before me, eyes brimming with suspicious scrutiny as I crawled into a corner. Curling into a ball now, my world went black.

Sometime later, a sharp tone pierced my consciousness: "Red One!"

Startled, I awoke to the sight of Prunus and Ette, flanked by a group of wind-rumpled hair mages.

They all looked seriously pissed.

"Yes, Persica?" I sat up.

"We need to talk to you. Now."

I swallowed. "Have a seat, then."

"Why don't you stand up?" he snapped.

"Watch it, soldier," I warned.

No one moved. I couldn't have stood if I tried.

"Why are you so exhausted?" he demanded, towering over me.

Seriously? "We *just* came out of battle."

"Why couldn't you see where the lung mages went, when I asked?" he pressed. "Why did you order Brun to lead the strike?"

I looked away.

"With your spectrum, you could've practically restrained the entire sandstorm by yourself," Ette piped.

"The medicine men said that Brun will stay diffused for at least a week," Prunus growled.

I looked at poor Ette, who was indeed as infrared as a Nordic. "I'm sorry," was all I could say.

"We're waiting for some answers, Red One," Prunus insisted.

"Hey, back off, everybody!" Fair emerged from the crowd. "Let's give the Multi-Source Enchant some space!"

"It's okay, Fair," I spoke quietly, "I can handle this."

"We're not going anywhere until she explains what the hell is going on here," Prunus shot.

Folding her arms, Fair glowered back at him. Great. She was getting into an argument with the guy she liked, on account of me. So, I wasn't just an inept war leader, I was a lousy best friend, too. "Our commander is tired," she snarled, "so, we're all going to show her some respect and quit breathing down her neck."

"She hasn't earned the right to be tired!" Prunus yelled. "She hardly used a photon, the whole battle!"

"You have no idea what you're talking about, thickskin," Fair seethed. "Scarlet gave this battle every photon she's got!"

The entire cabin went silent. Fair's face turned from brown to yellow.

"Red One?" Ette whispered, suddenly stricken with worry. I stayed silent.

"Are you sick?" Prunus dropped to his knees beside me, all rage apparently vanquished.

"Wounded?" Ette asked, also kneeling. She gently touched my arm.

I shook my head.

Countless times, I imagined how I'd break the big news to my Reds. But, somehow, none of the scenarios I pictured involved such a dramatic confrontation as this. An anxious hum slowly overcame the room. I understood their concern;

it would indeed be a serious problem, for the Multi-Source Enchant to suddenly lose her powers without cause.

I had no choice but to spill the grisly truth, now.

"I'm," I began weakly, as everyone held their breath. "I'm," I repeated, nausea escalating by the millisecond. Colors spinning before my eyes, I doubled over and vomited on the floor.

Fair decided to end the suspense: "She's pregnant."

There it was. My secret was out.

A buzz flared as every eye widened. Cheeks pink, Ette and Prunus backed away, bowing and murmuring apologies. I just stared at my sandals.

Fair stood in front of me, protectively. "Alright, folks, show's over. If you're done getting checked out by the medicine men, it's time to go back home to your strongholds. Move it!"

Once the crowd abated, Fair mopped up my puke then settled beside me, on the floor. I buried my face in my knees.

She stroked my limp hair. "They were going to figure it out on their own, sooner or later," she softly breathed. "Better they hear it straight from the source before rumors start flying, right?"

I sniffled. "I know you have feelings for Prunus; I'm sorry to put you at odds with him, like that."

"You, my sister, are far more important to me than any man." She draped an arm around my shoulders. "I may give you a hard time every now and then, but it's only because I care about you. Don't ever doubt that. Okay?"

I nodded.

"Time for bed." She helped me to my wobbly feet, pulled off my dirty robe and led me to my tarp. I literally collapsed into it. "I think you should take a break from battles until the baby's born, alright?"

I hummed and shut my lids, too weary to argue.

NURTIC LEAVESLEFT

October fourth. College move-in day. Classes would start on the seventh.

Little Ree enjoyed every minute of our flight over, occasionally squealing at the turbulence. I was amused by her excitement; after my service in the fleet, a beeline across calm skies wasn't exactly my definition of a thrill. When we landed, I bounded onto the tarmac, restless and ready to carry her stuff to her dorm room on the seventh floor. But, she just sat immobilized in the passenger seat, headset still on. Right. I'd forgotten how sensitive civilians were to things like elevation change. I gave her a moment to stabilize, then helped her out of the cockpit... to the sight of countless students flocking to the blacktop like paperclips to a magnet, eager to get a closer look at the 'cool plane' that just landed in the housing area.

"I can tell you guys are freshmen," retorted an upperclassman flagger. "This is a *runway*. Deliveries and such land here, all the time. There's nothing special about *this* plane. Soon enough, you're all going to hate living here because of the constant engine noise."

Apparently, the crowd still managed to find something special about our landing.

Me.

"Oh, my goodness, *Nurtic Leavesleft* goes to this school?" cried a willowy blonde.

"Did *she* fly here with him?" asked a swarthy brunette, noticing the headset in Ree's hands. "Lucky!"

Great. We'd been at the University of Vita for all of three minutes and things were already getting weird. Was *this* what college was going to be like? I'd been looking forward to a fresh start, a normal life.

I should've known better.

Indeed, within a couple days, my worst fear was well-confirmed: I was never going to make any real friends around here. It seemed like, everywhere I went, I was constantly stalked by opportunists who just wanted to bask in my limelight… until discovering how 'boring' I actually was.

"C'mon, you don't *act* like a kickass soldier," a suitemate named Shawn Sordid now told me, over dinner. It was the eve of the start of classes. "Aren't you supposed to be a big hotshot pilot, or something? Why not take more chicks up on your wings? If I were you, I'd be giving, like, ten rides a day. Followed by plenty of *other* rides, if you know what I mean."

I rolled my eyes.

"Man, Sleevey," he went on, "you could have all the girls you want."

That was another thing I already couldn't stand about college life: the stupid epithets. Literally overnight, I became 'Sleevey'—or, worse yet, 'Leavey-Sleevey.' Apparently, everyone had seen me on TV, barging into Lechatelierite's court-martial with the stripes torn off my left sleeve. Blend that with my last name and you got… well, a really lame nickname.

"What about that sexy mixed chick you came here with?" Shawn asked. "I mean, if you don't want her, I'll gladly take her to the mile-high club, if you know what I mean—"

Before I could think the better of it, I found myself on my feet, grabbing his collar and knocking over his chair. The entire dining hall fell silent.

"You stay away from Linkeree, you hear me?" I roared, throwing him to the floor and kicking him in the gut. "If you so much as lay a finger on her at any point over the next four ages, I'll kill you. Got it?"

Shawn writhed, coughing blood onto the tiles. I turned to the door... and saw Ree standing there, white-faced with shock.

"Nurtic?" she gasped, trey trembling in her hands.

I pushed past her and headed out into the night.

When I got to my dorm, I curled in bed, put my hands over my face, and cried.

* * *

October seventh, eighteen o'clock.

On my way out of the lunchroom, I spotted Ree at the end of a long table, hunched over her food, curly brown hair hanging over her face. Taking a deep breath, I marched over.

"Hey," I quietly greeted her.

She wordlessly stared up at me with those giant hazel eyes of hers.

"Ree... I'm really sorry," I awkwardly began. "I don't know what came over me, last night."

"You really scared everyone, Nurtic," she whispered.

"I'm... sorry," I repeated, plopping down across from her. How empty those words sounded compared to how I felt!

"So, you're the kind of guy who starts cafeteria fights, now?" Her voice shook. "The kind of guy who makes death threats while kicking a man on the ground until he literally pukes blood?"

"No, Ree, I just—"

"This is college, Nurtic," she spoke louder, "not the trenches. Shawn isn't an enemy soldier, he's your classmate. Drawing his blood doesn't preserve national security. It just makes you a bully. Or, worse, a criminal."

I looked away, overcome with anguish and self-directed hatred. "I know."

Silence.

"Nurtic," she piped, "are… are you okay?"

Another long pause ensued.

"You can tell *me*," she gently added.

"No," I finally admitted, shaking my head, "I'm not."

Concern brimmed in her gaze. "You want to talk about it?"

I shrugged, trying to swallow the growing grenade in my throat. "I don't know… I guess what it boils down to is… I'm just having a harder time adjusting to all of *this* than I thought I would." I gestured to our surroundings. "Serving in the fleet, living on the run across enemy lines, watching my best friends die, slaughtering mages left and right… it's a lot to have to suddenly push aside, you know?"

"I can't imagine," she breathed.

"I came home less than four months ago and it's like everyone here expects me to instantly pick up where I left off, living a regular student life, without a care in the world," I went on. "It's like I'm supposed to act like I *didn't* just spend the last two ages destroying everything I touched."

"Is that really how you think of your time in the military?" she asked, looking heartbroken on my behalf. "As a chapter where all you did was destroy everything you touched?"

My lids scrunched. "When I find myself having violent outbursts against civilians, unable to deal with normal-people problems without getting physical… then, yes, that *is* how I see what the Ichthyothians have done to me. It's like I've been reprogrammed into someone else—someone who responds to any situation with force. You know the saying, 'if the only tool you have is a hammer, everything looks like a nail'? Well, I guess, to me, everything now looks like a punching bag." My fists balled, on the table. "And, no matter how many times I tell myself I'm in a new life stage, away from the world of war forever, I still don't know how to shut off that aggressive persona and be my real self again."

It was Ree's turn to shake her head. "I think you're seeing yourself all wrong. You aren't the monster you're describing—not by a longshot—and your service in the fleet entailed far more than just destroying stuff. If you keep beating yourself up like that and discounting all the great things you've done for your country... well, no wonder you're not in the mood to tolerate Shawn Sordid—or *any* aspect of college life, for that matter." She toyed with her fork. "How about this: whenever you're tempted to start self-flagellating, instead of dwelling on what *you* think of yourself, focus on what *I* think of you. Does that make sense?"

I blinked. "What do you think of me?"

She hesitated for a moment, chewing her lip. "I think you're an all-around good guy—altruistic, genuine, kind—who's understandably experiencing some reverse-culture-shock with returning to civilian life after two intense ages of self-sacrifice. I think anyone would be a little traumatized and messed up, in your shoes. I think it's alight to cut yourself some slack, allowing yourself enough time to recover and readjust."

I didn't answer. She made me sound so... normal. Like it was okay to struggle with what I was dealing with, right now. Like my issues didn't make me a bad person. Like these past two ages didn't change the core of who I really was. Even after watching me beat down on a twenty-one-age-old civilian in a fit of unjustified rage, Linkeree thought I was a good guy. She made me feel accepted, unjudged.

"Don't trust your self-perception for a little while," she concluded, "and come to me whenever you need to be reminded of how awesome you actually are. Sound good?"

I nodded, chest a little looser than when I first sat down. There was something refreshing about being truly vulnerable with someone, for once. I'd lived the last two ages continually on my guard, inside a shell.

"Well, I should probably head to class, now," I told her. "Thanks for listening and for saying all that nice stuff."

"Anytime, Nurtic. I mean that."

"I appreciate it, Linkeree."

"Of course." She smiled. "I just have one small condition."

"Name it."

"Don't call me that."

"Call you what?" I asked, nonplused. "Linkeree?"

"Yeah."

"But… you're Linkeree."

"No, I'm Ree."

"What's wrong with Linkeree?"

She cocked a brown brow. "Um, well, for one, my last name is Link."

"So?"

She stared. "You don't see anything wrong with *Linkeree Link?*"

"Nope. I like it."

"Oh. Well, that makes one of us," she chortled. "Anyway, I only really let family members use it. So, you're not authorized, sorry."

I chuckled. "Know what this reminds me of?"

"What?"

"I had a comrade named Krustallos Finire the Seventh, but Lechatelierite always insisted on calling him 'Seven.'"

"That's pretty cool."

"Apparently, Finire didn't think so. I wasn't around to actually witness anything myself, but Arrhyth once told me that Finire and the Commander were always at each other's throats about it. But, you know what? After Lechatelierite passed away, Finire willingly adopted the epithet as his own."

"Really?"

"Yup."

"Wow."

"So, maybe, you'll come to like 'Linkeree' someday."

She smirked. "I highly doubt that."

"Maybe, if I called you by it enough times, it'd grow on you."

"You don't have that kind of power over me."

I stood, slinging my backpack over my left shoulder. "I commanded a fleet of hundreds into battle, but I can't persuade an eighteen-age-old college freshman to like her name?"

"That's right."

And, we laughed.

SCARLET JULY

October seventh.

I lay beneath my ragged blanket, shivering violently, face and arms prickly-numb. Head throbbing, my tongue grew thick in my mouth. Unable to ignore my bladder any longer, I struggled to unsteady feet and warbled out into the night. I made it to the outhouse after what felt like hours of dizzy meandering. I shut the door and fumbled with my robe, blood pounding in my ears. Before I could sit, the floor slanted and sharp pain shot through my head.

I woke up some time later in my tarp, a fuzzy patch of brown and white hovering over me. Dawn light filtered through the windows.

"Scarlet?"

It was Fair. I wanted to greet her, but my lips wouldn't move. Instead, I drooled on myself like a baby.

She cupped my slack face in her hands. "Tincture, Scarlet, what's going on?" She sleeve-wiped my dribbling saliva. "A moment ago, I found you passed out on the floor of the latrine. I'm getting help, now. And, like it or not, I'm telling the medicine man that your pregnancy is covalent."

I moaned in protest.

"For Tincture's sake, he needs to know what he's dealing with!" she retorted. "I promise I won't mention Cease's name." She jumped up. "I'll be back as soon as possible—I just need to track down a healer. I hate to leave you here, but you won't be alone for long; a handful of folks will be arriving at seven-thirty for a meeting. Hold on." And, she was off.

All morning long, I lay there, cold and immobilized, listening to the sound of people arriving and setting up shop, on the other side of the wall. For them, it was just another day of work.

I heard the front door violently bang open.

"Where's the Red One?" came Ette's frantic voice, piercing through the hubbub.

No one knew the answer.

"What about Gabardine, then?"

"She's not here, either. She left a little while ago, to fetch a medicine man," Prunus replied.

"Why, what's going on? Who's sick?"

"She wouldn't say."

A toddler's noisy wails filled the cabin.

"It's okay, Ash," Ette cooed, worry puncturing her tone.

A mix of fear, adrenaline and spectrum shot through my frame, miraculously giving me the strength to tap on the wall and croak, "Brun, in here!"

With a series of thumps and bangs, Ette came bounding in, Ash in her arms and Pha Rynx at her heels. The boy was bound up with diffusion rope.

Ette goggled at me, dropping to her knees while still cradling Ash. "Red One, are you alright?"

Never mind me! "W-what's wrong with Ash?" I choked. "Why's he tied up?"

As if on cue, his sobs escalated to howls. Pha forcefully clamped a hand over the poor kid's mouth.

"All morning, he kept trying to fly away," Ette quickly explained. "I caught him with my hair a few times, thinking he was just playing around… until he violently slashed me with his wings." She indicated where the cut must've been before it got spectrally healed. It stretched all the way from her palm to her elbow. "When I asked him what's the matter, he just screamed the same word, over and over: traitors." Oh, Tincture. "That's why we had to restrain him. He's seen too much; if he escapes, he could be a security threat." She paused for a moment. "That's not all. Other cabins have reported similar incidents in the last twenty-four hours. At least seven other mages have been acting like Ash."

My heart hammered in my throat. "Who?"

"Penni, Manus, Violet, Aureate, Regalli, Articulatio and Cubital."

"Children," Pha breathed. "They're all children."

"Except Regalli," I interjected. Regalli was seventy-five and on the brink of death from various age-related illnesses. "So, children and the elderly." I inhaled, chest trembling. "It's impacting those whose auras are dying or still developing."

"It," Ette echoed. "Then, you think so, too." She swallowed. "They're falling back under the System mind-suppression."

"Yes."

Her face went pale. "But, how? What about what Crystal's End did?" As my warriors often called me 'Red One,' they'd reverentially christened Cease 'Crystal's End.' Whether Red or System-supporter, most Conflagrians didn't care much for Nordics. Except Cease. Everyone had an opinion on Cease. The Reds, for the most part, loved him and honored his sacrifice. His name was legend, among us. Accordingly, the System hated him the way we did Ambrek Coppertus.

"What Cea—Crystal's End did was an isolated incident," I thought aloud. "Yes, he severed the problematic frequencies, but what's stopping them from being replaced? What's to prevent the System from manipulating the web, all over again? There's nothing permanent about Lechate-lierite's work. There's no force *maintaining* it. And, as the System gradually re-configures the Crystal's emissions, it makes sense that the weaker wavelengths—those belonging to kids and old people—are impacted first."

There was a long, tormented pause. Then, Ette, on the verge of tears, whispered, "Red One, what are we going to do?"

I was silent. For once, I didn't have a trick up my sleeve. Never before had I considered the possibility of something like this.

"We should destroy the Crystal," Pha fiercely declared, "before the System finishes what they started."

I shook my head. "We can't live without spectrum, Rynx."

"We did, before."

"Yeah, but our bodies were degenerating. If the System didn't restore the Crystal, all of magekind would've eventually perished. It was only a matter of time." I wrung my frigid hands. "Besides, it takes an aura like mine to destroy the Crystal, and I'm mostly diffused."

"How come *you* aren't falling under the mid-suppression, then?" Ette asked.

"I said, *mostly* diffused. I still have my eidetic memory. The spectrum in my mind must be protecting me."

"You know, I still don't understand why you're refusing treatment," Pha growled, entering dangerous territory. "If you just got complementary-color therapy, you wouldn't be going infrared like this."

The door opened, saving me from this discussion, at least for the time being. It was Fair, with the medicine man.

"Scarlet, meet Heil Olea, a healer who specializes in diffusive illnesses and—" She stopped dead. "Whoa, what's going on, in here? Why's Ash tied up?"

Olea cleared his throat.

"Sorry," Fair said to him, dryly. Apparently, the tragic answer to her question would have to wait.

Pha and Ette left, Ash still thrashing about like an angry snake.

Olea strode forward, giving off a blended air of importance, nonchalance and impatience. He dropped a hefty book on the floor with a dust-stirring thud. Then, he squatted beside me, placing both hands on my belly.

"Symptoms?" he demanded, fingers painfully probing.

I told him.

He nodded. "Your friend here says that your son is a half-blood."

At the sound of the derogatory term, fury flared in my chest. I glared.

"Well? Is he covalent or not?" Olea snapped.

"Yes," I resigned, "he is."

The man didn't miss a beat: "Without complementary-color therapy, your aura will continue to coagulate, putting you at risk of stroke."

"Stroke?" Fair squeaked.

"If you do have a stroke, chances are, it'd occur within twenty-four hours of this morning's episode."

"So, if I make it until tomorrow morning, I'm out of the woods?" I asked.

Olea cocked a feathered brow. I supposed he didn't understand the Nurian expression.

"If I last through the night, I'm safe?" I reworded.

"You'd be very lucky. The only reliable preventive treatment is complementary-color therapy, to dislodge and liquidate your spectral clots. With covalence, however, full irradiation would likely poison the fetus."

I toyed with Cease's Silver Triangle, concealed by my robe. "I... I want to do whatever's best for my child."

"Miss July," his voice went sharp, "in an emergency during a high-risk pregnancy, it's the consensus of the healing community to put the mother's life first. Do you understand me?"

I gave him a hard look. "I do, sir. But, this decision is mine. And, *my* priority is my son."

Fair gave me a venomous glower.

"Very well, then," Olea sighed. "In that case, I recommend light irradiation. The clots won't dissolve entirely, but they'll shrink somewhat, decreasing your symptoms and increasing your chances of making it *out of the woods*."

"I'll do it."

"But, if you receive *full* therapy, your odds rise from fifty to ninety percent."

I was silent.

"Miss July," he pressed, "I daresay there are many on this island who'd value *your* life far above that of an unborn baby. You have certain… responsibilities."

Unmoved, I solemnly replied, "Sir, if I'm meant to fulfill the prophecy, I will. I won't die until it's done. That's how it works."

He folded his arms. "Is that so?"

I didn't blink. "Yes. Because, if covalence takes my life, then that means I was never the one, to begin with."

Was that rage I saw effervescing in his olive eyes?

"Fine. We'll do light therapy under partial anesthesia."

"No anesthetic magic, at all," I protested, knowing how dangerous those numbing frequencies could be to Commence, especially considering my already-fragile health.

"Impossible," he objected. "No one can handle irradiation without it, especially in your condition."

"I can and I will."

Several tense seconds passed.

"My scabrous is outside." He stood, snatching up his book.

"Wait!" Fair rushed forward, bending to envelop me in a rib-crushing embrace. "Fifty percent?" she cried. "Scarlet, how can you do this to me?"

I put a trembling arm around her. "I'm sorry."

"I love you," she whispered. "Please don't die."

I stared over her shoulder. "I won't, Fair." Commence was counting on it.

KRUSTALLOS FINIRE VII

A complete and utter waste of time. That's all this war's been since May. It was dragging on unnecessarily, with neither side accomplishing jack. Preoccupied with the Magic Wars, the System only managed to toss us an occasional flame. And, as we were on the defensive, we scarcely picked fights ourselves.

Commander Inexor Buird and I must've proposed a dozen different peace treaties by now, but the System declined them all. It made no sense. They hadn't won a single battle since the Crystal's end. Continuing the war was obviously hurting them more than us. So, why did they press on, refusing resolution? What did they possibly have to gain?

"Time," Inexor said to me, one evening. "They're buying time."

Time. Time for what? What were they anticipating?

Sometimes, I wished Ichthyosis could just take the offensive already and bomb the living photons out of Conflagria, ending everything once and for all. But, of course, we couldn't actually do that; we cared about Scarlet and her people. And, after the 'Cobalt-60 Project' fiasco, the public believed it'd be a show of utter moral depravity to snub the Reds and blast their island to bits just because they happened to share it with the bad guys. So, we had no choice but to sit back and hope that Scarlet's uprising would triumph, so we could present our peace treaty to her rather than Principal Tiki Tincture.

It followed that the Red Revolution quite literally shared our own seventeen-age deadline; it was an emergency that should warrant our intervention. But, that was something the civilian world, the Trilateral Committee and the Alliance Committee refused to understand, no matter how much the Diving Fleet shouted and screamed. Though tempting, even I knew that a coup d'état was a bad idea. Sacrifice had its limits—we weren't willing to start a war on our own turf just to cure one overseas. So, we waited.

When not in battle, we kept busy with the ongoing Spectral Hurricane Relief Effort. It was expected that Nuria, Ichthyosis and Oriya would be drowning in the aftermath of *that* not-so-natural disaster for ages to come.

The months passed slowly. I used the time to restore my soiled reputation. I became the perfect soldier. Confident, but not cocky. A wellspring of off-the-wall ideas, but only when appropriate. Responsive to orders. Willing to fulfill any task without complaint, no matter how lowly.

I hacked Scarlet's old logs from the weeks following my infamous battle loss and read how worried she was that I'd 'break.' I discovered, from prowling Lechatelierite's old entries too, that Inexor himself once experienced temporary disillusionment, after his captivity. For months, Inexor could hardly function in combat anymore, blowing every chance Lechatelierite offered him, until he found himself at the bottom of the chain-of-command. But, despite all odds, he bounced back, over time. Fully. Whatever trauma he endured in Conflagria apparently didn't break him; it only bent him for a little while.

After what I did, I could've easily receded into depression, anxiety or post-traumatic stress disorder. Scarlet believed that'd happen. Inexor also watched for it, over the past few months. He wondered, how would I respond to costing a hundred Ichthyothian lives during my very first battle: would I manage my internal turmoil constructively? Would I learn my place without becoming castrated?

As the summer passed, it became clear to the world that the answer to both questions was a resounding yes. For the first time in my life of simulations and mock-battles, I finally learned that my actions had serious real-world consequences.

So, one night a few weeks ago, mere hours after our current Second got killed in a stupid skirmish in the Briny Ocean, Inexor called me to his quarters. I marched over happily, already smelling a promotion.

But, alas, the moment I set foot in his room, he blurted, "Seven, what do you know about Commander Ecrof Ecreoc?"

I blinked. The honest truth was: not much. Compared to the greats—Terminus Lechatelierite, Rai Zephyr, Oppre Sive, Rettahs Slous and Cease Lechatelierite, of course— Ecreoc was nothing special. The Childhood Program curriculum hardly gave him the time of day.

So, I blandly rattled off the few vital stats I still remembered—his birthdate, some stuff about the key conflicts he won, when he died—but, apparently, Inexor was after something else entirely.

"Don't tell me *when* he died, but *how*."

Well, that wasn't exactly unique: "In combat."

"Yes, but *how*?"

Um. "You want tactical specifics?" I asked, incredulous. I'd studied that battle at age eight; I could hardly recall the details anymore. What did it matter, anyway? "I believe Ecreoc's strategy fell apart, leaving Cease Lechatelierite in command…"

"Close," Inexor said, "but, incorrect. Yes, Ecreoc's strategy was sloppy, but it didn't *leave* Lechatelierite in command.

Lechatelierite *took* command without permission, leaving Ecreoc exposed. That's why the man's craft got shot down."

I stared, dumbfounded. The legendary Cease Lechatelierite made the same mistake… as me?

Inexor smiled. "Even the best of us are full of crap, sometimes. And, you, my crappy little comrade, have slowly become the best soldier to walk this base since Cease Lechatelierite and Scarlet July." He opened his palm, revealing four cobalt-blue bands—two for each sleeve.

I accepted them, saluting firmly. "Thank you, sir."

He saluted back. "Don't let me down, Second. Dismissed."

Nodding, I marched to the door.

But, as I touched the knob, I gave into the sudden irrational impulse to turn and spurt, "I guess that means all *three* of us eventually bounced back. Right, sir?"

Inexor's face stayed deadpan. "I believe I've dismissed you, Seven."

* * *

That night, I gathered my stuff and made my way to my new quarters, where Scarlet July used to live. The first drawer I tried to open was jammed. No matter how hard I pulled, it wouldn't budge. Frustrated, I looked down at my hands and saw they had turned bright red, as though sunburnt. I felt the metal again and, sure enough, detected a steady warm pulse.

Spectrum.

Instinctively, I recoiled. I'd never touched spectrum with my bare flesh before. In combat, we always wore bodysuits.

"It's okay; it's *Scarlet's*," I reassured myself, aloud. This magic didn't belong to some random fire-savage. It was Scarlet's. Scarlet was one of us.

Brazenly, I went ahead and grasped the bar again. It suddenly grew as hot as a ship engine. I jumped back, unable to contain my fear and disgust any longer. Who cared if this magic was Scarlet's? It still originated from the Conflagrian spectral web. Which was alien. Unnatural. Dirty. I went to the bathroom to wash my hands.

As I lathered up, I wondered how Lechatelierite had the courage to touch Scarlet, a mage of all mages, the way he did. I mean, he didn't just handle her in battle or practice like the rest of us, he really *touched* her. Intimately. Inexor and I were probably the only ones who knew. I wasn't sure how Inexor found out, but our conversation after the State-of-the-War Address back in June made it pretty clear that he did.

In February, I'd entered Lechatelierite's quarters to the jaw-dropping sight of he and Scarlet kissing rather intensely. Three months later, on the eve of the Second Infiltration, I was on night-watch in the south wing when I caught sight of Lechatelierite cradling Scarlet in his arms, her face buried in his neck. Holding my breath, I'd quickly ducked into an adjacent corridor, stricken to learn that their February canoodling session apparently wasn't an isolated incident. When I peeked around the corner, I saw Scarlet bring her lips to his ear. When she whispered something, he smiled.

I stared. A smile. On Lechatelierite's face. Not a strained, thin-lipped purse. But, a real smile, filled with emotion. He seemed… happy. Joyful, even. It was beyond weird. The look didn't suit him. It was wrong. The whole scene just seemed so wrong. Lechatelierite was supposed to be aloof, impervious. Untouchable.

Scarlet slid her arms around his neck and, the next thing I knew, their faces were smashed together like February on steroids. My palms turned sweaty as my insides squirmed; it was extremely unsettling to see two esteemed officers violate the Laws of Emotional Protection so blatantly and aggressively, not just in the solitude of their own quarters, but out in the open, in the base halls.

I believed in the LEP. I believed they existed to save us from ourselves and preserve the fleet's coherence. I knew I should've confronted then reported Lechatelierite and Scarlet. At the very least, I should've lost all respect for them. But, oddly enough, I did none of those things. Because, in the end, I decided that Lechatelierite was still Lechatelierite and Scarlet was still Scarlet—incredible soldiers whom I trusted with my life and with the fate of the northwestern hemisphere.

NURTIC LEAVESLEFT

UVA made me captain of the coed varsity swim team, though I was just a freshman. I neither asked nor applied for the responsibility. The school just dropped it in my lap. I supposed the Office of Student Athletics figured I was probably qualified enough to handle a bunch of college kids in a dinky chlorinated pool.

It felt strange, to swim just for the sake of swimming. To swim just for the sport of it. To swim just to see who could go faster, so that person could get a title and a medal. Back in high school, those accolades meant everything to me. But, now, they seemed a little silly. What did it matter if Shawn Sordid could freestyle faster than Alex Bold, if neither of them were going to use their skill for anything beyond competing in more races and accumulating more awards? It was pointless. The logic was so circular, I sometimes wondered why I even bothered with the team in the first place.

I remembered the answer, every time I dove. Apparently, the Diving Fleet had changed me into someone who couldn't live without the water. And, the only way to secure regular access to UVA's Aquatic Fitness Center was to join a competitive team.

College swim team practices were downright chaotic. Everyone spoke out-of-turn and laughed at everything. People would randomly show up late, with neither explanation nor apology. They took breaks after a mere hour or two, without asking. I found myself constantly on the brink of losing my cool. Was everyone at this school lazy and uncommitted or was *I* the one expecting too much of their discipline and performance? Whose perspective needed to be adjusted, here?

When I expressed my frustrations with the Office of Student Athletics, they suggested I get some advice from the previous captain, an alumnus with a rather First-Earth-sounding name, Michael Swift. Apparently, UVA made it to the national championships under Swift, presumably without him cracking any whips.

I called his cell phone.

"Hello?" he answered.

"Hi, there, this is Nurtic Leavesleft. May I please speak with Michael Swift?"

"This is Mike—whoa, wait a minute, did you say *Nurtic Leavesleft?*"

"Yes." I was used to this sort of thing, by now—not that it had become any less agonizing. It seemed so absurd for anyone to get star-struck on account of me. It was just *me*, for crying out loud. Not a superhero, not a movie-star, but an overaged college freshman from Alcove City.

"Are you pulling my leg?"

"No, I promise."

"Wow," he breathed. "Um, to what do I owe the privilege?"

"I'm the new captain of UVA's coed varsity swim team," I began.

"No surprise there."

"And, I was just hoping to get a few pointers from my predecessor."

There was a pause.

"Uh, yeah, sure, but… why on earth would *you* ask *me?*"

For heaven's sake. "Well, believe it or not, prepping a college team for competition is turning out to be a whole lot different than commanding a navy in combat."

"Ah, I think I can sense what's going on," he laughed. "You've gone all drill sergeant on your crew and they're about ready to throw you overboard. Right?"

"You could say that," I chuckled. "I don't know how to get through to my comrades."

"Teammates, man. Teammates."

I blinked. Teammates. Right.

"I can see the problem already," he chortled. "Sure, I'd be happy to give you some pointers. But, wait, does this mean I can tell people I got to advise a war hero?" he eagerly asked.

What was with civilians and bragging rights? Why was that so important to all of them? Well, perhaps, it was because, in their world, there was no clear universal ranking-system. In the military, no one had to wonder where they stacked up—we literally wore our worth on our sleeves.

"Of course, Swift; go right ahead."

"Awesome! And, uh, you can call me Mike, you know. Normal people don't do the whole formal last-name thing, remember?"

We talked for half an hour after that, my spirits sinking deeper with every passing minute. While Arrhyth and Dither were halfway around the world, saving lives and defying death, here I was at a cushy college, learning how to go easy on bunch of guys and girls who were older than the majority of my former fellow divers.

And, that's when I realized what was really wrong with me. Why I was so discontent, all the time. Why my fuse was a fraction of its original length. Why my chest ached whenever I perched at the edge of a diving board.

I actually missed being in the fleet. I couldn't believe it. I never thought I'd want that grueling life back. I never thought I'd *need* such an intense routine or demanding purpose, just to feel satisfied. Since leaving Icicle, I was continually agitated and guilt-ridden... because the war still raged on and I wasn't lifting a finger for it, anymore. I wished there was some way to continue my college education *while* working on resolving the international crisis. It felt so selfish to spend all my time and energy on making good grades and participating in a bunch of frivolous campus organizations when there were larger problems out there. As long as the northwestern hemisphere was in turmoil, what did it matter if I had a stellar GPA or a jam-packed resume? Would my grades save the alliance from ruin? Would my resume stop mages and Nordics from continuing to slaughter one another?

College life wasn't enough for me. I was still a soldier, through and through, whether I liked it or not. The real question was, what could I possibly do about it, now?

* * *

Restless and exasperated, I stayed late after tonight's practice, repeatedly diving from the highest board and completing laps until I lost count. My skin shriveled and my eyes burned. Those were aspects of civilian swimming I hadn't readapted to, yet—in the fleet, our arrhythmic suits always provided total protection from the elements. We could stay submerged for hours without actually getting wet.

Today, Ree waited for me, doing some homework poolside, so we could walk back to the dorms together afterward. Not that we lived anywhere near each other. Though a freshman, I was assigned to live in upperclassman housing because I was twenty... and because upperclassman housing was a little nicer and the Office of Student Life was probably a bit shy to stick a so-called 'war hero' in an overcrowded, un-air-conditioned building by a noisy runway. What the university *didn't* know was that I'd actually prefer to live by the runway since I flew deliveries all the time.

Anyway, after a couple hours of solitary swimming, I urged Ree to jump in with me. It still felt odd to swim alone; in the fleet, we always worked in groups. Ree obliged. But, it wasn't long before I started getting frustrated with her. No matter what we did—racing, water-hoops, Marco Polo, whatever—I had to go ridiculously easy on her, lest there be no competition at all. And, Ree was one of the stronger athletes on the team, too.

After about forty-five minutes together, I sort of... momentarily forgot where I was. It was like I had a flashback or something. I suddenly thought I was in the Septentrion Sea, with Scarlet instead of Ree. So, I tried to spin-toss her. Which scared her half to death. It was a miracle she didn't pull, break or twist anything. After I caught her, she wrenched herself from my grasp, scrambled out of the water, grabbed her pink towel, murmured something about being late to Art Club and fled the AFC still in her swimsuit.

So, I paddled to the deep-end, curled into a ball, exhaled and sank to the very bottom. I sat there until my lungs burned like the Fire Pit.

What have the Ichthyothians done to me?

FAIR GABARDINE

Scarlet came home twenty-four hours later. To my great relief, she didn't arrive in a burlap body-bag, but strapped like a ragdoll to Olea's dragon. Alive.

"She's a real fighter," the medicine man said, eyes bleary and tone breathy. He cradled her unconscious form in his arms. "Anyone else would've quit or opted for anesthesia after maybe a minute or two of trying."

Overcome with emotion, I wordlessly took her from him, in exchange for a couple heavy bags of taro. Then, I scurried inside, lay her in her tarp, sat at her feet... and sobbed for twenty straight minutes.

I wished the rest of Conflagria had put up as valiant a fight as Scarlet, over the past twenty-four hours. In a single day, the window of mental freedom narrowed considerably. Now, only those between the ages of thirteen and fifty-five were safe. I didn't look forward to sharing that bit of chilling news with Scarlet when she woke up.

Exhausted from waiting on hobnail pins to see if my best friend would survive the night, I now crumpled onto my mat and zonked out in seconds.

I awoke some time later to the terrifying sound of our room door violently unhinging. In came a boy I didn't know. He was obviously a leg mage, and definitely young enough to be firmly under the Crystal's spell. Before I could even sit up, he sprinted with remarkable speed to Scarlet's beside and viciously kicked her swollen belly. Falling to the floor, she shrieked like a scabrous at the slaughterhouse. In a flash, my locks snagged his neck, dragging him to the living-room. Now what? The child had seen too much, so I couldn't just throw him out—he'd be a security risk. I didn't think I could stomach killing him, either. He was just a kid, after all. My heart sank as I realized that I had to take him prisoner.

He struggled wildly in my grasp, thrashing with super-mage strength that could only come from illegal spectral steroids. And, suddenly, he swiveled around, my hair involuntarily yanking his head clean off.

Blood sprayed from his open neck as his body collapsed with a sickening squish. His head rolled across the wood, trailing crimson like a grotesque shooting star. His lifeless blue eyes found my face.

My world froze. I'd never slaughtered a juvenile before. I didn't have a clue how many adults I'd slain in combat since becoming a warrior but, as far as I knew, I'd never killed anyone younger than myself. Until now.

I ran back into the bedroom, screaming like a wounded throat mage. Scarlet lay spread-eagled beside her tarp, moaning.

"Fair," she wheezed, terror in her emerald gaze, "h-he's dying, I can f-feel it." She stroked her abdomen. "Oh, Fair, p-please help him!" Tears trickled down her pink cheeks.

I stared. I never wanted Scarlet to have that baby. But, now, moments after accidentally decapitating a pre-teen, all I longed to do was save a life, any life.

I dropped to my knees, wound my locks around Scarlet's midsection, and gave life to the son of the man who had tortured me without reservation. Once the fetus was 'out of the woods,' as Scarlet would say, I doubled over and wept, yet again.

For the next several hours, Scarlet held and comforted me. I cried myself to sleep in her arms.

NURTIC LEAVESLEFT

It made headlines everywhere: the Ichthyo-Conflagrian Wars were being introduced into the curriculums of all Nurian public grade-schools. It was about time.

Within a week of the announcement, I received a letter from the local 'Vitaville's K-12 Academy,' inviting me to speak at an assembly. Since my homecoming, I'd ignored every interview request the media threw my way. But, this one seemed different. The school didn't want me for ratings and hype, but for education. They were looking to me for help.

Aside from the nebulous phrase 'age appropriate,' I wasn't given many solid speaking guidelines. What exactly would be appropriate for an audience ranging from five to eighteen, anyway? Also, the letter specifically requested that I 'dress for the occasion, in attire that represents your unique journey.' Surely, they knew I wouldn't have my ceremonial uniform, anymore? The alliance was in crisis, which meant Icicle couldn't afford to let retired veterans keep precious textiles just for sentimental purposes. So, I planned on wearing a plain button-down shirt, some slacks and my Silver Triangle.

However, I wound up having to complete a cargo run *right* before the assembly—landing mere minutes before I was supposed to hit the stage—so, I found myself at the school in my Frost's Delivery Service flightsuit with zero time to change. From the critical way the staff regarded me as I walked in, I could tell they weren't amused. They were probably expecting me to look more like the dramatic pictures circulating the internet—all dressed in stark-white and cobalt-blue, left sleeve frayed where the stripes were torn off.

Nonetheless, I was greeted by thunderous applause from an auditorium of about thirteen-hundred. As soon as the clapping died down, many murmurs became audible.

"*He* was a big navy commander?"

"Oh my gosh, I don't think I ever realized how *young* he actually is."

"He's only like a couple ages older than the seniors, right?"

"He looks so much younger in real life than in the pictures."

"He's hot. How tall is he, seven feet?"

"He should play basketball."

"He'd be even cuter in uniform. What in the world is he wearing, anyway?"

"Is he a delivery guy?"

A boy in the front row shouted, "*Wow*, will you look at that scar on his cheek? Cool!"

No, not cool, I thought. There was nothing 'cool' about getting hair-whipped in the face by a mentally-enslaved mage.

Feeling slightly self-conscious, I took the microphone from its stand. After a brief introduction, I asked the kid who commented on my scar to join me onstage. Shocked and excited, he bounded up the steps.

"Someone, get a picture of this!" he cried, waving his arms. Laughter swept the hall, followed by several cellphone camera flashes.

"What's your name and grade?" I asked him, holding the mic to his lips.

"Cuous Inno, second grade."

"Cuous," I said, "may I ask you to repeat the comment you just made about my scar?"

He looked taken aback for a moment, then yelled, "It looks cool!"

The auditorium chortled again. It was going to be a long afternoon.

"Do you know how I got it?"

Without skipping a beat, he started making explosion noises.

More chuckles from the crowd.

"So, what do you like to do for fun, Cuous?"

He kept making explosion sounds.

"Come on, answer the question!" his teacher called.

"I did!" he replied. "I like to blow up stuff, at the arcade." He peered at me. "You used to too, ya know. Your high score is still stuck in the sub game, but it won't be for long 'cuz I'm gonna beat it. Blowing up stuff is fun! I also wanna be a Iktheeeotheeean soldier when I grow up, so I can blow up stuff for *real!*"

The laughter crescendoed.

"Thank you, Cuous. You may return to your seat."

"Yesssssssssssiiiiir!" he hollered, saluting sloppily and running off.

I clasped my hands behind my back. "I got this scar during the four months I spent stranded in the South Conflagrablaze Captive. The hair mage I hid out with attempted to decapitate me when she momentarily fell back under the Crystal's dominion. I dodged, so she just wound up cutting my cheek, instead."

Suddenly, the room went silent enough to hear the coughs of a girl in the twentieth row.

I began to pace, slowly. My original intention in asking Cuous about his free time was to create a segue to the subject of how the Childhood Program students spent *their* not-so-free time, but Cuous wound up giving me a totally different lead.

"There was a time when I also thought 'blowing up stuff' was fun. As a teen, I spent a lot of evenings at that arcade, dreaming about what it'd be like to do it all for real. War seemed glorious and exciting to me. But, now, after two ages in the Nurro-Ichthyothian Diving Fleet, I've come to realize that there's nothing glorious about a civilian skyscraper getting firebombed, a spectral hurricane leaving thousands homeless or dead, nor the political and magical subjugation of an entire nation." I thought of Ecivon and Tnerruc. "There's nothing exciting about sending your two best friends to the hull of a System ship, only to discover minutes later that you've delivered them to their demise—that their necks got snapped by the hand-mage pilot." I thought of Fair and all the other POWs we kept at Icicle, at one time or another. "There's nothing fun about torturing or killing mages just to draw information that'll be used to torture and kill more mages." I thought of Scarlet and Lechatelierite. "There's nothing fun about watching your commander burn alive in the Fire Pit, his diving suit melting and curling off his blackening flesh as he screams his last words—" I took a sharp breath, wondering how a scene I *didn't* witness just popped, clear as life, into my mind... and, involuntarily, out of my mouth. I stopped walking and scrunched my lids, for just a moment.

But, the image was so fresh and terrifying, it wouldn't leave me.

It seemed as though not a soul in the auditorium dared to breathe.

"War is far from an arcade game," I forced myself to press on. "Arcade games are exhilarating and entertaining, from start to finish. Real war is characterized by long stretches of monotony and intense periods of extreme terror. You're well aware that every moment you spend in combat could be your last. While the mere thought could drive anyone mad, you must swallow your fear and maintain constant vigilance. Because you are a soldier and your nation is counting on you."

Every person in the audience—student and teacher, alike—was completely transfixed. Except one. There was a white-faced boy in the first row whose woodchip-pale eyes reflected an odd mix of boredom, irritation and deep-seated exhaustion. I'd never seen a kid look quite like that, before.

Wrenching my gaze away, I plodded on: "This war's been going on for seventeen ages. That's three ages shy of my lifetime. Longer than most of you have walked this earth. And, while I've only been involved in it for the last couple ages, there are many in this world who were born into it. Hundreds of Ichthyothian children have been raised by island-wide military programs, taught to fight and kill from their toddler ages. One such soldier was Commander Cease Lechatelierite, hailed as the greatest military leader Second Earth has ever seen. Amazingly, it was this same man who eventually tore down the CP, liberating hundreds of students and saving future generations from oppression. It was a true honor to serve under him, during my time abroad. I'll be speaking more about him, later on. But, first, I'd like to take everyone here on a little journey into the daily life of an Ichthyothian child-soldier. Please, close your eyes."

I waited. All the elementary and middle-schoolers immediately followed my instructions. Some of the youngest ones even put their hands over their faces. The high-schoolers only obeyed after waiting a few seconds to see if their friends would too, for fear of looking uncool.

"It's seven o'clock," I began. "You wake up in the barracks to a trumpet blare. It's still dark outside. Though a snowstorm pounds the windows, you know practice won't be cancelled. Florescent lights snap on. Everything is white—the walls, floor, furniture, sheets, clothes, everything. You're in a winding hall of bunks, surrounded by hundreds of other young kids, but it's perfectly quiet. You have three minutes to dress and meet outside—yes, outside in the blizzard—for glacier-surface drills, until nine. All the while, as you're skiing and skating, a monitor adorns your chest; if your heartrate drops below the minimum requirement for even a moment, you'll have to complete an extra workout while your comrades shower and eat breakfast from nine to nine-thirty. After that, classes run until twenty-five o'clock. Yes, that's fifteen and a half hours, with a meager fifteen-minute pause for lunch somewhere in the middle. At age six, your courses include pre-calculus, nautical science, physics, leadership skills, diving, pilotry, tactics, geography, military history, mage culture, Ichthyothian language and Nurian language. At twenty-five o'clock, you head out to diving practice until breaking for dinner at thirty-one o'clock. Dinner is exactly like the last two meals—something along the lines of salmon paste, crackers and plain yogurt, to be eaten in silence. Lights'-out is at thirty-six o'clock. Until then, you scramble to complete mountains of homework. And, as you head to bed, you realize that, all day long, you only ever opened your mouth to answer questions in class or collaborate with your peers in practice. There's no socializing. No friendship. No dating. No families. No recess. No weekends. No vacations. Every single day, it's the same intense routine. When you're fifteen to seventeen—if you make it that far without getting expelled, injured or killed—you're branded with a barcode and sent off to war. Open your eyes."

Everyone looked thoroughly disturbed... except for the pallid child with the uncanny gaze.

He got to his feet.

"Excuse me, but diving practice ended at thirty-two o'clock, not thirty-one, and most six-age-olds were in calculus, not pre-calculus," he half-shouted.

I stared.

His eyes raked my face as he growled, "I suggest you do some research before standing up there and talking about things you've never experienced yourself."

"Comat, sit down! You're being disrespectful to our guest!" cried his teacher, at the end of his row.

Comat glared at me for a moment longer before obliging.

I blinked, pausing to regain my train-of-thought. Inhaling deeply, I finally continued: "My former Commander was sent to war at age ten, because he skipped a few grades. *Ten*. Think about that for a moment. Who here is ten?"

About a hundred children raised their hands.

"Those with your hands up, imagine piloting and surface-riding in the Septentrion, fighting for your life with the weight of the world on your shoulders. Do any of you feel ready for that? *Should* anyone your age be ready for that?"

They all shook their heads, whispering fearfully.

"Thank you; you may put your hands down. Now, who here is fifteen?"

A large group of ninth and tenth-graders seated closer to the back of the auditorium raised their hands.

"Lechatelierite became the Leader of the Ichthyothian Resistance at fifteen," I said. "Can you imagine what it'd be like to not only command dozens at sea, but also deliberate with heads-of-state several decades your senior on decisions that impact every man, woman and child in the northwestern hemisphere?" I scanned the crowd. "It's true, I was never a child-soldier myself. But, I *did* serve alongside hundreds of young men who once were. And, I could tell, just from the way they spoke and carried themselves, how truly hurt and broken they were, on the inside."

I resumed my pacing. "Under the System—Conflagria's dictatorship—magekind has suffered similar oppression. Mage society was spectrally indoctrinated for eras. I want all of you to think about it, now—I mean *really think* about what it'd be like to lack control over *your own thoughts*. As I briefly mentioned earlier, I spent four months stranded across enemy lines with a hair mage named Fair Gabardine. Though Fair's mind was protected by the aura of the Multi-Source Enchant, she still sometimes struggled with powerful violent impulses. Impulses triggered by the System's manipulative magic. Impulses to kill me, her only ally." I took a deep breath. "In a country like Nuria where freedom and equality are legally-protected rights, it can be difficult to fathom any lifestyle but our own. In a world that propagates isolationism, it can be hard to accept Ichthyosis and Conflagria as our responsibilities. But, they are. They have been since the Second War Pact was forged in the ninety-second age."

I talked for sixty more minutes, delving into some of my personal experiences on the frontlines. Then, I opened the floor to questions. The first several inquiries I got were from juniors and seniors who were considering applying to the Nurian military academies. Many of them seemed a bit unsettled as they asked if student life at the domestic schools bore any resemblance to that of the Ichthyothian Childhood Program.

"I'm not going to lie: you will be challenged mentally, emotionally and physically, beyond the furthest reaches of your imagination," I answered. "But, you will be treated with dignity and esteem—things that the Childhood Program did not afford its own. If you want to become a soldier, please don't be discouraged by any of the scary tales

I told in the last hour. Trust me when I say that there's a whole lot more to defending your country than fear and pain. War itself may not be glorious nor fun, but knowing that you helped protect millions of civilians back home is something you can't put a price-tag on."

* * *

With a burst of applause, the assembly was finally over. I stepped off the stage, sleeve-wiping my forehead. On my way out of the auditorium, the defiant ice-eyed boy passed in front of me… and, before I could think the better of it, I blurted his name.

"Comat?"

He spun on his heel. "Sir," he spouted, which sounded rather odd from someone so young, "if you're going to ask me to apologize, the answer is hell no."

Thoroughly startled by his rapid pendulum-swing from respectful to rude, my brows jumped. "My, aren't you inde-corous for an Ichthyothian diver?"

Surprise flickered through his countenance.

"What do you want?" he snapped.

"Just to ask you why you're here, in Vitaville."

Hands stowed in his pockets, he grumbled, "I was sent to live with my 'parents' in Aventurine City, after the Childhood Program shut down. But, when their house got destroyed shortly thereafter in the Spectral Hurricane, we had no choice but to relocate overseas. We got placed in a shelter around here."

I nodded, heart aching. "I'm sorry you lost your home."

Anger struck his flaxen face. "It wasn't my home; it was my parents'. I was forced to leave *mine* months before, thanks to Commander Lechatelierite."

I stared, daring to understand. He missed being a child-soldier?

"And, now," he growled on, "I'm stuck in *second* grade, with 'kids my age,' because the administration won't let me take any high-school placement tests for another month."

"I'm sorry, Comat," I repeated. "But, look on the bright side: at least this arrangement gives you a little time to actually enjoy being a kid, for once. While high school is certainly no military academy, it's still no walk in the park, believe me. So, enjoy this break while it lasts."

He glowered. "Speaking of military academies, that was *some* dramatization you made, about my upbringing. What exactly were you trying to incite, pity? We don't want your pity," he spat.

"There was no dramatization," I mildly replied. "Aside from the two minor errors you so graciously corrected, everything I said was unembellished fact and you know it. I'm sorry if sympathy is the emotion that normal human beings feel upon hearing about your former enslavement."

"*Close your eeeeeyes,*" he mocked, waving his arms. "*Try to imaaaagine!*"

"Comat? I've been looking for you." His teacher came scurrying in our direction.

"I'm sorry, ma'am," I greeted her, "it's my fault; I'm the one who pulled him aside."

As the woman regarded me, all color instantly drained from her cheeks. "Thank you for coming to our school today, Mr. Leavesleft. Your presentation was… something."

Something?

"Ah, I see that Mrs. Termag got to him first," came a man's voice. It was the school principal, Jim Johnson. Uh oh. "Mr. Leavesleft, I'd like a word with you in private, please."

I swallowed, following him to his office.

"Mr. Leavesleft, if I recall correctly, our assembly invitation clearly indicated that there would be primary-grade students in attendance?" he began, settling behind his desk.

I could see where this was going already. "Sir, I'm really sorry; I didn't mean to scare anyone." I perched in the seat across from him. "But, this is *war* we're talking about. War isn't something that should be sugar-coated. After everything that's happened to me, I'm simply unwilling to lie about it."

"I don't believe anyone ever asked you to lie, Mr. Leavesleft," he said, testily. "But, for your information, three of Mrs. Termag's students are currently awaiting parental pickup for dissolving into hysterics."

Alarmed, I breathed, "Sir, I honestly meant no harm; my intention was just to… to give the students some… I don't know… food for thought, or something."

"Oh, believe me, you gave them enough food to feed their nightmares for the rest of their lives. Some of the things you said terrified the wits out of *me*." He peered at his notes. "And, I quote, 'There's nothing fun about watching your commander burn alive in the Fire Pit, his diving suit melting and curling off his blackening flesh as he screams his last words.'"

I winced. "I, um, actually didn't plan on saying *that*," I explained truthfully, aware of how stupid and unconvincing I sounded. "I didn't even witness that particular incident myself. But, when I was speaking, the image just suddenly… came to me."

Johnson dropped his legal pad with a dull thud.

"I agree; I shouldn't have described Lechatelierite's passing and I sincerely apologize for any alarm it may've caused," I quickly said. "But, just to be clear, that's the only thing I'm sorry for, today. I stand by the rest of my presentation. If you wanted dry facts and statistics, your students could just read some textbooks. You don't need me for that."

The principal was taken about fifty steps aback. "Mr. Leavesleft—"

"Learning about war in a purely academic manner just breeds complacency. War isn't something anyone should ever get comfortable with. It should never become an acceptable status quo. We *need* to stay shocked and horrified by it. Emotional appeal is what gets through to people."

"*People*, Mr. Leavesleft? They're children!"

"Yeah, children whose futures are wholly hinged on how this war unfolds over the next seventeen ages before we're all doomed to severe economic depression. Children who may be the only reason any of us get out of this mess alive." I folded my arms. "From all the questions I got today, it seems like many of the high-schoolers are toying with an interest in political or military service. We need to foster that. I can't stress that enough. Because, as of this moment, the alliance has *no idea* what to do next. None. But, for all we know, the next Cease Lechatelierite was sitting in that auditorium, waiting to be motivated. Can you blame me for wanting to light a little fire under those kids?"

He exhaled through his nostrils. "Did you plan on indicting me right now, or did that motivational speech just come to mind as spontaneously as the graphic images of your Commander's death?" He clasped his hands together. "You sure know how to captivate an audience, I'll give you that."

"Thank you. And, again, I never meant to cause a stir. Please, let me make it up to you."

He paused, cocking a brow. "What did you have in mind?"

"My college major requires the completion of a long-term community service project. Maybe, there's something I could do for this school."

"You want to volunteer here?"

"Why not? I promise I won't talk about war, anymore... unless you want me to."

"We don't want you to." His face grew pensive. "But, since the Spectral Hurricane, we've absorbed a lot of transfers...

Mrs. Termag, in particular, has acquired an exceptionally large class; she's been asking for a teacher's aide since the semester began."

"I'd be happy to do it." I smiled. "When can I start?"

NURTIC LEAVESLEFT

"You're kidding," Termag breathed, looking at me in disbelief. A week had passed since my presentation. "*You're* my new aide?"

Grinning, I nodded. From the back of the bustling classroom, Comat stared daggers at me.

"Alright, then." She cupped her chin in her palm. "I just hope I don't get any angry parental phone calls about this. What you said at the assembly made the *Alcove City Post*, you know."

"I know," I sighed, "I read the article. Rest assured, I didn't come here to 'relieve my inner turmoil at the expense of the children,'" I quoted, rolling my eyes. "But, to be honest about my speech, ma'am, I'd like it on record that I'd say it all again."

Her brows constricted. "*Really?* You didn't learn your lesson?"

"More like, the other way around."

She froze for a moment while that sank in, then huffed, "Alright, well, I suppose I shouldn't keep the class in suspense, any longer."

She turned, clapping for attention. I had a hunch it'd take solar flares to actually get it. The principal sure wasn't joking when he said that this class was unusually large. I counted *fifty-two* children, bustling about. As the teacher whistled and shouted, the hubbub gradually died down… until the kids noticed my presence.

"Oh my gosh, it's *him!*"

"C'mmander Leeeeeavesleft's back!"

"Cool!"

While most squealed like I was their favorite uncle, Comat still looked about ready to kill something. I could tell already that it was going to be an interesting semester.

"Class, I'd like to introduce you to our new teacher's aide, Mr. Nurtic Leavesleft. You may remember him from our lovely assembly last week." Lovely. Uh huh. "He'll be working with us part-time for the rest of the school-age. Please give him a warm welcome."

* * *

"Everyone doing alright, over here?" I asked, stopping at the next desk-cluster. The kids were working on multiplication problems.

A girl with blonde pigtails shook her head. "Without the table, I can't remember what seven times eight is. And, it'd take *eras* to count out on my fingers."

"Here's a trick: five, six, seven, eight."

"Oh, I get it!" she excitedly exclaimed. "Five, six, seven, eight... Fifty-six is seven times eight!"

Comat, who had finished his worksheet within the first minute, sat rigidly in his seat, woodchip eyes transfixed. From time to time, kids in his circle leaned over to peek at his answers. Comat was obviously aware of the cheating, but apparently didn't care. Probably because the assignment took him no effort. People only protected what they actually valued.

"Hey, there," I greeted him cheerily. "Done? Can I take your paper?"

He shrugged.

I picked it up, scanning his perfectly-formed numbers. Naturally, every answer was correct.

"Well, since you did such a fine job, I'm going to give you a special privilege," I told him with a smile. "You get to walk around the room like me to help out your classmates."

Nodding mechanically, he stood.

"Psssst! Hey, Comat!" hissed a boy nearby. "What's seven times four?"

"Twenty-eight," he replied, monotonously.

"Thanks, man!"

"Don't just *give* them the answers," I told Comat, quietly. "Help them figure it out on their own."

"It's single-digit multiplication, for crying out loud," he responded, acidly. "There's nothing to 'figure out'—it's rote memorization."

"Then, offer some memory tricks."

"I don't *know* any tricks. Those are dumb. I just *memorized* it straight-up, like anyone with half a brain cell," he growled, stalking away.

A quarter-hour later, I heard raised voices from across the room.

"Quit being such a moron, already! Anything times two is just twice the number itself, you dimwit. If you're too idiotic to multiply, then *add!*"

"What's going on, over there?" I interjected, bounding toward them.

Comat wheeled around. "Sir, I can't help out, anymore. I can't handle it. They're too stupid."

The girl beside him had tears in her eyes.

I bent so my face was level with Comat's.

"You listen here," I spoke in Ichthyothian, voice low. "If I hear *one more* nasty word from your lips, I'll personally see to it that your placement tests get delayed until next age. Got it?"

The boy was visibly frightened. "You can't threaten me like that," he whimpered, also in Ichthyothian. "Adults can't bully kids, around here. We aren't at Icicle, anymore."

"Really? Well, then, you should be the first to quit acting like we are."

The other kids stared at us, in awe. This was likely the first time any of them heard a foreign language, up close. And, it was probably the first time anyone really put Comat in his place, since his military discharge.

Finally, it was time to collect everyone's worksheets. When I handed the stack to Termag, she glowered at me and demanded, "What did you tell Comat? I won't tolerate the use of secret languages in my class!"

Secret languages? "I'm sorry, but if his peers understood me, it would've embarrassed him, which doesn't help anything—"

"Are you terrorizing my students?"

Great. I'd been a teacher's assistant for all of thirty minutes and I was already wreaking havoc. Maybe, Ree's perception of me was the incorrect one and all I really did know how to do was mess stuff up.

"What, no, I was just—"

"I'm not saying you don't have the right to take disciplinary action when a student's behavior warrants it, Mr. Leavesleft, but the punishments we typically dole around here fall along the lines of reduced recess and parental phone calls, nothing worse. Understood?"

Please. "Those are suitable punishments for normal seven-age-olds, sure. But, missed playtime and tattling to mommy won't have any impact on someone like Comat. He's a *child-soldier*. Growing up, the kind of repercussions *he* often faced were in the stratosphere of fifty extra laps in ice-water, sans diving suit."

Her jaw unhinged.

"Of course, I'm not advocating child-abuse or anything," I quickly added, "but, I do think Comat needs to be handled a *little* more firmly than his peers."

"No, absolutely not." Her arms crossed. "I'm not giving anybody special treatment. Comat needs to learn that he's just the same as everyone else."

"But, he *isn't*. He's tougher, smarter, angrier and harder to influence. In other words, he's military. Why should we expect civilian cookie-cutter methods to work on him?"

"Mr. Leavesleft, you're a teacher's aide to a second-grade class, not a drill sergeant at boot-camp! I will not permit you to push anyone around or make threats—"

"I didn't *threaten* Comat; I was only doing what needed to be done, to get through to an ex-child-soldier. I endangered something he actually cares about—not recess, but how long he has to wait to take his placement tests."

"Goodness, no," she breathed. "I want him out of here, as soon as possible, for everyone's sake. He'll be much happier when he's academically challenged, and *we'll* be much happier without the scenes he causes on a regular basis."

"He causes scenes on a regular basis?"

"You've already witnessed one and you haven't even been here for an hour. He rarely *starts* them, but he *sure* knows how to end them, if you get my meaning." She sighed. "And, here I thought the military would've taught him some discipline."

I shook my head. "Ma'am, his ages of emotional abuse have gone unaddressed since his discharge; can we really be surprised he's acting out? He can't just jump into the civilian world overnight after growing up a soldier; he needs some time and resources to adjust." I shrugged as I added, "Maybe, I can help him with that."

"If he's going to get help, it should come from a licensed therapist," she retorted, dryly, "not some college student with a save-the-world complex."

I chose to let that dig slide. "Nuria may object to isolationism, but that doesn't change the fact that it—like the rest of Second Earth—is a product *of* isolationism. Would any therapist in Vitaville know what to do with an ex-child-solder?" Realization hit me in the face like a glacier-thawing lance. "And, what about all the other kids out there, in Comat's position? I think the alliance should establish a transitional program for *all* discharged child-soldiers. Huh. Maybe, I could get in touch with the Trilateral Committee and—"

"Hey, you already have a service project," Termag shot. "*My* class!"

I grinned. "Don't worry, I can handle more than one project at a time. I think the Diving Fleet afflicted me with terminal restlessness."

"If you say so." She checked her watch and suddenly handed the worksheet stack right back to me.

"You grade these. I need to start the social studies lesson."

"Sure."

"I'm teaching on the First Fire Pit Infiltration of the ninety-third age," she added, warningly, "which means you aren't allowed to open your mouth. I don't need my children to hear any graphic play-by-plays of how your Commander disemboweled the guard at the gate, or anything."

I blinked. "I was the getaway pilot on that mission, that's it. I didn't witness any of the action on the ground."

"Didn't stop you before, did it?"

Right.

With that, I sat at her desk, red pen in hand. Comat's paper was at the top of the pile.

"Comat Acci," I read aloud. Acci? I bit my lip. Why was that name so familiar?

Of course. Tose Acci was my old friend and comrade. He was the kindest base-raised diver I ever met. One of my piloting protégés. The soldier whose mangled corpse I found floating in the Fervor Gulf, during the Second Infiltration.

Tose and Comat were probably brothers. I chewed my pen's cap as I thought about their parents. The war was particularly unkind to them. Ichthyosis, with its low carrying capacity, had strict population laws: married couples were only allowed two children each. I wondered how the Accis coped with losing both of their kids—the only kids they could ever have—to the military. Their oldest son came home in a body-bag. And, their youngest...

He was also lost, in a way. But, not for long, if I could help it.

* * *

I breathed a sigh of relief; I was through with my first day of volunteer work. But, there was no time to rest—I had physics class in less than half an hour, back at UVA. Ironically, though I had a plane at my disposition, I didn't own a flivver. So, right now, I had no other way to get back to campus than to take public transit. I hurried across the street, to the city-bus-stop. As I waited, I was surprised to hear some Ichthyothian chatter amongst the Nurian hum.

"Those ice people should learn to speak *our* language, if they're going to live here," snarled a Nurian woman, standing to my right.

"Their language is so *ugly*," her companion agreed. "Like mouthfuls of broken glass. Is it *all* consonants?"

To my left, I heard a different lady say, in Ichthyothian, "So, when's your son taking the placement tests?"

"The administration is forcing him to wait a little while," another Ichthyothian voice replied. "He's been restless and disgruntled in second grade; I'm hoping the transfer will sooth his anxiety."

Alarm bells went off in my mind. Before I could think the better of it, I turned and blurted, "Hello, are you Mrs. Acci, by any chance?"

She stared. She didn't need to ask who *I* was. "Y-yes, I am," she answered, faintly. "How did you…?"

I grinned, sheepishly. "I didn't mean to eavesdrop. I'm a teacher's aide for your son's class." I stuck out my hand. "Nice to meet you."

"Likewise," she breathed, shaking my hand. "Your Ichthyothian is very good."

"Thank you, ma'am."

"Call me Consci," she revealed her first name. "I, um, wasn't aware that Mrs. Termag even had an aide, let alone one so… renowned."

"Well, it's my first day."

There was a pause during which Consci frowned at her scuffed shoes. "You were there, weren't you?" she half-whispered.

I blinked. Where?

"D-did you see when Tose…?"

Of course. "No, I didn't. Scarlet July and I arrived at the scene after he'd already passed. But, we could tell he put up a brave fight."

She sniffled.

"Consci, it was an honor serving with someone so loyal and courageous," I solemnly said. "Tose wasn't just my comrade; he was my friend."

She just nodded, miserably.

"Well, it's great that your youngest got to come home safe," I went on, hoping to bring the conversation to a brighter place.

Wishful thinking.

"No," she croaked, "he's dead, too. Dead to the world." I was stricken by the harshness of her words. Comat must've really hurt her, more than I could ever imagine. "He doesn't even love his own mother!" And, with that, she burst into noisy tears.

Shocked, I stood and stared, unsure what to do next. Everyone around us, Nurian and Ichthyothian alike, glared at me. For heaven's sake, I just couldn't stop wreaking havoc everywhere I went, could I?

"I'm sure Comat does love you," I assured, feebly. How pathetic my words sounded! "He just doesn't know how to express it."

She shook her head, vigorously. "Besides rage and indifference, I'm not sure he has anything left in him to express."

"He does, I promise. I've served alongside hundreds of base-raised soldiers, so I'm positive: there's no emotion we've experienced that they haven't. Comat just needs to learn to let it out."

She wiped her eyes in her sleeve. "But, I don't know how to encourage him in that. No one does."

At that moment, the bell rang and students began pouring from the school. The city bus arrived when Comat did. The kid gave his weepy mother a passive glance, refused to take the hand she offered and clambered onboard without looking back.

NURTIC LEAVESLEFT

Walking across the schoolyard, I caught sight of a kid who looked no older than seven or eight, shirtless and spread-eagled. His bookbag and sweater lay in a heap, beside him.

"Hey, there," I called, approaching. "Everything okay?"

He rolled over as though basking on the beach, exposing the glacier-white skin of his back. It was, what, forty degrees out here? Not exactly sunbathing weather.

"I'm fine, and no, I'm not cold," he answered in accented Nurian, voice muffled by the grass. "It's not even snowing."

I stood over him, blocking his sunlight. I knew what was going on, here. I felt my heart ache.

"Come on," I urged. "Get dressed and come with me."

He didn't budge. "I don't want to go back inside," he murmured. "I don't *ever* want to go back inside that school."

Squatting, I gently pulled him to his feet. His forehead was smeared with mud.

"How did you stand it?" he half-whispered, eyes moist.

"Stand what?"

"Living overseas." He sniffled. "I mean, weren't people mean to you for being different?"

"Yes," I answered, honestly. "But, I didn't let them discourage me from what I knew I was there to do—serve the alliance as a diver. I stood my ground and proved myself. And, eventually, my comrades came to respect me for it."

Well, *that* was an oversimplification to end all oversimplifications, but what else could I say to a tearful Ichthyothian kid who skipped class to go tanning so he could look more like his bronzed Nurian peers?

He pulled on his hoodie. "I wish I could be like that," he mumbled.

"I believe you can." I put a hand on his shoulder. "Now, let's head to class. I'll get your tardy excused; don't worry."

This boy obviously wasn't an ex-soldier. He didn't suffer the intense emotional abuse that rendered people like Comat wholly unable to function in civilian society. No, he probably grew up in a suburban Ichthyothian town not unlike Vitaville, attending a regular public school, enjoying all the freedoms of normal life. And, yet, Nuria became a living hell to him, all the same. Because his skin was a different color, and this was an isolationist world that condemned even the smallest of differences.

* * *

When I arrived at Termag's classroom, her students had just returned from gym. Cuous Inno bounded toward me, yelping, "I did three pull-ups!"

I smiled. "That's great."

He punched the air. "Pow, pow, pow! I'm gonna grow up to be a big bad soldier like Leeeeeavesleft!"

Ashley, the girl Comat had insulted during the math lesson yesterday, ran up to me and hugged my legs, for no apparent reason. I'd spent, what, two hours of my life at this school, thus far? Children sure formed attachments fast.

"Can you be our aide forever?" she asked. I noticed that she had a bandage around her upper arm that wasn't there yesterday.

"I did more pull-ups than *anybody*," Cuous declared. "Well, except for *him*." He pointed at Comat. "He would've kept going on forever and ever and eeeever if I didn't push him off the bar."

I stared at Cuous, alarmed. "That wasn't very nice of you. You should apologize to him."

"It's not *fair*," he pouted. "Ichthyothians are freaks of nature; I mean, it's not like he has to try hard at athletic stuff like the rest of us normal people. He clawed Ashley's arm when she asked if everyone on his island hides from the sun in igloos all the time, you know, since he's pale as paper. So, I pushed him while he was doing pull-ups. He should get on a sub and go back to his stupid frozen wasteland and leave all of us regular people alone."

* * *

After class, I went to see Principal Johnson. I expected him to be somewhat rattled by the magnitude of racial tension and hostility occurring amongst second-graders but, instead, he just gave me an exhausted look and said, "I can tell you haven't been working here for very long, Mr. Leavesleft."

"Sir?"

His tired eyes blinked. "Since the Spectral Hurricane, this school has acquired one-hundred-twenty-five Ichthyothians, eighty-seven of whom are ex-child-soldiers. What you witnessed in your class today is nothing special. The student body is just having some difficulty adjusting to the newfound diversity."

Nothing special? Around here, racial slurs and physical aggression were run-of-the-mill reactions to 'newfound diversity'? Was he serious?

I went ahead and told him about the tearful Ichthyothian kid I caught sunbathing in forty-degree weather, earlier this morning. But, that didn't seem to faze him, either.

He shrugged. "Maybe, you haven't seen children act like this before because you grew up in an ethnically-homogeneous environment yourself."

Ethnically-homogeneous environment? Was he implying that segregation would be an acceptable solution to this mess? I couldn't believe it. He was advocating the doctrine of isolationism without even realizing it. Isolationism wasn't the answer here, *education* was. Antagonism between people who looked or spoke differently wasn't natural or normal; it was a learned response, a product of the toxic doctrine that was tearing this world apart.

"You need to be patient with them," he went on, sipping his coffee. "You've been around Ichthyothians before; it's not new to *you*, anymore. But, it's still fairly new to everyone outside the military. And, as I'm sure you know, the development of tolerance takes time."

Tolerance? What exactly were we *tolerating*, here? Was the mere presence of non-Nurians at Vitaville so outrageous and offensive, we needed to put time and effort into *enduring* it?

The Nurian public overwhelmingly supported the reestablishment of the Nurro-Ichthyothian Alliance. The 'Support Our Brothers of the North' campaign was all the rage. How? How was that possible when our society was *this* prejudiced? It was almost as if we liked the *idea* of breaching isolationism… just as long as we didn't have to do any actual integrating ourselves, on a personal level. Just as long as the average Nurian citizen could still live happily-ever-after in an 'ethnically-homogenous environment.'

"Well, Mr. Leavesleft," Johnson plowed on, "I'm glad you came to see me regardless, because there's something else I've been wanting to talk to you about. We have a service project for you."

I blinked. *Another* project? College life may've made me restless and all, but there were still only thirty-six hours in a day. "What did you have in mind, sir?"

"The Trilateral Committee just issued a notice to all Nurian public schools, demanding that we bolster student interest in the military academies, right away. They claim to be in serious need of immediate manpower."

Wait, what? I sat up straighter. "Why, what's going on?" I asked, voice an octave too high.

"I don't know."

My pulse quickened. I needed to call the Trigon Center, asap. They'd clue me in, wouldn't they? I was the former Leader of the Nurro-Ichthyothian Resistance, after all. That had to mean something to them. Right?

Johnson's fingers drummed the desk. "Anyway, in compliance with the Trilateral Committee's request, this school will soon be starting a junior military program for those fourteen and up. You're the single most qualified person in the country to spearhead it. What do you say?"

NURTIC LEAVESLEFT

The Trigon Center had an automated answering system expertly engineered to keep callers pushing buttons indefinitely, without ever speaking to a live person. It took two full hours and a whole lot of aggravation to find my way to Admiral Oppre Sive's secretary.

"Admiral Sive's office," chimed a young female voice, "whom do I have the pleasure of speaking with today?"

"Nurtic Leavesleft, the Ex-Leader of the Nurro-Ichthyothian Resistance."

"The Admiral is currently unavailable," she immediately spouted. "May I take a message or transfer you to another extension?"

"No message." Because I'd never get a callback.

"Alright, then, sir, who may I patch you through to, instead?"

"Anyone who can answer my questions," I pressed. "You work closely with Admiral Sive, so maybe you can."

There was a pause. "Um, well, sir, I—"

"Great, thanks, I appreciate it. Firstly, I need to know why the TC is so desperate for enlistments, it felt the need to ask the Nurian public schools for help. The civilian world has been led to believe that the war's winding down. That's what the media says, every day. So, what's the emergency, now?"

There was a long, uncomfortable pause.

"Sir, I-I'm not authorized to divulge that kind of information," she finally sputtered.

"May I speak to someone who is?" Ugh, wait, why didn't I just call Inexor?

"I can connect you to Commodore Slous's office. One moment, please."

There was a click, followed by a hiss.

"Good afternoon, Commodore Slous's office; may I ask who's on the line?"

"This is Ex-Diving Commander Nurtic Leavesleft calling for the Commodore, and no I won't leave a message."

"There's no need to be rude, sir. He *is* available."

Well, would you look at that. "Thank you."

"Hello?" came a gruff voice.

"Hello, Commodore, this is—"

"Nurtic Leavesleft, yes, I heard you being rude to my assistant."

"Am I on speaker, sir?"

"No, I just have exceptionally good hearing." So, yes, I was. "I don't have much time to waste with chatting up *civilians*, so let's cut the small talk and get to the reason you're disrupting my busy day."

Well, this conversation was off to a fantastic start. "My apologies, sir. I have two quick questions for you. First, I need to know why the alliance is desperate for manpower when the war's supposed to be waning."

"I can't disclose that to you, Mr. Leavesleft."

"I was the Leader of the Nurro-Ichthyothian Resistance, sir."

"*Was* is the operative word, here. Not to mention, it's an empty title, regardless."

"Really? Was it empty when Commander Cease Lechatelierite had it?"

"Contrary to what you may believe, Commander Lechatelierite was barely more than a foot-soldier," he sneered. "His authority was strictly limited to coordinating the military's three branches in the next stage of combat."

"With all due respect, sir, that actually *does* sound like a lot of power to me."

He chortled. "He was a tactical leader on the battlefield, nothing more. He was without legislative influence."

"Ah, okay, now I see how things work," I growled, feeling a wave of the same scary rage that compelled me to beat up Shawn Sordid in the cafeteria. I never experienced these frightening surges before my service in the fleet. "To have *real* power, you need to be sitting in an office, behind a desk, safe and sound. Not actually out there on the front-lines, risking your life."

"How dare you!" Slous erupted. "I'm a decorated veteran of the First War! I've been to battle decades before you were even born!"

"And, I'm a decorated veteran of the Second War, sir. My Silver Triangle looks a whole lot like yours. I'm not trying to belittle your service; I daresay I know a little something of what it may've cost you. I'm only suggesting that, compared to those lowly foot-soldiers on the field, you may be a bit out-of-touch."

I could practically feel his anger, seeping through the earpiece.

"I won't tolerate indecorum, Mr. Leavesleft," he reeled. "And, may I remind you, though Lechatelierite was a gift-ed strategist, he was also a war criminal with zero respect for the law."

Zero respect? That seemed a bit harsh. "His charges were cleared." Well, temporarily, anyway. "The court accepted his appeal."

"I'm referring, of course, to his flagrant disregard of the Laws of Emotional Protection."

My heart pounded against my Adam's apple. How on Second Earth did Slous know anything about that? I thought I was the only diver who had a clue. I saw Lechatelierite and Scarlet kissing once, over an age ago. But, surely, their affectionate farewell wouldn't constitute a 'flagrant' disregard of the LEP? Then again, I had no idea what became of their relationship since then. Just how far did they take things, in the end? And, more importantly, how in the world did Slous find out?

"I see I've rendered you speechless," the Commodore commented with much satisfaction; I could almost hear him smile. "Commander Inexor Buird recently found something that used to belong to Lechatelierite; we now have solid proof of his grievous crime. He and… Miss Scarlet July."

Inexor *found* something? What could that be? What sort of 'solid proof' would an illegal military romance leave behind? Love notes? Surely, Lechatelierite and Scarlet were never so dumb as to leave a paper trail of their lawbreaking. Moreover, why would Inexor hand over whatever it was to the Trilateral Committee? Why wouldn't he cover for his dead best friend?

"May we get back on topic, sir?" I asked, voice smaller.

"Please."

"Sir, I think your effort to bolster recruitment would have more success if the public were made aware of the reason for it. If there's some sort of emergency going on, knowing about it could motivate people to action."

He didn't speak.

"Commodore," I pressed on, "I may be retired now, but I still care about the war. A lot. I just want what's best for the alliance. That's my only incentive in contacting you today."

Silence.

Irritation prickled my chest. "Sir, anything you don't tell me, I'll ask of Commander Buird, so how about you save us the time and trouble, right now?"

"Buird would never reveal a thing to a *civilian*," he spat. "Now, did you say there's a second reason you called, or can I get back to my full schedule?"

Fine. I supposed I'd bother Inexor, after all. "Sir," I took a deep breath, "I wanted to see if the Trilateral Committee would be willing to cooperate with me in an endeavor to help its own. I'd like to start a recuperation program for the child-soldiers who've been sent home. Civilians and retired veterans could work together to assist these kids in making the transition to—"

"Sorry, I'm afraid we can't help you."

"Why not?"

"Special circumstances have necessitated the reconstruction of the Childhood Program. The child-soldiers who've relocated overseas are exempt from the callback for practical purposes, but those living here in Ichthyosis will return to duty by January. The press release is scheduled for the end of the week."

It was as though lightning struck my entire frame. "You... you can't do that," I babbled, stupidly. "Commander Lechatelierite tore that program down, fair and square."

"Commander Lechatelierite isn't... here."

His words were like knives in my ear. "So, you're just going to trash the agreement you made with him because he's dead?" I roared. "Is that how you honor his memory?"

"Watch your tone, Mr. Leavesleft."

"Why are you doing this?" I demanded. "What are the 'special circumstances'?"

Slous exhaled; the phone rattled. "Well, there's no doubt you were going to go behind my back and wrangle it from Commander Buird anyway—heaven knows the man can't keep his damn mouth shut—and I'd prefer if you didn't rile him up any more about this, since he's already quite upset… so, here it is." He cleared his throat. "While the Trilateral Committee can't be completely positive yet, we have sufficient reason to suspect that the System's thought-control is progressively resurfacing across Conflagria. Our spectrometers are detecting a rise in the particular frequency we believe is responsible for it."

My stomach disappeared. "What?"

"The war may appear to be dragging and tapering *now*, but once the System's magical dominion returns…"

"No." This couldn't be happening. I refused to accept it. "When did you first start detecting the frequency, sir?"

"In July."

"*July?*"

"The so-called 'Red Revolution' lately requested aid from us, but we declined because they're doomed anyway—the System will likely have Conflagria completely re-enslaved by the end of the age. It would be futile to pour any additional resources into Scarlet July's rebellion, now."

"Do the Reds know why you turned them down?" I breathed.

"We never shared our findings with them. But, by now, they're probably already experiencing traces of the Crystal's influence."

Holy crystallines. "And, the alliance has just been sitting around, doing nothing about this, since the summer?" That really didn't sound like Inexor. Maybe, the Trilateral Committee, Alliance Committee, Air Force and Ground Troops all didn't give a lick of salmon paste for the Red Revolution, but the Diving Fleet sure did. They genuinely cared for Scarlet and her people. They'd do everything in their power to save magekind.

"We only alerted the foot-soldiers yesterday." Of course. Why *not* leave your own men in the dark for months? Typical TC.

"I don't believe this." I wanted to scream, cry, vomit and punch something, all at once. "You should've told both the Reds *and* the wartime bases as *soon* as your suspicions were piqued, then you should've invested everything you had into helping them figure something out! Keeping secrets just wastes time!"

"Conflagria is a hopeless case."

"How can you say that?" I yelled. "How can you just write off a whole population like that?"

"Mr. Leavesleft, this isn't a moral determination, these are the facts. The Crystal's oppression is returning and there's nothing anyone can do about it but make sure we have sufficient manpower to defend against an inevitable upsurge in enemy attacks by the start of the ninety-fifth age—"

"There *is* something that can be done! Scarlet July may not know how to replicate what Lechatelierite did in May, but she can destroy the entire Crystal!"

He didn't miss a beat: "We've *also* recently discovered that mages can't live for very long without spectrum. Their bodies literally degenerate, over time. And, after the public-relations disaster of the 'Cobalt-60 Project,' we're not about to ask the Multi-Source Enchant to basically commit genocide."

"How very benevolent of you."

I sank to the floor of my dorm room, knees unable to support my own weight, any longer. The phone felt slippery in my hands. This was a nightmare, worse than I ever imagined. Lechatelierite's death was in vain. The war was headed right back to square one. Every mage on Second Earth except Scarlet was becoming slowly re-enslaved.

And, there was nothing I could do about it.

NURTIC LEAVESLEFT

Comat started shielding his answers, not because he actually cared for them, but because he discovered that doing so annoyed his classmates. He even refused to cooperate in group projects.

"I'm not asking to copy," a boy named Ecino now said to him. "I just want to know *how* you figured that out, so I can do it, too."

Comat shook his head.

"But, this is a team assignment. We're all getting the same grade, no matter what," Ecino whimpered.

"I don't care. I'm transferring out of here in a couple weeks, anyway."

"Selfish paleface," Ecino muttered.

Comat rose from his seat, calmly walked over to Ecino and punched him in the stomach so hard, the kid threw up on the spot. While Termag called for a nurse and a janitor, I grabbed Comat's wrists and ushered him out into the hallway.

"Stop it!" he screeched like the little boy he pretended he wasn't. "This is child-abuse! I'm only seven!"

"Really? Most seven-age-olds *I* know don't go beating up on each other because they don't want to do a group project," I said. "And, you know what? Neither do soldiers. If you think you're acting like a big bad soldier, you're sorely mistaken. Soldiers have discipline, and they know how and when to work as a team. You're not acting like a seven-age-old civilian *or* like a soldier. You're acting like a bully."

He tried to kick me then, but in a flash, I'd passed both his wrists to my right hand and caught his foot in my left.

"Comat, look at me," I demanded, forcing him still.

He didn't meet my gaze.

"I can hold you here, all day," I warned.

He knew I wasn't joking. He reluctantly obeyed.

"Talk to me. What's going on? Why are you so upset, today?"

He didn't answer.

Releasing him, I squatted so we were eye-to-eye. "You haven't acted out in days, so I know something's up. What changed? What's wrong?"

"I want… I want to go to high school," he blurted.

I shook my head. That definitely wasn't it. "You're taking the tests in, what, two weeks? You should be thrilled that you're getting exactly what you want, so soon."

He chewed his lip.

"Come on, Comat, what's really on your mind?"

Studying the floor, he finally murmured, "I want to go home."

Home. Icicle Academy. Last night, the Trilateral Committee publicly announced the reinstatement of the Childhood Program. Of course, that news would strike Comat to the core.

His lids scrunched. "Why do the kids in Ichthyosis get to go back, but not those of us stuck out here in Nuria? I don't wanna be exempt. It's not fair."

Sighing, I briefly brushed his shoulder. "Serving your nation is a wonderful thing, Comat. Believe me, I know. But, so is enjoying the benefits of others' sacrifice. Our lives give the soldiers something to fight for."

"I don't *want* to give them something to fight for," he protested. "I want to be the one to do the fighting."

"Well, then, wait until you're a senior and apply to the Nurian Diving Academy. In the meantime, enjoy what you have, now—your childhood. Because, once it's gone, it never comes back. There's a lot to love about being a kid. There's a lot to love about civilian life."

"No, there isn't." His arms folded. "It's all meaningless."

"Really? Then, why do the soldiers bother defending it?"

He was silent. But, I could practically hear the gears turning in his mind.

"I became a soldier because I love my country," I went on. "The core of military sacrifice is patriotism. So, how can you be a patriot to a society you don't yet know a thing about? How can you decide to give yourself up for a people you've barely begun to interact with? Civilian life isn't meaningless, but I'll tell you what is: the sacrifice the Childhood Program was forcing you to make, *precisely because you were being forced to make it.* Wouldn't it mean a whole lot more if you got to choose to do it, *after* getting the chance to integrate with your own culture?"

Comat stared at me. And, his expression was neither blank nor angry, as it usually was. Rather, he seemed... scared. After all, I'd just picked apart the noble self-delusion that Icicle fed him since birth.

Right now, he really did look like a child. A frightened vulnerable child. The sight of him, helplessly blinking and gaping, made me want to protect him. To embrace him. But, I couldn't. I knew he wouldn't respond well to an affectionate gesture. Not yet. It was too soon.

Or, so I thought.

Without warning, he threw his arms around my neck for a couple seconds before turning on his heel and scurrying back inside the classroom.

* * *

That night, I got a phone call from Consci Acci. She was crying, hard.

"What's the matter?" I asked, alarmed.

"He hugged me," was all she said.

PART II
THE TRI-NATION CAMPAIGN:
A WORLD IN REVOLT

---

*"The soldier, above all other people, prays for peace,
for he must suffer and bear the deepest wounds and scars of war."*

—*General Douglas MacArthur*

SCARLET JULY

November first of the ninety-fourth age.

It was time, I decided. Time for Conflagria to spear-head the World Revolt against the Second Earth Order. If only a brief stint of mental sovereignty remained, mage-kind needed to get the dragon egg rolling, now. We needed to rapidly gain enough global support for the rebellion to soon carry on without us.

So, the moment dawn broke, I initiated the process of spreading the word across the island. Long-distance com-munication was cumbersome. It literally entailed sending throngs of leg mages running from cabin to cabin. No kid-ding. I sure missed Nordic technology, sometimes.

Fair was currently staying at Third Cabin, tending to the battle-wounded Ichthyothian soldiers temporarily housed there. (Last night, the System shot down an Air Force jet flying over the Dunes, and some Reds from Third managed to extract the pilots from the wreckage, alive). As much as Fair hated Nordics, her Ichthyothian fluency landed her a caretaker job, just for a day or two, until Ich-thyosis sent a plane to pick up their men. I wondered how she'd take my announcement.

Turned out, I didn't have to wait very long to find out. By midday, she'd made her way to Headquarters on sca-brousback, white hair swinging.

"You've gone mad!" she now greeted me.

"Good day to you, too," I replied.

She hastily dismounted, stirring clouds of dust. "Scarlet, how could you think we're ready for something like this? We haven't even completed *this* revolution!"

"Fair—"

"How could a tiny, struggling war-torn country become the leader of an international rebellion? You should've talked to me before making such a call! Have you become Tincture? Is this a dictatorship?"

"Fair, we don't have time to waste," I insisted. "The Crystal will have everyone in shackles in a matter of months, if not weeks. We have to get things going while we still can—going strong enough to continue without us, momentarily."

Her lips parted. "So, that's it, is it? We're a hopeless case?"

"I didn't say that. Of course, we won't stop looking for a solution to our problem. But, while we're at it, we can't be totally selfish. We still need to pay some mind to the world outside our window."

She threw her hands up. "We can't afford to divide our attention like that! And, saving our own society from cerebral enslavement and political tyranny isn't selfish!"

I cocked a brow. "So, to the hell with the billions of other human beings on this earth? Sometimes, individual sacrifice is necessary for the greater good—"

"How very noble of you, Scarlet," she cut across me, nostrils flaring. "But, guess what? Your people never consented to being sacrificed. And, even if we did, how do you expect to convince the whole world to join our crusade when we're about to collectively drop off the face of the planet?"

Blood churned in my ears. "No one's *dropping off the face of the planet*. Even if the System regains spectral dominion, our society will still *exist*. We'll still be here, for all the world to see. Maybe, the horror of watching an entire nation succumb to slavery will motivate our new allies even more. Maybe, *they'll* be the ones to figure out a way to save us, down the line. Getting their attention and allegiance now, before we're totally helpless, can only—"

"Come on, Scarlet, face it: there's no way the World Revolt will survive our disappearance! If you don't believe me, just look at the Nordic military."

"What about them?" I asked, coldly.

"Ichthyosis and Nuria are within an *inch* of their war's finish line. So, why haven't they completed the race, yet? Why's the alliance just sitting around like aged scabrouses, letting the conflict drag on forever for no good reason? Because they lost their one good commander—the only player on their team who ever had a clue. Since the Second Infiltration, the System has been focusing *all* its attention on us, rarely tossing Ichthyosis and Nuria a flame, yet the Nordics haven't done a damn thing to take advantage of that... because Cease isn't around to tell them what to do. Likewise, what do you think'll happen to the global rebellion when it loses Conflagria?"

"*I'll* still be here," I squeaked. "The rest of the Reds may not be, but I will."

To my surprise, she suddenly scrunched her lids and whimpered, "Scarlet, I'm scared. Out of my mind. We all are. Your announcement today sounded like an admission of defeat." She opened her eyes, and they were moist. "For most of our comrades, joining *this* revolution was the biggest sacrifice they've ever made. So, to hear that, all along, our own leader thinks we've been fighting for nothing..."

"So, I don't have anyone's backing on this," I concluded, bitterly. "The World Revolt is a no-go."

"Oh, we'll do it," she spoke to her sandals. "Tincture knows we'd follow you into the Fire Pit, blindfolded. All I'm saying is, while we're at it, we're on the brink of pissing in our robes."

I touched her shoulder. "I know, Fair. Don't you think I'm also scared? I'm downright terrified, for all of you. Terrified of losing you. Terrified of the possibility of going on without you."

She let out a quivering breath. "I know. I'll miss you, too. And, I'll miss fighting for what I believe in."

I searched her unblinking stare. "This doesn't have to be the end. Like I said: if we don't manage to save ourselves in time, the nations whose support we win over now could come back and rescue us, later on."

She shook her head. "Sure, we may win them over, *now*. But, what about an age from now? Five? Ten? When we're nothing but an enormous indefinite pain in their asses, how long will they remember that they're supposed to like us and fight for us? Everyone will eventually forget that we're supposed to be innocent. It won't be long until they're crying for our blood. It'll be Hitler's Holocaust, all over again. Mage extermination. Suddenly, dirty bombs won't sound so scandalous, anymore."

"Fair, *I* won't let that happen!" I exclaimed, horrified.

She snorted. "How much power do you think you have?"

"I-I'll make them listen," I piped, frantically. "I won't let them do this to you!"

"To *me*? Will *I* even be around when the dragon dung hits the fan? Will *you* be around forever, to guide the course of mankind?" She swallowed and abruptly switched tracks, cutting to the root of all our fears: "Scarlet, are the spectroscopers onto anything, yet?"

Most spectroscopers in the Red ranks now worked, day and night, on finding a way to stop the System from regaining control over the Crystal. Since I couldn't go off to battle anymore, I spent most of my time toiling with them, though I was no spectroscoper—I knew far more hard science than I did magical theory. That left Fair, my co-leader, in charge of military operations. It was obvious that each was more suited for the other's role but, all things considered, we couldn't exactly swap.

"No," I answered.

"Well, they need to, like, yesterday," her hair twitched, "because I just witnessed some thirteen and fourteen-age-olds complaining about their thoughts starting to stray—there were several kids crying about it when I got up this morning, at Third Cabin."

My stomach disappeared. "*Fourteen*-age-olds?"

She nodded. "Scarlet, *we're* only seventeen. Not to mention, most of our warriors are only in their early twenties." Her oil-black gaze dropped to my swathe. "And, what about your child? Once he's old enough to realize there's more to life besides eating, sleeping and pooping, wouldn't he also become susceptible?"

My pulse quickened. "Not if he's a multi-sourced enchant."

"Well, what if he isn't? He *is* covalent, after all."

My heart hammered harder.

"When we all lose our minds, where are you planning on going, anyway?" she pressed. "You obviously can't stay here."

I shrugged. "I could always return to Ichthyosis, I guess. Inexor would take me back."

"But, if your son can't control his thoughts…?"

A twinge of panic pricked my chest. What *would* I do with Commence, in that case? Would I take him to Icicle anyway, forcing him into a POW's life? A lump the size of a hobnail egg rapidly formed in my throat. No, I couldn't do something so unbelievably awful and selfish. I'd have to leave him behind; that was the less-cruel thing to do. He'd be an orphan, but at least he'd be free to lose himself in the Crystal's spectral ecstasy.

Then again, if he *did* stay here, his mind and magic would inevitably become weapons in the enemy arsenal.

So, the bottom line was, if Commence didn't have my special spectral gifts, he'd be condemned to some capacity, no matter what.

Fair noticed the fresh tears tickling my lashes. "I'm sorry, Scarlet," she said, softly. "Just when you think war can't suck any more than it already does... it does." She stood. "Well, I shouldn't keep you from the spectroscopers. I'm going back to Third Cabin, now. Okay?"

I silently nodded, though we both knew that nothing in this world was really 'okay' anymore.

NURTIC LEAVESLEFT

November first, thirty o'clock.

I hunched, spreading my physics notes across my bed. It was really hard to concentrate on vector math when the suite right outside my thin room walls always sounded like a rock concert blended with a wrestling match. It was so noisy now, I hardly noticed when my cell started ringing. When I halfheartedly glanced at the screen, my heart stopped.

It was the number of Scarlet's plane. In June, I'd stored my contact info in its computer and told her to call if she needed anything.

I grabbed the phone like it was a shard of the Core Crystal. "Hello?" I squeaked.

"Nurtic?"

"Scarlet!" I gasped. My roommate, Spii Pord, promptly removed his earbuds. "H-how've you been?"

"No matter, that's not why I called," she said, voice uncharacteristically crisp.

A little taken aback, I sputtered, "Um, a-alright. What's up?"

And, like a crystalline on full throttle, she was off, chattering away. The more she spoke, the more excited I became.

"So, basically," she went on, "we would gather our intellectual, technological and magical resources to broadcast persuasive information around the world, spurring an international revolt against isolationism. Our ultimate goal would be for nations to secede from the Order—submitting to voluntary blacklisting—until the planet as a whole finds itself with no choice but to erect an entirely new system of moderate globalism."

"Wow," I whispered.

"Inexor assured me that he can get the alliance on-board. So, Conflagria, Nuria and Ichthyosis will essentially spearhead this project together." She inhaled, then dryly chortled, "Three nations down, six-hundred-ninety-seven more to go."

"Like a… tri-nation campaign," I commented.

"Nice," she brusquely replied. "I think that's what we'll call ourselves."

My cheeks heated. Thank goodness she couldn't see.

Suddenly stricken by a frightening thought, I found myself stupidly babbling, "But, Conflagria can't be the epicenter for long, because…" Oh, shoot. I bit my tongue.

"So, you know," she said. "You know what the System's doing to the Crystal."

There was a lengthy pause.

"Yes," I finally admitted. And, I certainly didn't mean to bring it up so casually and callously. My offhand remark was so insensitive, I couldn't stop cringing.

"How?"

I swallowed. "The Trilateral Committee… they found out months ago."

"Months," she echoed. "How many?"

She wasn't going to like the answer. "Uh, about… four."

"So, since *July?* Oh, Tincture, I don't believe this," she growled. "This is why I'm turning to Inexor and the Diving Fleet to bring the allied nations onboard, not the Trilateral Committee. We can't trust the Trilateral Committee."

"Yeah, no surprise there." I shifted the phone to my other ear. "Scarlet, how much longer do you all have before…

you know?" I wished Spii would stop staring. He was so blatant about his eavesdropping. Shameless.

"I don't know. Right now, it's only impacting kids and old people. The window of freedom ranges from about twelve to fifty, though those on either extreme are living with difficulty."

Yikes. "Does anyone have any ideas yet on how to reverse this thing?"

"No good ones." She exhaled loudly—my earpiece buzzed. "So, you can see why I'm in a hurry. Can I count on you to help me with the Tri-Nation Campaign?"

That's when I realized, she was essentially calling me back to service. Military service. This was what I'd been waiting for, since college began.

"Yes," I breathed, sitting up straight as a lance, "of course."

"Not so fast," she shot. "Do you realize what I'm asking of you? I'm asking you to drop... whatever you're doing... and return to duty."

"I'm a freshman at UVA," I said, "and I can juggle both."

"Are you sure?" she pressed. "Because, once you give me your final answer, I won't let you go back on it."

"My final answer is yes." My palms grew sweaty. "I'm sure."

"Alright, Nurtic," she said, seriously. "As of this moment, you're my soldier."

"Okay," I piped.

"First order of business: I'm going to need you to attend our kickstart briefing at Red Headquarters on November seventh. Can you manage transportation or do you need the Ichthyothians to pick you up?"

The *seventh?* That was in under a week. I nearly dropped my cell. "I-I've got my own wings."

"Good."

After relaying the coordinates of Headquarters, she abruptly hung up. I sat still for several minutes, homework completely forgotten. All the while, Spii still watched me, dumbfounded.

Then, without a word, I got up and went to central campus to get the proper paperwork to reduce my courseload.

NURTIC LEAVESLEFT

On the afternoon of the sixth, after I'd successfully secured approval from UVA to switch to part-time student status, I went to Vitaville's 'K-12' to inform Termag and her class that I, regretfully, couldn't be their TA anymore. Then, I went to Principal Johnson's office to let him know that I wouldn't be able to lead ROTC next semester, after all.

"But, without you, how will we raise interest and support for the program?" he asked.

I laughed, until I realized he was totally serious.

"I'm really sorry," I feebly croaked. "You have my permission to say, as often as you'd like, how much I believe in its mission," I joked.

He blinked. "Can I get that in writing?"

When I left Vitaville's, I went to the UVA Student Health Center to load up on inhalers and allergy medication. Conflagria sure wasn't the best environment for someone sensitive to dust.

And, last but not least, I had to tell my parents and friends I was leaving… tomorrow. I typically wasn't one for procrastination, but I supposed there was a first time for everything.

Once evening fell, I called home, insisting that both my mother and father get on the line. Naturally, this request stirred a bit of alarm.

"What's going on, Nurtic?" dad pressed, the moment mom picked up.

I spilled the beans, and because they were parents of a war veteran, they actually understood the gravity of what I was about to do. They were stricken.

"When you said you had big news, I thought you meant you were getting engaged or something," dad responded, hollowly.

What? "I don't even have a girlfriend."

"Can you visit home on your way?" mom asked, voice quivering. "We'd like to see you one last time, in case…"

"Come on, mom." How could I put this in gentler terms? "I'm not going to die."

"You don't know that," she squawked. "For heaven's sake, Nurtic, I thought we were through with being a military family."

"I'm really sorry." How empty those words sounded! I sure felt like I uttered that phrase a whole lot, these days. After twenty more painstaking minutes during which I repeatedly explained that I wouldn't have time to stop in Alcove City on my way tomorrow morning, they finally let me hang up.

And, now, for the hardest part of all: telling Ree. Without preamble, I word-vomited it out, about ten minutes into dinner.

She stopped chewing, frowned and said, "But, I thought you were done being a soldier."

Of course, she wouldn't understand. Those who'd never been in uniform simply couldn't. Those who'd never experienced the life-altering terror of battle couldn't possibly comprehend the concept of 'once a soldier, always a soldier.' When I joined up, I essentially committed my mind, body and soul to a different way of thinking and being. But, how could I convey this to Ree? How could I get her to grasp that I was essentially responding to a call of duty? That shirking duty wasn't a viable choice, for a man with soldier blood?

She stared at me, expectantly.

"I'm really sorry," was all I managed to say.

"Quit apologizing, all the time."

"I'm—" I bit my lip, realizing that I was on the brink of apologizing for having apologized. "Look, I… I just… have to do this."

We ate in silence for a long while after that, until I glanced at my phone and noticed that only about fifteen minutes remained until my evening math class on the opposite side of campus. I stood, swinging my backpack over my shoulder.

"Well, see you later," I mumbled.

"So, that's it, you're just going to go?"

I paused. "I have a night seminar."

"No, I mean, you're just going to blurt, 'oh, I have to go start a world revolution tomorrow,' then hop on a plane and vanish across three seas? You aren't going to tell me why you 'have to' leave school, four weeks into your freshman age?"

"I'm not *leaving school*," I objected. "I'm taking isolated leaves of absence."

"But, why?"

"It's a call of duty," I automatically spouted.

"I don't get it. I thought you retired."

"Scarlet called me back."

"Scarlet isn't your commander, anymore."

I exhaled, heavily. "Look, Ree, this isn't optional for me, okay? I don't know how else to put it. You wouldn't understand, anyway."

Oh boy, did *that* come out all wrong. She inhaled sharply, as though slapped.

"I don't mean *you*, in particular," I quickly added. "I mean, *no civilian* can understand the notion of 'there's no such thing as an ex-soldier.' And, that's perfectly fine. It'd be unfair to expect you to." Goodness, that sounded so lame, so unconvincing.

"Why didn't you tell me sooner? Like, when Scarlet first called you, a week ago. I'd come to *you* with something this big, right away. You're one of my best friends."

I felt horrible. Of course, civilians would be sensitive to this sort of thing. Why didn't I see it coming? Stupidly, I was subconsciously expecting Ree to take the news more like I would; I'd been trained to cope with all manners of loss quickly and without objection. I didn't consider what an impact my sudden disappearance would have on someone like Linkeree—an eighteen-age-old girl who just started her college experience a month ago.

"Am I the last to know?" she squeaked.

I studied my half-eaten bowl of clam chowder. "Yes."

"Why?"

"I don't know."

"Come on, Nurtic."

Fine. Here it was: "Well… I guess… saying something earlier would've made leaving more difficult."

"For you or for me?"

"Ree—" I reached out to touch her shoulder, but she popped from her seat and marched to the trey-return without looking back.

* * *

Morning came too soon.

Considering the length of the trip, I knew I should've left at five or six o'clock, but I decided to wait until Ree woke up at her usual six-thirty to try and make things right between us first. I went to her building at the crack of dawn and found Alexandra Bold sitting in their suite lounge with a textbook on her lap.

I rapped on the window and she pretended not to notice. Ree must've told her what went down between us, last night. So, I decided I'd keep on knocking and knocking and knocking until Alex got worn down. After only four minutes and thirty-two seconds, she caved. Sheesh, I'd forgotten how easily civilians gave up on things.

"Go away," she now greeted me.

"Good morning, Alex," I replied, mildly. "I'm just here to see Linkeree."

"That's too bad, because she's not interested in seeing you. Also, don't call her that. Her name's Ree."

"Alex, I really need to talk to her. It's urgent; I have to leave for Conflagria, like, right now."

She gave me a sour-honey smile. "As I've heard. Goodbye." She started to close the door, but my leg blocked it. It hit hard, but I didn't even flinch. Fear flashed across her face.

"I'm not leaving until you let me in," I firmly declared.

"I need to study. I have a test in a couple hours."

"Then, move aside and I'll never bother you again."

She obliged. Well, that was easy. A soldier would've put up far more of a fight.

I tapped on Ree's door. It creaked open, and there she stood, clad in pink pajamas, corkscrew curls all tangled up.

Her sleepy eyes went wide. "Nurtic? What are you doing here?"

"Look, I'm really sorry about everything," I launched. "You should've been the first to know. I promise I won't do anything like that, ever again. Can you please forgive me? I don't want to leave the country without knowing we're okay first."

She regarded me for a moment then nodded. No resistance, like a true civilian.

"I'm so glad you came," she breathed, throwing her arms around my neck. I hugged her back, relieved. When she finally pulled away, she said with a sad smile, "Have a good flight. I hope the kickstart goes well."

"Thanks." I grinned. "Miss you already."

NURTIC LEAVESLEFT

I arrived to Red Headquarters at ten past noon. Mortified by my lateness, I burst into the cabin at top speed.

And, a millisecond later, I found myself face-down on the floor, restrained by several magical limbs and tools—hands, feet, hair, wings, diffusion rope, the list went on.

Fair Gabardine ran over, shouting a vowelesque garble at my captors. They reluctantly released me.

"Sorry about that, Nurtic," Fair greeted me in Ichthyothian—the one language we had in common. "Knock next time, will you?"

Shaken up a bit, I slowly got to my feet. I smiled sheepishly at the mages still staring daggers at me, feeling like a total imbecile. I bowed a couple times, knowing it was the Conflagrian thing to do, but all that did was raise more brows.

Where was everyone, anyway? I expected a much bigger crowd for the kickstart. There was no Scarlet, no Inexor, no Arrhyth. Only about a dozen random mages. What on earth was going on, here?

Fair stuck out her left hand. "Sorry, forgot my Nordic civilities," she chuckled, rolling her eyes. "If you're going to bow to us like an awkward idiot, the least I could do is shake your hand."

"Wrong one," I said. "We shake with the right."

"But, you're lefty, so I'm accommodating," she replied, seriously.

I suppressed a laugh. "Um, that's not quite how it works, but I appreciate your thoughtfulness."

Though it'd only been about six months since we parted ways, Fair looked different. There were still bags of exhaustion under her eyes, but her hair was thicker, her cheeks were fuller and her aura was brighter. I was glad to see how well she'd recovered from our time on the run. I hoped Scarlet was doing as well.

"I'm sorry I'm late," I apologized. "So, uh, where is everybody? Isn't the meeting supposed to be, like, right now?"

"Scarlet's been phoning you all morning, but all she ever got is your overly-chipper, incredibly-dorky voicemail greeting."

"Yeah, I don't get signal at thirty-thousand feet."

"The meeting's been postponed until tomorrow."

"Why?"

"The Ichthyothians called. They're in battle."

"Oh." I blinked. So, I was missing class today for nothing? "Where's Scarlet?"

"She's with the spectroscopers in the other room."

I nodded. I knew what they were working on; I wouldn't dare interrupt.

Inhaling the steamy air, I took a good look around. The floor was cluttered with worn books, crinkled parchment, splintered scrolls, frayed quills, cracked ink bottles, unstrung bows, bent arrows, rusty swords, dirty multicolored robes, broken tarps and chairs, half-rolled floormats, and a lot of other weird objects I couldn't begin to identify. The wooden walls were intermittently punctured and patched, as though the cabin got repeatedly torn apart and reassembled. Accustomed to associating military facilities with the crisp monochromatic sterility of Icicle, I found this topsy-turvy setup rather unsettling. It was easy to look at the vast, fortified, organized, fluidly-functioning Ichthyothian diving base and confidently think: *this* is a stronghold of war. But, Red Headquarters? I didn't know what to expect, but this wasn't it. This was supposed to be the nucleus of a global effort? The epicenter of two major revolutions? The fulcrum of an organization that was going to topple the world government?

It was a shack that looked like it'd blow over in the next sandstorm.

"Well, make yourself at home." Fair curled on a mat. "Brought something to do?"

"Homework," I answered, "and lots of it. I'm a college student, now."

"I thought Scarlet said you left school."

"I didn't *leave school;* I just switched to part-time."

She shrugged. "If you say so."

I waded through the clutter and sat on a wadded yellow robe. Fair introduced me to the mages all around us, speaking their rainbow names. Then, for the rest of the afternoon and evening, I got lost in a world of anti-derivatives and trigonometric functions, occasionally gnawing hunks of burnt dragon meat and sipping on smelly water that'd probably give me violent diarrhea tonight.

The sun began to set. It seemed a bit early for the day to be ending. I worked by candlelight now, stuck on the same question for the last thirty minutes. This assignment was turning out to be a lot harder than I anticipated... maybe, because it was supposed to follow an actual instructional lesson. A lesson I skipped, today.

Fair's group started to wrap things up and head off to their own cabins, for the night. The spectroscopers slowly began to follow suit, emerging from the adjoining room and briefly passing through the lobby on their way out. Every time their door cracked open, I peered anxiously, hoping to catch a glimpse of Scarlet.

"Nurtic," Fair spouted, "I'm going to go check up on Scarlet, okay?"

"Okay." Any reason I couldn't come with? I'd been dying to see her, all day.

"She probably won't be able to meet with you until tomorrow. She really needs to rest." Fair looked a little tense.

I sat up straighter. "Is she okay?"

"Of course," Fair snapped. "I only said she needs rest. It's been a long day, after all. Aren't *you* exhausted?"

It was only twenty-three o'clock—fairly early in the evening for one accustomed to thirty-six-hour days. But, to Conflagrians, it was nearly midnight. Despite the dizzying heat, I wasn't tired enough for sleep, quite yet. Calibrating my internal clock to cope with commuting between differing day-lengths was sure going to be interesting.

"Um, I'm getting there," I politely answered. "So, where'll I be staying, overnight?"

She spread her arms wide. "Here, with us."

I surveyed our disastrous surroundings, once more. "Right. Of course." I smiled.

"You haven't changed one bit, have you?" She smirked. "You're just as obnoxiously courteous as I remember."

My lips drooped. "I don't mean to come across as obnoxious. I really am thankful for your hospitality."

"I know you're sincere—that's exactly what makes this situation totally ridiculous. We're forcing you to leave school in favor of a dusty oven and you're thanking us for it."

"I didn't leave school," I repeated, "and I brought my inhaler, this time." I glanced down at my half-finished worksheet. "I love college and all, but I'm actually pretty relieved to be doing something like this, again. Something greater than coursework and swimming laps in cramped pools. I'm sure I'll be fine."

She rolled her parchment. "I wish I shared your confidence in this little crusade."

I froze. She wasn't excited about the World Revolt?

"But, Fair," I said, "we need to gain momentum as quickly as possible, so the Tri-Nation Campaign can survive once—"

"Once Conflagria loses its mind, yes, I know. Scarlet's going to love you; you've already got her mantra memorized." My cheeks grew hot. "And, it's nice to know that you've also already written off all magekind, like her," she added, sourly.

The few folks still hanging around abruptly forgot all about packing up and going home. Instead, they watched us intently. They probably didn't understand a single word we said, but it didn't take a linguist to figure that things were on the brink of escalading into an argument.

"I said no such thing," I answered, calmly.

"*Some* of us think it'd be wiser to channel *all* our time and energy into the Crystal restoration problem," Fair plowed on, arms folded. "Maybe, *after* that disaster is mitigated and *after* the Red Revolution succeeds in bringing democracy to Conflagria, *then* we can dare to set our sights on the Order. Dividing our attention now isn't going to accomplish squat."

Something suddenly popped in my mind: "Fair, aren't *you* a spectroscoper?" Why wasn't she working with them? "I mean, you engineered the Underwater Fire and the Spectral Hurricane, right?"

"Why, yes, I am responsible for the System's most lethal magical advancements to date; thank you for the reminder," she retorted, acidly.

"I meant that as a compliment to your genius, not an accusation. I know you were under the Crystal's influence when you did those things, so you're not accountable. I didn't mean to offend—"

"Of course, you never mean to tread on *anybody's* toes, not even for a second, do you, Nurtic? You're just so damn civil all the time, so eager to please, always ready to throw yourself under a rampaging pack of hobnails for the sake of everybody else. I mean, all it took is a two-minute conversation with Scarlet to get you to drop everything and leave school—"

"I didn't leave school!"

"—So you could gallop in on a white pine-dragon and save the world!"

"Fair," I said, firmly, "I'm not doing this to please Scarlet." Though, that was a nice added bonus. "I'm doing this because I really believe in the cause. Because, after only one month in college, I realized I can't just turn my back on the world to solely pursue my own success. I want to be a part of something greater than myself again. I've missed that, since leaving the Diving Fleet."

Fair's hair autonomously leapt over her shoulders. "Tincture, I can't even have a proper argument with you. Your over-the-top kindness drove me crazy when we were marooned, you know."

"Sorry about that. I promise I'll be mean and nasty, next time we're stuck for a third of an age with no company but each other." While it wasn't easy handling Fair's temper all those months, losing patience with her would've just soured our already-miserable circumstances. I had no choice but to stay calm through her storms. "Well, anyway, as I was saying: if you're the best spectroscoper around, why aren't you working on the Crystal restoration problem?"

"I'm the Red Co-Leader. Scarlet is already busy with the spectroscopers around-the-sundial, so I can't be. It's called division of labor. Someone needs to take charge of planning and executing military operations."

"Scarlet would be great at that. Why don't you two switch roles?"

"Because I can't fight, right now," came a voice from the doorway.

I turned, and there she was. Scarlet July strode forward, ruby hair squirming, green gaze alight… and stomach protruding. Every molecule of oxygen in my lungs instantly evaporated.

"I won't be able to fight until the end of February." She smiled her florescent smile. "I don't leave the cabin much these days, lest the System discover *him*." She patted her belly.

Him. Her son. It had to be Lechatelierite's, I knew. I'd always wondered what happened to their illegal romance since I caught a glimpse of them kissing in the mess hall, over an age ago. I supposed I had my answer, now. Despite all odds, they managed to keep their affair going strong. All the way to covalence.

I fought to keep my face still, suppressing the irrational urge to punch holes in the walls.

At that moment, Scarlet's vitreous eyes locked with mine. "Nurtic," she breathed. And, before I could even stand up properly, she scurried my way and literally threw herself at me. I wasn't expecting such a warm reception; she was so cold over the phone. I put my arms around her delicate frame.

I only let go of her when she let go of me. That took a while.

SCARLET JULY

Fair left to spend the night at Fifth Cabin. I showed Nurtic to Ambrek's old room, then went to crash in my own tarp. After about ten minutes of staring at the ceiling, I felt Commence kick. I abruptly sat up, literally trembling with excitement. He never did that before. There came another kick. And, another. How badly I wanted to share this special moment with someone! But, Fair wasn't around. And, I realized with a sinking feeling that, even if she was, she likely wouldn't reflect my enthusiasm.

More than anything in the world, I wished Cease were here. My throat tightened as I imagined him sitting beside me, stroking my belly, smiling with his eyes. I wiped my face in my left sleeve but, no matter what, it wouldn't dry.

There came a light knock at the door.

"Come in, Nurtic," I croaked.

He entered, holding a torch. "Hey, Scarlet, just thought I'd bring you some fire before you go to slee—"

He stopped dead upon noticing my tears.

"Are you okay?" he breathed.

I swallowed and sniffled. "Yes, it's just that... my son's kicking, for the first time."

Instantly, a big grin broke out on Nurtic's face. He lit the fireplace, snuffed out his torch then hurried over to me. Before he could ask, I grabbed his left hand and pressed it against my swathe.

"Wow, that's incredible!" he exclaimed. "Too bad Conflagria doesn't have soccer teams; he'd be a star for sure."

I couldn't help but chuckle at that, even as my eyes continued to water. To everyone around me, my pregnancy was a terrible scandal. But, Nurtic treated the news with excitement and joy.

When Commence finally settled down, Nurtic took a long draught from his inhaler.

"Sorry for making you come to the dustiest nation on Second Earth," I sheepishly apologized.

He laughed heartily which, of course, led to a coughing fit. "It's okay," he mustered, as soon as he could breathe again. "At least, I came prepared, this time. When I was marooned, things were way worse, believe me."

"Thank you for agreeing to do all of this," I added, realizing I never did show him any gratitude or consideration when we talked on the phone, "especially since it involved leaving school and all."

"I didn't leave school! Why does everyone keep saying that? I'm going to do college *and* the World Revolt."

I smirked. "UVA's too easy for you?"

"Compared to the Diving Academy, any civilian university is a breeze. I'm only a freshman but I already figured out which majors I want to declare: Religious Studies and Physics."

I whistled. "Physics?"

"Blame the Ichthyothians. They're the ones who got me into the hard sciences. Otherwise, I probably would've done Religious Studies and Public Speaking, or something."

Huh? "Public Speaking?"

"Yeah, apparently, I'm good at that—but, only when I want to be morbid and terrifying."

How absurd. "Morbid and terrifying? *You?* I can't imagine that. You always know how to cheer people up." Thanks to Nurtic, I'd miraculously stopped crying by now.

"Thanks, Scarlet." He smiled, but more soberly this time. "It's really good to see you again. When I gave you my number in June, I didn't think I'd be so lucky to hear from you this soon."

"Well, I've been wanting to start this project for a while... pretty much, the minute I left Ichthyosis. And, now, it's more important than ever before, to get things moving quick."

He chewed his lip. "Are the spectroscopers onto anything, yet?"

I shook my head.

"Keep working on it; don't even *think* of giving up," he practically snapped.

I was taken aback by his sudden harshness. "No one's considering giving up, Nurtic."

"Well, Fair makes it sound like the World Revolt's onset is Conflagria's death-sentence."

"It isn't. We'll figure something out."

He didn't blink. "But, if you don't find a solution in time, just leave. Take your son and get far, far away from here, as fast as you can. Don't hang around and try to... to fix anything or fight anyone, all on your own. Okay?"

Well, whether or not I'd take Commence abroad depended on a few key things, but I didn't need to scare Nurtic with any of that stuff, now. "Of course, I wouldn't stay here all by myself, among an entire population who'd be out for my blood."

"Good. And, don't do anything that could backfire on you either, even if you think it'd be a big blow to the enemy. Don't be a Samson," he insisted. Samson was a biblical figure who willingly took his own life because he knew his opponents would go down with him. "Promise me."

This was getting weird. "Nurtic?"

"Just… go to Icicle and let the fleet decide what to do. Don't take matters into your own hands. If you don't want to go to Ichthyosis, then come to Alcove City and stay with my parents. They'd take good care of you and your baby. Okay, Scarlet?"

"Nurtic, you're really starting to freak me out, right now."

His hazel eyes wrenched from mine and settled on the floor, instead. It was like he suddenly snapped out of a frightening trance. "Sorry," he murmured, "I'm just a little worried about you, that's all."

"Yeah, I can see that." I drew my blanket. "I can also see why people would say you're a moving speaker. You got my heart pounding without a clue what you're even talking about."

He chortled, lightly. "Sorry, got a bit carried away."

I leaned against the wall, legs stretched across my tarp. "You know," I began cheerily, hoping to dispel his nerves with stupid humor, "when I get my powers back, I could always just destroy the Crystal and let Conflagria do away with itself. That'd save the rest of the world from one long, slow nightmare."

He turned pale.

"Nurtic?" I asked.

He didn't speak.

I touched his arm. "Nurtic, I'm not *really* going to blow up the sustenance of my own people."

"O-of course, not. That was… funny. Heh."

For Tincture's sake. "It's nice to know my Second-in-Command can take a joke."

His blonde brows lifted. "Second-in-Command? I thought I was just a Nurian liaison."

"You are, of course, but you're also going to help me lead." I thought I had made that clear over the phone, but I guessed not. "Is that alright?" At this point, it better be.

"Yes, sure, of course," he breathed. "Wow."

"It's not as glorious as it sounds, believe me. Running a rebellion involves plenty of grueling work. Like, I'm going to need you to handle many of the practical aspects of the information exchange—you know, smuggling stuff across borders."

"Well, I did come here in a delivery plane; I'm a professional cargo-hauler."

"It'll be a lot riskier and trickier than working for a civilian transport service. Regularly flying through Conflagrian airspace will likely attract the System's attention. Which is one of the many reasons I wanted *you* for the job—as far as I'm concerned, you're the best pilot to ever walk Second Earth."

His tan cheeks went red. "Th-thank you, Scarlet."

"The Diving Fleet has already agreed to loan you an arrhythmic suit and a well-armed and shielded convertible. There's no way I'm going to let you co-lead the World Revolt in a polyester jumper and a winged tin can."

"Thank you," he said, again.

"Don't thank me—thank the Ichthyothians when they get here."

He studied the fire, face pensive. "You said Dither and Arrhyth are coming, right?"

I nodded. "Along with Inexor and Seven."

"Nice. It'll be great to see them again."

"Yes, it will," I agreed.

"It's really great to see *you* again."

I yawned. "You already said that."

Aura coagulating heavily, my extremities began to prickle. Rubbing my hands together, I hopped off my tarp and toddled closer to the fireplace, shivering.

"Everything alright?"

I only nodded, wondering if I should tell him about the dangers of covalence and why I couldn't get proper medical care. Gnawing my lip, I decided that, no, I wouldn't dump my personal worries on him quite yet, not when the whole world was still so fresh on his shoulders. I'd already turned his universe totally upside-down, overnight. I stole him from college. From civilian life. From the normal, safe twenty-age-old existence he deserved.

But, apparently, Nurtic was already pondering my myriad of private problems, because then he said, "Scarlet, raising a child by yourself in the middle of a civil war and an international rebellion... that's going to be beyond crazy. Since I'll be around all the time anyway, why don't I help you out with the baby? I can be like... like a father-figure or something, you know?"

Wait, what? I whirled around, stricken by the weight of his words.

"No," I replied flatly, "I can't ask you to do that. Absolutely not."

"You didn't ask," he unblinkingly objected. "I'm offering."

"And, I'm touched by your offer," I spoke loudly, "but, the answer's no."

"Why? You and your son are going to need all the help you can get. You want to do what's best for him, right?"

"Not at the expense of a single, unrelated twenty-age-old college student, I sure as hell don't," I shot.

"Scarlet—"

"You have enough on your plate already, Nurtic. Not to mention, *I* got myself into this," I poked my abdomen, "so, I'll clean up my own mess."

"You didn't 'get yourself into this' alone." His voice seemed to resonate from the walls, despite its low volume. I didn't know he could do that—yell while still speaking softly, somehow. Cease, with his throat-mage abilities, could do that too, though he typically didn't bother, as he rarely shied from shouting whenever he pleased.

"Yes, but *you're* not the one who got me into it."

He didn't miss a beat: "It's not your fault the father of your child is dead."

So, he knew it was Cease. How?

"It's not your fault, either," I pointed out. "Look, Nurtic, once the Tri-Nation Campaign really gets rolling, you're going to be too busy to breathe. So, as much as you'd like to help me out, the bottom line is, you won't be able to. And, that's okay."

I knew Nurtic was a loyal friend with a big heart, but seriously, why on Tincture's island would he make such an outrageously-sacrificial offer? His proposition went far beyond friendship's call of duty.

When I met his warm eyes, I got my answer. Of course. Why didn't I see it before? Nurtic had feelings for me. Oh, Tincture. I wasn't okay with that. I was still in love with Cease. Moreover, if things got weird between us, it'd be harder to work together on the World Revolt. After Cease and Ambrek, Tincture only knew that I'd had my fill of awkward, high-tension 'workplace' romance. When Cease and I were comrades, it was like every move we made and every word we spoke to each other was rife with sexual tension. Our private strategizing sessions were liable to turn into intense episodes of kissing and touching, or arguing about our relationship... or, getting faux-married and sleeping together...

"What's his name," Nurtic's voice pierced my thoughts, "your son?"

At once, it dawned on me that, since Qui Tsop Lechatelierite, no one had ever asked me that. Not even Fair. Everyone called my baby 'him,' or worse yet, 'it.'

"Commence," I answered. "Commence July Lechatelierite."

And, now, there were three souls on the planet who knew my baby's name: Nurtic, Qui and me. That was it.

He smiled, cheeks dimpling. "Crystal's beginning," he breathed. "That's beautiful."

I beamed. "Thank you."

"Mind if I pray for Commence?"

Chest aching, I choked, "S-sure, go right ahead."

Nurtic took my hand, scrunched his lids and began to speak, voice barely above a whisper. He asked God to strengthen and bless Commence in the months and ages to come, protecting him from any enemies he may encounter. His words were simple, yet powerful. By the time he finished, the fireplace was out. I was glad, because that way he couldn't see the fresh tears glazing my face.

NURTIC LEAVESLEFT

It was noon on November eighth. The Headquarters lobby was packed with chattering mages, their colorful auras tinting the humid air. I stood up front with Fair and Scarlet, awaiting the arrival of Inexor, Seven, Arrhyth and Dither.

Without warning, a throat mage named Pha Rynx came bounding into the cabin, loudly garbling in vowelly Conflagrian. Apparently, the Ichthyothians called Scarlet's plane an hour ago and left a message saying they were stuck in battle. The *same* battle they were in yesterday. They'd been at sea for fifty hours and counting.

Scarlet decided to hold the meeting anyway since mages from across the island—not to mention, a college student from Nuria—were already gathered and rearing to go. Fair served as my translator, throughout. I blushed furiously when Fair relayed that Scarlet introduced me as, "Nurtic Leavesleft, the best pilot I ever had the honor of serving alongside. He will be our World Revolt Co-Leader as well as our primary liaison to Nuria."

Immediately after the meeting, Scarlet dished out my first real assignment: head to Icicle to relay intel and material from the kickstart.

The flight over was a real fiasco. I was met by only one System craft… but, it was armed while I wasn't. Extensive evasive maneuvering wound up costing a lot of fuel. A *lot*. I was literally gliding on empty by the time I made it to base, crash-landing on the runway. Great. The plane wasn't even mine. I had a feeling, when my boss said I could use the company craft how I pleased off-hours, that didn't include demolishing the left wing and half the hull.

I laboriously extracted myself from the cockpit, miraculously unharmed. How on earth was I okay? I wasn't even wearing an arrhythmic suit, just a lousy sack of polyester…

I inhaled the frosty Ichthyothian air. While not a fan of subzero temperatures, I was definitely glad to be away from the desert for a bit. Marching up to Icicle's front gate, a small smile tugged the corners of my lips. I never thought I'd have reason to return here, especially so soon.

I was greeted at the door by Illia Frappe, who acted like he didn't know me. With dark bags beneath his eyes, he looked dead-alive. Of course, he was fresh from the endless battle. Sure enough, everyone I passed in the corridors was also a total zombie.

"Nurtic Leavesleft." Inexor saluted me as I entered the great hall.

"Commander, sir," I saluted back, "good to see you, again. How've you been?"

"We won," he numbly answered, lids half-shut.

I grinned. "That's great!"

Inexor just continued to stare, silently and without expression. Base-raised divers were never good at small talk.

It was time to cut to the chase, I supposed: "Well, I brought literature on the World Revolt for everyone; when can I give a briefing, sir?"

"Now's fine. I'll assemble my men."

"Thanks! And, um, I also have a little favor to ask," I added, uneasily.

"What's that?"

"I sort of… crashed my plane…"

His cool blue eyes slowly blinked. "We're well aware of that. We already consented to loan you an armed craft."

"Yes, Scarlet told me, and I'm very grateful. But, you see, the plane I came here in, it isn't exactly... mine. It belongs to my employer, Frost's Delivery Service."

"We can't afford to pay for a replacement, if that's what you're asking."

"Oh, no, I wouldn't dare ask that," I said, quickly. "I was just wondering if Icicle could tow the remains for me?"

"What, you think we're just going to leave your scrap-metal on the runway? A team should be clearing it off, as we speak. We can recycle the parts."

My stomach jumped up my esophagus. "What? No!"

"What's wrong? I said we're loaning you a better plane—a convertible, actually. You don't need your ridiculous winged flivver, anymore."

"I just told you, it doesn't belong to me!" I cried. "I have to return the damaged property!"

His arms folded. "Do you have any idea how much it'd cost to tow a ten-ton aircraft fifteen-hundred miles to southern Nuria? If you haven't noticed, we're in a steep recession."

Frost's was going to fire me. And, perhaps, sue me. Why, oh why didn't I think to refuel on my way so I'd have a bit of wiggle room while traversing the Septentrion, knowing how dangerous that sea could be? I couldn't imagine committing such a careless oversight when I was a diver. What did five months of civilian life do to me?

* * *

As the hall emptied after my presentation, Arrhyth Link and Dither Maine rushed over to greet me.

"Crashing on the runway?" Arrhyth hooted. "Ladies and gentlemen, I present to you Nuria's very first Silver Triangle recipient!"

"Looks like the alliance's pride and joy forgot a few basic principles of pilotry," Dither cheerily chimed, "like, you know, planes can't fly unless you put gas in them?"

I smiled, weakly. It was way too soon for me to laugh about the crash.

"It's great to see you, again," Arrhyth said, embracing me. That's when I noticed the stripes on his and Dither's sleeves.

"You've been promoted, both of you," I breathed, hugging Dither next.

They beamed.

"I'm the officer of unit twelve and he's got thirteen," Arrhyth proudly declared.

"Congrats, guys, that's great!"

"Sorry to interrupt this lovely reunion," Inexor growled, popping in from nowhere, "but, could one of you go to the storage garage to get Leavesleft an extra-large diving suit?"

"Extra-large or just extra-long?" Dither snorted.

Inexor was already walking away. "And, make sure his utility belt has a PAVLAK," he called over his shoulder.

"Right away, sir," Dither responded, taking off.

PAVLAK. It was here! The computer system had been in development for nearly a decade. I'd anticipated its release since setting foot in the Nurian Academy and was sorely disappointed when my service ended before its launch. But, alas, the time had come!

"What does the acronym stand for?" I'd always wondered about that.

"Portable, Adaptable, Visual, Linguistic, Auxiliary, Kinesthetic system," Arrhyth immediately spouted.

Say, what? "Um, wow, that's quite a mouthful."

He reached for his belt and, with a flourish, retrieved a thin white rectangle. "Engineered exclusively for the Nurro-Ichthyothian military, you won't find these babies anywhere but the wartime bases. They're insanely expensive, so just officers get them, for the time being. We're giving you the only spare we've got, so guard it with your life."

I stared. *"That's* a PAVLAK?" It sure didn't look like a revolutionary top-of-the-line piece of tech to me. More like an old-fashioned flip-phone that'd been squished flat. "Who sat on your great-great-great-grandmother's cell?" I joked, dryly.

"Oh, go ahead and laugh it up, my friend, but it's like something straight out of a science-fiction novel. It does everything we thought it would and more. Let me show you."

With a push of a button, his unit unleashed a vivid hologram. He then loaded various applications, explaining each, one at a time.

"So, as you can see, the PAVLAK can act as a spectrometer-slash-homing-beacon."

In awe, I beheld the enormous three-dimensional projection of Icicle. A tiny figure labeled 'Dither Maine' was making its way to the storage area.

"Incredible," I breathed.

Arrhyth cast me a grave glance. "If we had this when you went MIA, we would've been able to find you, right away."

I frowned. "Just missed it by months."

He went on: "It can also video-call other soldiers."

"Other soldiers with PAVLAKs," I pointed out.

"It's got maps of every landmass and water-body on Second Earth, from Anich to Zenus. It even has historical First Earth atlases with animated recreations of old battles." He loaded a very realistic rendition of a creek swarmed by dozens of mini figures. "Here's a clip from the battle of Antietam, from the American Civil War. McClellan versus Lee. Of course, a lot of the detail is speculative." He tapped a spot in the air. "Now, *this* is the battle we just finished off."

Immediately, Antietam got replaced by a vast hovering mass of cobalt-blue, infested with vitreous silicas, dragon ships, crystalline shuttles and surface-riders.

"How many units are there, now?" I asked, trying to keep track of all the whizzing shapes and colors.

"Twenty, of forty divers each. Except unit one—Seven's got a special-ops team of fifteen."

I watched as simulated Underwater Fire consumed a crystalline.

"This went on for fifty hours?"

"Sixty-something," he corrected. "I'm surprised I'm still conscious, right now." He flicked off his PAVLAK, tucking it away. "I keep the projection on at full magnitude, whenever I pilot. All the officers do. Much better than our old radars. Someday, all our crafts will have PAVLAKs already built in them."

"That's cool," I commented, "but, I hope it doesn't become a crutch for anyone. Sometimes, a pilot still needs to turn his head and actually look out the windows, no matter how awesome his radar."

"The mapping function can also auto-strategize," he continued, ignoring my remark. "Just input your plan of attack and the computer will create a variety of anticipated retaliations. You can watch the battle unfold in, like, two-dozen different ways."

"Wow."

"I only told you about some of the PAVLAK's features; I'll leave you to discover the rest on your own."

I rubbed the back of my neck. "Goodness, I don't think I'll be needing so many bells and whistles."

"You never know. If you're going to fly through warzones on a regular basis, maybe it'll help you shake off pursuers before running out of gas."

I smirked. "Yeah, yeah, okay."

He grimaced. "The only thing the PAVLAK *can't* do is go online or call civilian households."

"You're kidding."

"It's like designing a fancy multi-purpose wristwatch that can't tell time."

Typical Trilateral Committee. "Well, I have a feeling those features were intentionally excluded."

He looked angry. "I don't see how communicating with Linkeree or my parents would cause any harm."

"Yeah, I don't understand the Laws of Emotional Protection, either," I sighed.

"Well, speaking of the world outside these walls, Nurtic, how've you been? How're you liking civilian life? What've you been up to, since you left here?"

"I'm a freshman at the University of Vita."

"Wow! How is it?" I could definitely detect a note of jealousy in his voice.

"It's only been about a month but, so far, so good."

"My sister has been in love with UVA since she was in diapers. I hate how I have no idea where she even is, right now."

"She's also at UVA."

He fist-pumped. "I'm so glad she got what she wanted! Not that I doubted she'd get in. How's she doing; do you know, at all?"

"Yes. She's doing great. A gazillion credit-hours, violin, swim team, archery, bible study, art club.... she's definitely keeping busy."

"Awesome. Can you pass my congrats to her, if you see her anytime soon?"

I shrugged. "Sure. That shouldn't be too hard to manage; I see her pretty much all the time."

His brow cocked. "Really?" He flashed a mischievous smile. "Big brother approves."

Oh, boy. "Arrhyth, we're not dating. We're just… really good friends."

His face fell. "Oh. Well, alright, then." He shoved his hands in his pockets. "So, how's Scarlet?"

My heart skipped a beat. "Pregnant."

His eyes went wide. "It's Lechatelierite's, isn't it?"

Wait, what? "How do you…?"

"Wait here for a moment," he spouted.

"Why? Where are you going?"

"Just hold up; I'll be back in a sec!" And, he was off.

What on earth?

He returned a couple minutes later, brandishing a folded scrap of paper.

"When Inexor Buird's laptop died—Dither spilled ice-water on it and *man*, you should've seen Buird's face— he dug out Lechatelierite's old one from storage and wound up finding this, wedged inside. He took it to the Trilateral Committee for proper validation. At first, they refused, of course. So, Buird got all the officers to breathe down their necks until they finally gave in. It took *months*. Here." He handed it to me. "We were going to give it to Scarlet at the kickstart. Since you'll see her before we do, could you pass it along? I think she'll be very happy to have it, now more than ever."

When I unfolded the slip, all air abruptly evaporated from my lungs.

Arrhyth grinned. "And, tell her she still owes me those Conflagrian-language lessons."

LINKEREE LINK

News of a Nurian cargo-plane accident on Ichthyothian soil reached Vitaville a few days after Nurtic departed. Channel Seven went on and on about how 'unexpected and shocking it was, that renowned pilot Nurtic Leavesleft would crash for no apparent reason.'

"It's not *no apparent reason*," Nurtic retorted on the evening broadcast, probably unaware he was being filmed, at all—the angle of the shot was suspiciously awkward. "I ran out of fuel after a dogfight." He stood in a world of white, wearing an Ichthyothian diving suit, helmet tucked under his arm. The wintry wind whipped his sandy hair into a frenzy. Gleaming on the ice behind him was a small military convertible—his replacement craft. I noticed that a cobalt-blue '7' emblazoned its left wing.

So, after that, whenever I heard jet engines revving outside the dorm, I made sure to take a peek out the window, checking for that iconic numeral marking. My roommate, Alex Bold, made fun of my jumpiness. While she mostly supported my crush on Nurtic, she sometimes took jabs at him.

"He's lucky that you still give a damn about him after the stunt he pulled," she once told me. "He was a total jerk to you, suddenly vanishing to the other side of the world on a crazy suicide mission without even telling you until the night before."

I wished she wouldn't say things like 'suicide mission.' Because, when Nurtic left, I knew it was a real possibility that he may never come back. The thought made my stomach turn.

After ten straight days of disappointment, I stopped eyeing the sky whenever I heard a rumble. And, I grew to hate that I lived so near to the runway, not because I was actually bothered by the roaring sound of takeoffs and touchdowns, but because every plane that landed reminded me of the one that didn't.

SCARLET JULY

For security and safety reasons, I hardly ever left Head-quarters anymore. When I had to, I was sure to stay disguised and accompanied. This morning, I was supposed to go with Fair to Fifth Cabin for a special meeting but woke up feeling too sick to travel. So, I stayed put.

However, those who came over at dawn weren't aware I'd cancelled my trip and was still in my bedroom. Which meant they also thought it was safe to gossip about me. I now heard their chatter, through the wall.

"I just don't understand why she's refusing proper pre-natal care," said Ette Brun. "That could be the end of her *and* her kid."

"I don't get it, either."

"Yeah, it makes no sense."

"And, it's inhibiting her powers."

"We *need* her powers in this war, dammit."

"Well, she must be declining treatment for a reason…"

"Yeah, the Red One never does anything without cause."

"What could that possibly be, though?"

"I don't know."

"No idea."

"Maybe, it has something to do with being the Multi-Source Enchant?"

"That makes no sense."

"I don't know; I'm not a spectroscoper."

"Neither am I."

"Perhaps, she's worried about poisoning her baby," came the voice of Pha Rynx.

"Spectral poisoning?"

"Why'd that be a concern?"

"Well… maybe, the boy's a mutt or something."

"A what?"

"A half-blood."

"Huh?"

"You're talking crazy."

"No, really, think about it," Pha insisted. "The math works out. She's, what, five or six months along? She wasn't here, half an age ago. She was still in the Nordic military."

There was a silence. Then, everyone seemed to burst at once:

"Covalence?"

"You think the Red Leader's son is part Nordic?"

"Oh, Tincture!"

"She's carrying a *covalent* child!"

"Keep your voice down! We don't know who might be outside."

"Neither of our leaders are supposed to be back until this afternoon."

"We have three leaders now, remember?"

"Oh yeah, I forgot about the new one."

"The tall blonde guy, right?"

"Yeah."

Pause.

"It's *him*, isn't it!?"

"What?"

"The tall blonde guy!"

"I think his name's Leavesly or something?"

"What a strange name."

"All Nordic names are weird."

"So, what about him?"

"*He's* the father!"

Another pause.

"What?"

"Tincture, you're probably right!"

"You saw the way they hugged when he arrived."

"Wouldn't let go of each other."

"And, she made him an admin on the spot, though none of us know a damn thing about him. Shouldn't we've gotten to vote on it?"

"You heard all that gooey stuff she said about him. Best pilot she *ever* had the *honor* of serving alongside. For Tincture's sake."

"He stays at Headquarters whenever he's around, right?"

"Uh huh."

"Overnight."

I'd had enough. I hoisted myself up, yanked open my door and marched into the lobby.

All talk abruptly ceased. I was greeted by a circle of guilty faces. Ette wouldn't even meet my eye, at all. She studied her sandals.

"Red One," Pha breathed, "we didn't expect you to be back, so soon."

I gave him a small smile. "I never left."

"Oh. Not feeling well?"

I shrugged.

"I'm sorry to hear that." He swallowed. "Would you like us to get you a medicine man?"

"No, thanks."

"But, if you're aura's clotting, he could help you."

Oh, didn't Pha think he was so clever.

"I already got treated for that."

"Yeah, *once*, when you were on the brink of stroke." He was gaining a little more courage. "You're supposed to get it weekly."

I was silent.

He took a deep breath. "I think you're avoiding treatment because you're afraid of poisoning your baby."

I kept my expression deadpan.

"Spectral poisoning, I mean," he went on, cheeks purpling. "Because your baby is covalent."

No one moved nor spoke.

I was spared having to address Pha's accusation by the very sudden, dramatic arrival of Fair and Prunus. Fair thrashed and wept in Prunus's arms, hair bound up with diffusion rope.

What the hell?

"Fair?" I ran over to them.

"Red One, stay back!" Prunus yelled.

"Persica, what's going on?" I demanded.

"I told her not to go into Ardor Village. No Red is to enter Ardor Village, anymore; it's too dangerous!"

"But, Seventh Cabin is in Ardor Village," Ette breathed.

"Seventh Cabin was evacuated, last night. The Crystal's emissions are too powerful, out there."

Brazenly ignoring Prunus's warning, I took Fair's trembling hands in mine.

"It's okay, Fair, you're safe, now; you're with us, far away from the Pit," I told her, examining her glossed-over gaze. "The thoughts in your head, right now—don't dwell on them, don't feed them. Think of something else. Think of…" Of what? What could I possibly distract her with, at a time like this? At that moment, I felt Commence kick. Yes, of course! Immediately, I pressed Fair's frigid fingers against my belly. "Feel that?" I asked her, grinning. "My son is kicking!"

Fair, still wailing, managed to nod. Good. So, she could hear me. I had her attention—a portion of it, at least.

"Isn't that exciting, Fair?"

"Mmm."

After several minutes during which Commence diligently kicked without ceasing, Fair's agonized cries gradually ebbed. At last, she lay still in Prunus's arms. Removing the cord from her locks, he set her on her feet. Immediately, she leaned in to embrace me hard, panting like she'd just outrun a semivowel.

The danger had passed. For now.

"Scarlet," she whimpered, "th-that was terrifying."

I thought back to when I'd touched the Crystal with my hair last age and got overcome by the urge to kill Cease. 'Terrifying' was too mild a word.

"Red One," Prunus croaked, "are the spectroscopers onto anything, yet?"

"No, they aren't." I got asked that question a gazillion times a day, and I hated it.

I also hated how the spectroscopers were fixated on finding a means to replicate what Cease did in May. I believed, even if we could recreate Cease's work, it wouldn't solve the problem in the long run; the System could simply begin restoring the mind-control, all over again. We'd be running in circles, and at a great risk to ourselves: repeatedly attacking the Crystal was insanely risky. If we accidentally inflicted improper damage—or, worse yet, destroyed it in entirety—we'd indirectly spurn a mage genocide. So, in my opinion, we shouldn't physically strike the Crystal, ever again. Instead, we needed to figure a way to manipulate the fibers of the spectral web themselves, reversing the System's alterations.

But, whenever I vocalized these thoughts, I got a lot of opposition because it sounded like I was advocating 'fighting the symptoms rather than the disease.'

"The spectroscopers aren't onto anything yet because they're still wasting time with pondering ways to harm the Crystal's physical form," I brazenly said now, and everyone but Fair shot me exasperated looks. They'd all heard me go off about this, at least a dozen times before. "The Crystal is a 'disease' we can't live without; we need to leave it alone for our own safety and focus instead on impacting the threads of the spectral web. After all, we just need to eliminate *one* of the many 'symptoms' that the Crystal causes: the mind-control. Nothing else."

"Not this, again," Pha grumbled.

"Red One, we've already been over this," Ette sighed.

"Impacting the Crystal is the *only* way to impact the web," Pha added, begrudgingly. "We can't manipulate the fibers independently."

"Hold the torch for a sec, people," Fair spoke up. "What if we got something to… I don't know… live *in* the web, actively binding and fortifying its strands, making them impervious to the problematic aspects of the Crystal's calibrations?"

"We'd need whatever it is to be sovereign, everlasting and insanely strong," Prunus interjected. "Like, strong enough to overpower the entire web, all the time, forever."

"Anybody got a spare god handy?" Ette murmured, dryly.

"Gabardine, the entity you're describing doesn't exist," Pha retorted, flatly.

There was a silence.

"Maybe, we could create it?" Prunus suggested.

"But, how?" Pha asked. "Out of what?"

I toyed with Cease's Silver Triangle, under my collar. "An aura," I breathed. "Don't auras live in the spectral web?"

"No," Fair answered. "Auras are sustained by the web, sure, but they're also anchored to our bodies. We can't just make one hop out of its host."

"What if the host is dead?" I asked.

Prunus blinked. "So, the next person to die donates their aura to the cause?"

Fair shook her head. "No, no, you guys have got this all wrong. Auras don't have control over themselves after their hosts die. Auras of the dead have no will, no independence, no distinct frequency nor color. They just return to the spectral web in the form of raw energy, dissipating into radical photons."

"So, what we'd need is a sort of... hyper-aura," Prunus mused. "One that harnesses enough of the Crystal's energy to both retain its sovereignty post-host-mortem *and* indefinitely bind the web."

"No one's aura is that powerful," Pha voiced, bluntly. "This conversation is stupid."

My heart pounded against my ribcage. What if *my* aura was that powerful? After all, Cease's aura, born from mine, already showed itself to have some measure of sovereignty after its host died: instead of fully dispersing into the spectrum, many of his photons immediately fled to me, giving me the second wind I needed to fight Ambrek. And, later, Cease's aura took on a physical shape to appear to Fair in a vision, vocalizing what Cease himself would've likely chosen to say in life.

I cleared my throat and feebly piped, "Um... my aura might be strong enough."

Everyone stared.

"What?" Fair blurted.

My face burned. "I mean, it probably isn't right *now*, but maybe after the baby is born?"

Silence.

Finally, Fair declared, "Well, we're not killing you in February just to test your theory, sorry."

* * *

Through the window, I watched as the skis of Nurtic's new plane neatly glided across the seashore's sandy slopes. When the craft came to a full stop, Nurtic hopped out of the cockpit, clad in a diving suit. Pulling off his helmet, he ran over to our cabin and knocked.

"Come in," Fair called.

He stepped inside, expression quizzical. "Um, you guys should really think of installing a lock or something. I know you all don't have fancy fingerprint scanners or keypads like Icicle, but at least you could put in a bolt."

Fair laughed. "Spoken like a true Nordic. Like a *bolt* would really keep out a mage. Our kind doesn't bother with locks."

"Seriously?" he gaped. "None, at all?"

"Of course not." Fair blinked. "At night, we post guards outside."

"What about during the day?"

She gave him a wry look. "There are always tenants during the day, and if an uninvited guest walks in on them, you know what happens."

"That, I do," he chuckled. "I have the bruises to prove it."

"Back before the Crystal's end, we didn't have to bother with watching over our safety or our stuff, at all," Fair sighed. "Theft, violence, murder—none of that existed under the System's dominion. You can see why Tincture still has plenty of supporters. With their astounding spectral prowess, the System could've accomplished great things. If only they used their mind-control moderately."

Nurtic shook his head, visibly shaken by Fair's words. "No, with free will, the door's got to swing both ways. Real freedom means having the choice to do good *and* bad. The moment a man isn't able to *consider* committing a crime, he's a slave."

She just shrugged.

* * *

Once evening fell, Nurtic asked to talk with me in private, face grave. I was alarmed—his face hardly ever went grave, even in the midst of tragedy.

He ushered me into my room, closing the door behind us. "Nurtic, what's going on?" I asked, fear prickling my scalp.

He wordlessly handed over a wadded slip of waxy Ichthyothian paper. And, when I unfolded it, my heart stopped.

It was my marriage form. The original document, with mine and Cease's signatures. Only, now, it was emblazoned with a stamp from the Icicle Base Retirement Center and co-signed by a judge named Dne Latsyrc. I couldn't believe it.

"Inexor found it," Nurtic answered my unvoiced question, voice low, "wedged in the Commander's old laptop. He and some of the other officers took it to the Trilateral Committee for validation." He gave me a small, sad smile. "Congratulations, Mrs. Lechatelierite."

I knew this paper carried no practical significance. The registration probably wasn't even legal, since death had long since done Cease and I part. But, nonetheless, just having the document in my hand—after nearly half an age of believing it was gone for good—triggered a confusing cascade of shock, grief, relief and happiness. Overcome, I collapsed into my tarp and wept. Nurtic sat beside me and let me cry on his shoulder as long as I needed.

LINKEREE LINK

Though I heard a rumble outside, I didn't bother to lift my eyes from my history textbook. I was through with getting my hopes up for nothing.

"Hey, Reeeee," Alex called in a sing-song voice, "*someone's* landing on the runway! His plane has a blue seven on the left wing, right?"

Yes, it did. "You better not be pulling my leg."

I scurried over to the window. Sure enough, there was Nurtic, clad in a white suit, climbing out of a grey military jet.

"Be right back," I said, grabbing my jacket.

"Have fun!" she giggled, winking.

Preoccupied with opening the cargo bay, Nurtic didn't even notice my approach. He now slung his school backpack over his shoulder—an odd contrast to his diving attire.

"Hey, Nurtic!" I exclaimed.

He swiveled around. "Ree!" His face broke out into a big dimpled grin. So cute. "Good to see you!"

"Likewise," I breathed as he scooped me up into a back-breaking hug. Once he put me down, I eagerly asked, "So, how was your trip?"

He shrugged. He actually *shrugged*. Seriously, was *that* his reaction to spending a full fortnight traversing the hemisphere in pursuit of saving the world?

"Come on, what have you been up to, these past couple of weeks?" I insisted. "What sort of things are the Reds having you do?" I noticed an odd sort of... sandy haze, hovering around him. What on earth was that?

"Fly, of course." He gestured to his magnificent craft. "The Diving Fleet got me some sweet wings."

"I can see that." I blinked. "So, you fly. That's your job in the World Revolt."

"Yup. I transport material and information. Sort of like a smuggler."

"Really?"

If that was all, Scarlet was seriously underestimating and underusing him. Yes, Nurtic loved to fly, but exclusively serving as an air-delivery-boy seemed like a waste of his many talents. I thought she'd want the Ex-Leader of the Nurro-Ichthyothian Resistance in more of a management role. Did Scarlet really need to stunt Nurtic's college career so he could haul cargo?

"I said yes, Ree." The subtle edge in his tone seemed to imply, *that's all I'm going to tell you, anyway.* So, he didn't trust me. I couldn't believe it. My heart sank to the pavement.

"How's Scarlet?" I asked.

Immediately, his enormous smile returned, but with more life than before. "She's busy learning languages in rapid succession, so she can translate media for global broadcast." I figured that my dad was the one supplying her with all the necessary multi-lingual teaching tools. I made a mental note to ask him about it, the next time we talked on the phone.

"Wow."

"Did you know that she taught herself Nurian in *one* night, when she was only ten, just by reading a dictionary and some grammar books? I swear, she just inhales language and exhales it back out."

"Amazing."

"So, how's school?" he suddenly switched gears.

I blinked. He barely shared two sentences about his international travels and he wanted to talk about *school?*

"Well, not too much has changed since you left," I answered, honestly, "except the swim team is in ruins, but you probably saw that coming."

He shrugged, again. "I'm sure they're happier without the ol' drill sergeant around; they'll be fine."

For a moment, I was stricken by his total disregard. Of course, why didn't I see it coming? He didn't care about UVA, anymore. College was now just a footnote to his glamorous life. He was no longer one of us. His concerns went far beyond campus classes and sports. What did it matter to him, if the swim team went to the dogs? He was a soldier again; the civilian world was inconsequential.

"What about your classes; how're they going?" he asked, blandly.

"You're going to like this," I said, excitedly. "The university's about to launch a series on the international wars. The one-oh-one class opens next semester: 'Intro to Ichthyo-Conflagrian Relations.' It's going to be a huge lecture!"

"Of course, it'll be." He glanced around the corner for the bus. "Everyone loves chasing a new fad."

Huh? "Fad?"

"A couple decades before First Earth got destroyed, there was a boom in foreign-affairs majors," he explained, tone bubbling with irritation. "The craze lasted for a few 'years' before everybody got used to having war as the status quo. Once violence became the norm, everyone lost interest in working to stop it." He shifted his backpack to his other shoulder. "After finishing the intro class, let's see how many students actually follow through with the whole series."

My voice went small as I chirped, "I think I would."

"Let me know how it goes, then."

I stared, dumbfounded. "You mean, you don't want to take them, too? Not even the first one?"

He shook his head. "I actually *went* to war; I don't need to hear the musings of a stodgy professor without a clue. Besides, I'm not interested in getting bombarded with a bunch of anti-Conflagrian, us-versus-them, all-mages-are-savage propaganda."

"Wait, what?"

"Just look at how the alliance is handling the Red Revolution, Ree. We're sitting back and watching Conflagria crumble, refusing to lift a finger for the very people who are currently sharing our burden by fighting our enemies. Why? Because of racial politics. Because we think that mages are less than human. Because we think that they're primitive while we're civilized, so they can't possibly be worth saving," he seethed. Aside from the time he kicked Shawn in the gut, I'd never seen him so riled up before. "Both Icicle and the Nurian Diving Academy teach their students to hate mages. I mean, really *hate* them. And, if you think UVA's going to offer anything less twisted, you're sorely mistaken."

Wow. "Well, then, maybe, you can be the one to shed some light," I suggested. "You've lived in Conflagria. You've got real personal relationships with mages. You can tell your profs and peers the truth. Dispel the stereotypes. That's a good enough reason to take the class, right?"

He shook his head again. "Normally, I'd agree with you, but now, I've got better things to do with my time and energy."

Better things to do. Like, saving the world.

I touched his shoulder, noticing how very slippery his suit was. What material was that? I'd never felt anything like it. "Come on, Nurtic. If anything, you should take the intro because it'll be a piece of cake for you. We'll be studying people you've met and events you've participated in. Aren't you in need of easy 'A's?"

He gave me a strained smile. "Come on, Ree, don't you know I'm way too masochistic for easy 'A's? Bring on the astrophysics with a side-dish of vector math. And, maybe, some organic chemistry for dessert. Mmmm."

At that moment, the bus arrived and he was off to the other side of campus.

Less than a week later, he was gone again, only sparing me a brief phone call before jetting away. I made it to the tarmac just in time to watch his plane disappear into the horizon.

AMBREK COPPERTUS

I woke with a start, head slamming into the bunk above. And, every image I just saw while asleep... fled my mind in an instant. Except one. Scarlet's face. A confusing mix of emotions unfolded in my chest whenever she visited my nightmares. Fear. Longing. Hope. Guilt. Satisfaction. Panic.

After months of mental terrorism fueled by my mysterious premonitions, I decided I was tired of it all. I was tired of bailing on missions near Red Headquarters, afraid I'd run into Scarlet. I was tired of looking over my shoulder wherever I went, fearful I'd unwillingly bring my horrific dream to life. I determined I was through with fleeing from her.

But, the problem was, the minute I decided to stop consciously avoiding Scarlet, it seemed like she'd all but vanished from the island. She never showed up in battle, even ones that took place in her cabin's backyard.

When I was her co-leader, she always insisted on storming the frontlines herself. Always. The Scarlet I knew wouldn't willingly abstain from combat, no matter how much the Reds wished to guard her life. The Scarlet I knew would never consent to being protected, letting others do the dirty work. The Scarlet I knew always fought like she had nothing to lose.

So, I concluded, there had to be a serious reason for the Reds to suddenly start hiding their leader. A serious reason for Scarlet to accept to be hidden. Perhaps, now, she did have something to lose. What could that be?

LINKEREE LINK

Under the captainship of Shawn Sordid, the swim team was going to the Fire Pit in a handbasket. I still couldn't believe Nurtic's choice of successor.

"Michael Swift told me to pick him," Nurtic once explained to me with a shrug. "Shawn's three-age record is solid. Seniority tends to be the way things work, around here." With him as the glaring exception, of course. "In the Diving Fleet, we didn't care about age or experience. Rank was awarded purely according to performance. It was a real meritocracy." Which explained how in the world someone as green as him got to be an officer within months of enlisting. "Believe me, if talent was the only factor I had to consider, I would've made you captain."

Coping with Captain Sordid was a real chore. For one, he despised Nurtic. No, 'despise' was too mild a word; Shawn downright hated Nurtic's guts. At practice, he'd casually refer to him by a variety of colorful names. Nurtic once told me that he had apologized profusely for the cafeteria incident a couple days after it happened, gleaning Shawn's immediate absolution. But, it was obvious from Shawn's current behavior that he didn't actually accept the apology, he only pretended to. Why?

Regardless of their history, to me it seemed rather unsportsmanlike and inappropriate for a team captain to start a loud vendetta against his predecessor the moment he stepped out. Sometimes, I wondered if Shawn were jealous of Nurtic. But, that seemed pretty dumb to me; who compared themselves to a war hero? That'd be like comparing myself to Scarlet. How absurd.

And, as anyone would guess, if Shawn hated Nurtic, he also hated me. Apparently, we were a packaged deal. I predicted I'd be warming the bench at many a competition, this age.

But, what bothered me most of all was the cowardly way Shawn was handling his anger. He was entitled to loathe Nurtic all he wanted—this was a free country—but, I believed he should do it to Nurtic's face rather than behind his back. Why did he pretend to be forgiving when he obviously wasn't? Why not confront Nurtic like a man instead of whining to everyone else on the team?

This was going to be a long semester.

* * *

Seeing Scarlet regularly again definitely fanned Nurtic's flame for her. That was fine by me. After all, the two of them had a ton of history. Moreover, it'd be really stupid for someone like me to envy someone like Scarlet. The more Nurtic talked about her, the more I understood what he saw in her. There was no other way to put it: she was amazing.

And, so was her work. Almost overnight, the World Revolt seemed to take the western hemisphere by storm, with its many masterfully-composed articles, slogans and videos. Regular news outlets tended to sterilize the war, never daring to broadcast a clip of say, an eight-age-old mage boy bawling at the sight of his family's demolished cabin. But, the Revolt didn't shy from revealing how much the war impacted not only Nordics but the so-called 'enemy race,' who were people, too. They didn't just show vids of bombers swooping in and out, but how things looked *after* the mushroom clouds cleared.

Thankfully, the Tri-Nation Campaign was also careful not to overdo it, avoiding the greatest pitfall of propaganda-making: heavy-handedness. *Too* much graphic horror would just motivate people to turn off their TVs and close their web browsers. The Campaign was likewise careful not to make the international state-of-affairs look too disastrous to be helped. Nothing would be gained if the world came to think of itself as a hopeless case. And, above all, the Campaign was sure to lucidly explain the complex racial ideologies lurking behind the façade of 'world peace through non-intervention.' Finally, the ugly bare bones behind the theory of isolationism were being unmasked, for all to see. The Revolt made it clear as day that the Order didn't prevent violent conflict as it was supposed to, but actually created the perfect environment for its onset and uncontrolled perpetuation.

The more I delved into Campaign media, the more I found myself wanting to become a part of it all. As a Link, I was already born with a passion for politics; regularly consuming World Revolt material only added fuel to the fire. For fun, in my scant free time, I started writing anti-isolationist essays. I didn't have any practical purposes in mind for them, until Alex suggested I share them with my social studies teachers. Hesitantly, I took her advice... and wound up really impressing them. One professor even asked if I was on staff with the Revolt.

"Because, if you aren't, you *should* be," Dr. Encour said. "It's a shame to let this kind of talent go to waste when they could clearly use you. At the very least, get something published in the school paper."

So, I picked a piece to submit to the *Vita Vision*. Almost immediately, it was printed in the opinion column. Soon thereafter, I got a ton of positive feedback from my peers.

And, so, tonight at dinner, I decided to go ahead and take the other half of Encour's advice: I asked Nurtic about the possibility of joining the World Revolt.

"Really?" he now replied, skeptically. He put down his fork. "Are you serious?"

"Um, well, yeah." Why was he so surprised? "I mean, look at who my dad and brother are—this sort of thing is right up the Link family alley, isn't it?"

Nurtic wiped his mouth. "Sure, we have hundreds of thousands of *supporters* across the hemisphere already, but most of them aren't part of the actual staff. Are you telling me that you *support* us or that you want to start *working* for us?"

I crushed a cracker into my tomato soup. "I want to work for you. I could produce articles, brochures, email blasts—anything you guys need. I can write persuasively, and I'm fluent in Star. I'm sure Scarlet would appreciate expanding the language base of her staff, instead of doing *all* the translating herself."

"Well, actually, Star isn't one of the languages that Scarlet handles, though she does speak it fluently." Of course, she did. "That's one of your brother's jobs."

"Arrhyth writes articles?" Arrhyth could do multi-variable calculus all day, but when it came to authorial prowess, I couldn't imagine him composing anything longer than a text message.

"No, he translates stuff that others write."

That made a lot more sense. "Well, if he's the only Star-speaker on the team thus far, then I guess you all could really use me."

Nurtic took a deep breath. Why was he giving me such a hard time? I thought he'd be thrilled to have his best friend onboard.

"Joining the Tri-Nation Campaign is... how do I put this?" He rubbed the back of his neck. "It's permanent. Like, rushing a frat or sorority—once you're in, you can never back out. But, it's much more serious than that; the stakes are higher. Kind of like joining the military. It takes priority over everything else in your life. It becomes who you are."

"Nurtic, are you trying to scare me off?" I asked in a small voice, stomach twisting a bit.

"No, Ree, I'm just being direct with you. Scarlet doesn't joke around with this."

"Neither would I," I squeaked, feeling a little hurt. When did I ever give Nurtic the impression I was flighty or flippant? And, for goodness' sake, I just wanted to draft a bit of propaganda.

"Fine." He sat back in his chair. "You can come with me to Conflagria over fall break, for vetting and briefing. Then, when we get back, I can help you plow through all the paperwork the university's going to throw at you, to reduce your credits—"

"Whoa, wait a sec, why do I have to do any of that? I only want to write some articles. Why do I have to travel, at all? Can't I just produce stuff here to send out with you, or something?"

His sandy brows scrunched. "No. This isn't the school paper, it's professional journalism. Journalists go out into the field. They write about what they see, firsthand. The information-exchange isn't a peripheral role in the Tri-Nation Campaign, it's central. It's who we are."

I hated to admit it, but Nurtic was starting to freak me out. Real journalism. I'd be taking leaves of absence from

UVA to venture into foreign warzones to find stories. I wasn't a veteran like him, I was a ninety-something-pound eighteen-age-old college freshman. Was I ready for all that?

Nurtic saw the doubt on my face. *Told you so*, his eyes seemed to say. He stuck a big forkful of pasta in his mouth.

"I won't mention anything to Scarlet until you've made up your mind," he mumbled through packed cheeks. "Take your time, think about it and get back to me, whenever you like."

Reading between the lines, he was basically trying to give me an easy out. He was essentially saying, 'Don't be embarrassed that you didn't understand what you were trying to get yourself into. We don't have to talk about it, anymore.' I didn't take that as a jab, necessarily. More like, he was trying to protect me. He clearly wasn't thrilled about my dumping normal college life for an intense, militant, life-consuming endeavor.

But, I didn't see things that way. I didn't see it as throwing away student life, I saw it as enhancing it. The Tri-Nation Campaign was a beautiful, heroic endeavor. Didn't every college kid dream about changing the world? How often did any of us get the chance to actually *do* it? Here was my shot to become a part of a mission that'd likely accomplish far more than any pretty-on-paper campus organization. Here was my chance to use my writing ability to achieve something more than just good grades.

"I don't need additional time to think about it, Nurtic; I've already made up my mind," I solemnly declared. "I want to do this."

Chewing, he silently studied my face. Finally, he swallowed and said, "You're going to miss a ton of class. You won't be on campus for more than a week or two at a time."

"I know." Believe me, Nurtic, I knew.

He plucked an ice-cube from his water glass and popped it into his mouth. "Alright. I'll call Scarlet tonight to arrange a meeting for you two, over fall break." He crunched, loudly.

"Wait a minute," I breathed.

"What, now?" he snapped. "You *just* told me that you're in. You can't change your mind once I speak to Scarlet, you know. You *want* to get me killed?"

Was Scarlet really *that* kind of leader? "No, no, I'm not backing out. I'm just surprised I have to meet with the head honcho *herself*." I pushed my trey aside, appetite vanquished. "I mean, how many people does she preside over? Does she really have time for *me*?"

"Yes. She knows her staff."

"You mean, she knows all *about* them."

He shook his head. "No, she *knows her staff.* Down to the last secretary and smuggler. Names, faces, strengths, weaknesses, what assignments they're on, when and to whom those assignments are due. She keeps tabs on everyone."

"That's impossible. No one's brain can hold that much information!"

"Her memory is perfect." Right. Of course, it was. "So, she'll definitely want to meet you and get to know you. Be sure to bring some writing samples and anything else you think she'd want to see. She's pretty tough on who gets to be a reporter; the World Revolt essentially *is* what our media makes it out to be. One bad piece can throw off the whole game."

My heart pounded in my throat. I had to knock the socks off of one of the most brilliant people in the entire world. *Me*, dazzle Scarlet July. Sure.

"After your interview, she'll watch you for a short while," Nurtic continued, "analyzing your psyche from the way you talk and act and respond to your surroundings—"

"*Analyzing* my *psyche?*"

"You know, to see if she wants your help at all, even if she likes your work and enjoys your company."

I cocked a brow. "Why wouldn't she want my help, if she likes me and my work? I thought revolutionary leaders want all the manpower they can get."

"No, *rabble-rousers* want all the manpower they can get," he objected, "because the strength of a mob is found solely in numbers. But, we're not a mob, looking to go on a rampage today before vanishing tomorrow. We're an organized mission with serious long-term goals. Scarlet needs to determine, before she gives you any responsibility, whether or not you're trustworthy and dependable. She's really learned from her mistake with Ambrek Coppertus; it's a lot harder to win her over, these days."

Ambrek Coppertus. The infamous twenty-one-age-old System soldier who used Scarlet to bomb the Nurian Trade Centerscraper and restore the spectral web. The same man who, less than half an age later, single-handedly killed the legendary Leader of the Nurro-Ichthyothian Resistance while outnumbered. I supposed it took someone like Ambrek to shake up someone like Scarlet.

"So, you'll be in a sort of… incubation period… until Scarlet makes her decision," Nurtic went on.

Great. "What exactly does *that* entail?" I croaked.

"Well, she won't let you stray too far from the cabin, nor attend any classified meetings, nor speak to anyone too important—that sort of thing."

"How long will all this last?" How long would I be isolated and scrutinized!?

"It depends on the person, but I wouldn't worry if I were you. Can't be more than a day, or so."

"A *day?* A single day to dissect someone's *psyche?*"

He answered my bewilderment with an amused smile.

A day wasn't a long time—especially, if that day were a Conflagrian one—but, I was sure it'd still *feel* like eras to me.

"The thought of undergoing an ordeal like that is enough to make the most guiltless squirm," I murmured.

He shrugged. "It's not like you'll really be aware of what Scarlet's doing with you, while she's doing it. You won't even notice when your 'incubation' starts or ends. It'll feel natural. You'll just be going about your business, tagging along with some lackey... then, the next thing you know, you'll be in important meetings and off on your first big assignment. It's not like Scarlet will stick you in a prison cell for twenty-four hours before announcing, 'Congratulations, you passed!' It'll just... *happen*. You'll be fine."

"Did you have to go through all this?"

His cheeks reddened. "No. She just called me up one evening and asked me to be her co-leader."

"You're her *co-leader?*" I gaped. "I thought you said you're a smuggler!"

"I am. But, I also lead the whole shebang, alongside Scarlet and Fair. We're a management trifecta."

"Wow!" I breathed. "Hey, you took Ambrek Coppertus's place," I observed, a moment later.

"Don't say that; I want my dinner to stay down," he groaned. "And, by the way, I really wasn't supposed to tell you all that, especially the part about my real job."

I laughed. "You make it sound like you're a secret agent, or something."

"Oh, believe me, after Ambrek's betrayal, Scarlet's a lot more uptight than any government agency," he said, dryly.

"The World Revolt," I echoed, thoughtfully. "I wonder how that'll look on my resume?" I joked.

"I don't know," Nurtic answered, darkly. "That depends on our outcome."

After fall break, my life would never be the same again. But, I drew comfort from the fact that, throughout this entire crazy adventure, I'd have my best friend Nurtic, right there with me. Even so, by now my stomach had grown so butterfly-infested, I doubted it could handle another drop of tomato soup. Nurtic, on the other hand, was still chomping through an athlete's portion of pasta.

"I don't mean to be rude, but do you mind if I did some homework while we ate?" he asked. "Down time isn't really a thing for me, anymore…"

"Sure, go right ahead."

He pulled his physics notebook from his overstuffed backpack, plopped it by his plate and started scribbling away. I glanced at his work. Though I hadn't taken physics since my sophomore age of high school, I still remembered that—

"Nurtic, force equals *mass* times acceleration. Not velocity."

What a weird error for an Ichthyothian-trained diver. It was as though a calculus professor forgot how to add two plus two while finding the anti-derivative of a multi-variable function.

He blinked. "Oh, yeah. Of course." His eraser scrubbed the page. "Thanks for catching that, Ree. Imagine if I'd turned that in. Another flunking mark is *just* what I need."

Another flunking mark?

I noticed then how very red and bleary his eyes were.

LINKEREE LINK

It was the last day of November. The last day of class before 'fall break'—a glorified three-day weekend. In other
words, it was the eve of my first Conflagrian excursion. As
night fell, my anxiety only escalated. Desperate to dispel
my nerves, I called Nurtic to vent.

"If this is code for 'I don't want to do this anymore,' my
answer is 'tough luck,'" he replied. "Scarlet is expecting you."

"I'm not trying to bail."

"Good. Because I won't let Scarlet down. I've really talked you up to her."

Did he, now? My cheeks burned. "Um, thanks."

"Scarlet doesn't tolerate mediocrity. None of us do. There
are no tag-alongs or passengers in our ranks. Only drivers."

"*Every*body can't be a leader."

"I didn't say leader, I said driver. As in, actively engaged,
at all times. Ever vigilant and hard at work."

I sat down heavily, on my bed. So much for calming my
fears. "What happens to those who do mess up?"

"Why do you ask?"

"I don't know," I squeaked. "I guess I'm just scared."

He sighed. "I think you're psyching yourself out for
nothing. A writer of your caliber doesn't have anything to
worry about. Plus, Scarlet's a fair leader. You'll love working for her. I know, I do." Of course, he did. "So, what are

you up to, tonight?" he abruptly changed the subject. "Anything special?"

"Packing, I guess. Why?"

"It's your last night of normalcy, before getting drafted into a magical cult," he joked. "We should do something fun to commemorate the end of college life as you know it. You know, celebrate."

A distraction sure sounded good to me. "What did you have in mind?"

"For one thing, let's forget the dining hall. Conflagrian cuisine almost exclusively consists of fired dragon meat and steamed taro root, which is pretty close to living on burnt shoe soles and chewy potatoes. So, you need to eat as much real food as possible, while you still can."

I laughed. "Alright, then."

"Also, a garish remake of a First Earth sci-fi classic just hit the theaters. It's called 'Galaxy Wars,' or something like that. Let's go and laugh at how calm and boring the characters' lives are, compared to our own."

A war movie? "Um, okay, if you're up for it."

Nurtic once told me that his military service zapped all the fun from violent films and video-games. He said, after experiencing real battle, most of the imitations were a mockery. And, the realistic depictions—the ones that actually did a decent job of portraying the horror and gristliness of combat—were even harder for him to stomach than the mockeries. Those brought back terrible memories of still-fresh traumas.

"I could really use some cheesy dialogue, digital explosions and a hero-wins-all ending—a refreshing break from the way war really works," he added. "Meet you at the bus-stop in ten?"

* * *

It felt nice to walk around downtown Vitaville with Nurtic again, but my enjoyment was intermittently punctured by waves of nausea. As the daughter of the Ex-Order Chairman, I'd traveled more than most Second Earthlings. But, never to a place as exotic as Conflagria. And, never to participate in a major revolution.

The entire evening, Nurtic's body language and behavior clearly communicated that we weren't on a date. At dinner, we each paid for our own meals. At the theater, he didn't even use the armrest between our seats. All night, he never so much as tapped my shoulder.

But, I didn't have to touch him to sense the bizarre way he seemed to just... *radiate* heat. Dry waves undulated from his body, accompanied by a strange sandy tint. I'd seen and felt that odd haze around him before, but never this clearly.

"Nurtic, are you sick?" I whispered.

He didn't even take his eyes off the screen. "No, Ree."

I brazenly placed a hand on his forehead... and it wasn't just warm, but scalding hot.

"You have a fever," I breathed, alarmed. "A really high one."

"I feel fine."

"Your forehead's like a stove."

At that moment, the couple in front of us turned and shushed, angrily.

The movie was corny and clichéd, but I liked it. Overall, I had a great evening. The best in weeks. Not once did we broach the topic of the World Revolt, nor the Ichthyo-Conflagrian War, nor the Red Revolution, nor Scarlet July. We were just normal college kids enjoying the start of fall break. I came back to my dorm past midnight.

"How was your date?" Alex asked, mischief in her smile.

"It wasn't a date."

She rolled her eyes. "Yeah, and I'm not your roommate, I just live here." She pulled off her socks, tossing them into her laundry-hamper. "I bet you two are going to wind up together."

Please. "Celebrities only date other celebrities."

"Bull," she grunted. "He's not a celebrity to *you*. You guys have been friends for eras."

"Exactly. Friends don't date."

She swooped her long hair into a high ponytail. "When he's not abroad, he's always with you. *Always*."

"Look, can we just drop the subject? Nurtic isn't into me like that, okay?"

"Really? You sure about that?"

"Yes, because I *know* who he likes."

She sat up straighter. "What? When has Nurtic ever spent enough time on campus to meet girls? I mean, girls who aren't you. Who is it?"

It felt so wrong, to talk about Nurtic behind his back. I needed to shut this conversation down, stat. "It's no one at UVA; don't worry about it," I answered with a shrug.

"Is it someone from back home in the city?" she pressed.

I unzipped my empty duffle. "Alex, we really shouldn't be gossiping—"

"You can't tell me this much then stop!"

"Alright," I wrung my wrists, "think of it this way: why do movie stars only pair off with other movie stars? Because they understand each other. They lead similar lives, facing the same challenges and stuff. You know?"

"So, he likes a fellow high-profile soldier?" After a brief pause, her jaw dropped. "It's *her*, isn't it! That prophet chick with all the crazy magical powers. Right?"

I was silent.

"Wow, he sure aims high." Alex blinked. "Eh, I still wouldn't sweat it, if I were you. Celebrity relationships never last. They'll probably break up, real fast. I'd give them a month, tops."

"Can we please stop talking about this, now?"

"No," she folded her arms, "because there's something else you need to consider."

I tossed my civics book into my duffle, though I doubted I'd really have time for homework on the trip. "What's that?"

"If you ever want to find a *real* boyfriend, you need to shed your Nurtic-shaped shadow."

Huh? "What do you mean?"

"You two are joint at the hip, every minute he's in town. And, now, you're going to start traveling together, too. While you guys may not be officially together, it certainly *looks* like you are, to the rest of the school. Guys won't ask you out if they think you're taken."

She was right. I stayed quiet, buried in my bag, wondering why her words didn't bother me as much as they should have.

NURTIC LEAVESLEFT

The shower stayed frigid, no matter how far I pushed the knob. Admitting defeat, I hopped into the next stall… and came across the same issue. Gritting my teeth, I made do with a quick cold wash. When I left the bathroom, shivering like a Conflagrian mage caught in an Ichthyothian snowstorm, I saw my roommate approach, towel slung over his shoulder.

"Brace yourself for a deep-freeze," I warned him.

"Great," he grunted. "We pay twenty-thousand bucks an age, yet UVA still can't buy us hot water?"

When Spii got back to our room, he said, "I don't know what you're talking about, Nurtic; the shower heated up just fine."

A few minutes later, I dug out my thermometer. And, sure enough, Ree was right. I didn't feel ill, at all. But, I had a fever high enough for a heatstroke.

LINKEREE LINK

An hour before dawn, there came a knock at my suite door. I opened up and there stood Nurtic, fully suited and ready to jet.

"You're super early," I greeted him, feeling intensely self-conscious about my bed-hair and morning breath.

"I know." He stepped inside. "I wanted to give you something before you finished getting ready."

"Before I started, you mean."

He cradled a small cardboard box. "This is for you. I *did* mean to pass it along sooner; sorry to be so last-minute." I stared at the blue triangle on the label, flabbergasted. "They couldn't exactly take your measurements," he went on, opening the package with his keys, "but, I told them you're about Scarlet's build, only a few inches taller, so hopefully they got it right or at least close." He pulled out something liquidy and white and handed it to me. It felt like a cross between steel and water, and it hardly weighed an ounce. "Your helmet awaits you in the cockpit. No utility belt nor flippers, though, sorry." He winked.

"Um, Nurtic," I said, faintly, "why do I need an Ichthyothian diving suit?"

"You're a soldier, now." He flashed me a big dimpled grin I didn't return. "But, in all seriousness, we *will* be living in a warzone, and this is the most durable and flexible piece of body-armor ever manufactured. Plus, it has a built-in air-conditioner, which you'll *definitely* need in the desert. Unfortunately, the Ichthyothians overdid things a bit by setting the maximum temperature to forty degrees," he grimaced, "but, in my opinion, it's better than the alternative."

Nurtic waited on the suite couch while I showered and suited up. I now stood before the restroom mirror, staring at my reflection with parted lips. Never in a million ages did I imagine I'd have a reason to wear Ichthyothian military garb. How absurd.

When I came out, Nurtic whistled, "Looking sharp, little Ree."

I squirmed. "Um, thanks."

"Fit alright? Comfortable?"

"Heh, a little *too* comfortable, to be honest." I rubbed my shoulders. "It kind of feels like I'm not wearing anything, at all."

"That's the idea. It's designed for diving, so it can't have drag."

"The only thing that's a little weird is the, uh, bottom part," I awkwardly added.

He laughed. "That's the catheter. You're probably not wearing it properly. It's supposed to be… well, attached."

"The *what?*"

"Catheter. It's so you can go to the bathroom in your suit, if need be."

"Why'd anyone need to do that?"

"Soldiers can get stuck in combat for days on end."

"Oh, right," I said, stomach knotting.

"You'll probably never need it," he reassured me.

"Have you ever used yours?" I asked.

"Of course."

We headed outside and boarded his convertible. I'd never been inside a warcraft, before. It looked a lot different than his old delivery plane and the private jets my family used to take on Order business. We were positively surrounded by dials, knobs, buttons, levers and screens. It was like something straight out of a science-fiction novel. How on earth did Nurtic keep track of everything?

Nurtic strapped in, totally at ease. I picked up my helmet and peeked inside. It was almost entirely filled with white foam.

"Where's my head supposed to go?" I breathed, stupidly.

"Just put it on; you'll see."

I obeyed, feeling as though I were sticking my head up a vacuum-cleaner. The fluff molded perfectly to my face.

"Without the shock-absorbent padding, divers would get knocked out, all the time," Nurtic explained. "But, with this, you can get hit by a flivver without losing a brain-cell."

"Your voice is inside my head!" I cried.

He chuckled. "Inside your helmet, you mean. Intercom. There's a switch on the mouthpiece that controls where your transmissions go. Since we'll only be talking to each other, you don't have to worry about that."

I'd barely caught a glimpse of Ichthyothian technology and I was already flabbergasted. One would think that a world with tech like this would also have flourishing space programs. But, no, the Order prohibited the establishment of any manned exploratory space programs on Second Earth; we just had necessary utilitarian satellites and such, in orbit. The Order's rationale for the ban was twofold. Firstly, they believed that a 'space race' could incite inter-country violence. Secondly, they believed that space exploration would open the door to finding intelligent life on other planets, which could also lead to war. (Never mind that, if there were hostile aliens out there, nothing was really stopping *them* from finding *us* and picking all the fights they wanted, regardless of the Order's stupid head-in-the-sand policies.)

Anyway, Ichthyosis had been blacklisted for seventeen ages and counting, so it technically could've been sailing the stars, by now. The problem was, Ichthyosis's isolation from the global trade network severely strained its resources, so whatever tech it *did* have got put toward the war. I could only imagine what Ichthyosis would accomplish if the world didn't turn its back on it, but fed and nurtured its genius, helping it finish off its conflict with the System so it could finally redirect some of its military production to other ventures, like space travel and adapting the PAV-LAK system for civilian use. Ichthyosis had some of the best scientific minds on the planet, but instead of designing rockets and ships to traverse the galaxy, these brains were preoccupied with engineering warcrafts and weapons for killing mages.

* * *

The flight to Conflagria was peaceful and picturesque. From our attitude, Nuria became nothing but a vast dotted expanse—the big buildings and bustling streets were mere flecks on a watercolor backdrop. I pictured myself down there, amongst the scurrying specs, going about my school routine. How small and insignificant that life seemed from up here. How small and insignificant *everything* seemed from up here. All the political struggles and violent clashes were suddenly so far away. No wonder Nurtic loved flying so much; it elevated you from all the chaos.

It wasn't long before we cleared the coast. The Briny Ocean's sunlit ripples were stunning. But, Nurtic once told me that he no longer saw any beauty in the sea. When he looked at the water, all he could think about was the battles it housed and the corpses it swallowed.

The longer we flew, the more certain I felt of my decision to join the Tri-Nation Campaign. I realized, the world was beautiful. And, it was worth saving.

* * *

We landed by Red Headquarters, near Conflagria's northern shore. Suit air-conditioner cranked to the max, I yanked off my helmet and inhaled the stale, dusty air. Having an eighty-degree difference between my head and body was one of the strangest and most unpleasant sensations I ever experienced. I sneezed and shivered and perspired, all at once.

Nurtic watched me, closely. "If you ever feel the discrepancy is becoming too much to bear, just put on the helmet for a while; that'll stabilize all of you to the same temperature. But, whatever you do, don't turn off the air-conditioner for more than a minute or two at a time. In this heat, you can't walk around in an unventilated bodysuit for long; you could have a heatstroke. If you find that you really can't stand the suit anymore and would rather brave the desert elements, change into something else entirely."

I nodded, murmuring, "Yessir."

As we made our way to the cabin, Nurtic excitedly whispered, "Scarlet should be waiting for us."

My heartrate jumped with anticipation. It was time! I was actually going to meet the legendary Multi-Source Enchant!

The door swung open and, before I could so much as *glance* at Scarlet, Nurtic had enveloped her in a tight embrace. I hung back, feeling awkward and shy, like I didn't deserve to be in the presence of such collective magnificence.

When the two of them broke apart, I finally got a proper look at her.

She was pregnant.

I resisted the urge to gawk. I couldn't believe it. In all of Nurtic's enthusiastic Scarlet-centered chatter, he never mentioned anything about a baby. In fact, because he bore such strong feelings for her, I'd assumed she was single and available. Of course, a pregnancy didn't mean she *wasn't* single, but it did mean that someone else had to have been in the picture, fairly recently.

"Ree, meet Scarlet July, our fearless leader," Nurtic said, grinning. "Scarlet, meet Ree Link, Arrhyth's sister and one of the finest writers I know."

I bowed to Scarlet, since that was the conventional mage greeting. But, simultaneously, she offered her right hand. At this, she and Nurtic totally cracked up. I also thought it was funny, but I was too nervous to join in. What would she think if I laughed? That I was a goofball? Then again, what did she think of my stoicism, now? That I was uptight?

Oh boy, I was going to drive myself crazy, this weekend.

I followed them inside. The place was a total mess. I could hardly see the floor. Everywhere I looked, there were crumpled shreds of parchment, torn robes, bent arrows, unstrung bows, broken clay pots and other unidentifiable trinkets. *This* was the epicenter of a military movement that was going to shake the world?

Before I could meet anybody else, Scarlet asked if we could have a 'little chat' in her bedroom. This was it. The interview. I gave Nurtic a nervous peek, afraid to go anywhere without him, quite yet. Beaming broadly, he handed me my essays, patted my shoulder and left me alone in Scarlet's doorway.

Scarlet sat cross-legged on the floor like an elementary-school kid, smiling and gesturing for me to join her. The absence of chairs and tables in the room sure made things interesting. I wondered, should I sit across from her, or beside her? Beside her seemed too friendly. We weren't friends. She was the one in charge here; I needed to show some respect. Sitting beside her could give off the impression that I was putting us on the same level. Sitting in front of her, facing her, would be more professional.

The next question was, how close should I sit? I wanted to be near enough to hand over my articles without excessive leaning or stretching—that wouldn't look very dignified. But, I didn't want to sit *too* close and wind up seeming forward or invasive. It was already unnerving that I physically towered over her. I was used to being smaller than most other young adults.

I decided the safest bet would be to settle across from her, at arm's length.

Her smile widened. "Oh, come over here, Ree," she chortled, patting the spot directly next to her. "I want us to be able to look at your essays together."

I scooted over, feeling like a total idiot. I chose wrongly, after all.

Scarlet then struck up some small talk, asking about college and what my dad thought of my interest in the World Revolt. I understood why she'd start off easy; she was giving me a chance to unwind a bit before hunkering down. After thirty minutes of small talk, however, I was starting to wonder when we'd get around to the actual interview.

Of course. Realization hit me like a flivver: this *was* the actual interview. Fear rippled through my over-air-conditioned frame. Scarlet was going to judge me by this *chit-chat?* That wasn't the way an interview was supposed to work. I was supposed to receive a concrete set of questions, not a jumble of straying dialogue. Like this, how was I to discern what she wanted from me? How could I determine the right words to say to prove I was sincerely committed to the cause and worthy of the job?

Goodness, she was smart. She really knew what she was doing. She didn't want textbook answers, so she made it impossible for me to give them to her.

The entire time we spoke, her astute gaze didn't leave my face. Never before had I interacted with someone so alert. Having the Multi-Source Enchant's undivided attention made me feel… important. Interesting. Worth listening to. She hardly blinked; her enormous eyes continually examined, measured, calculated. But, her stare carried more than just intelligent scrutiny. I saw compassion. Warmth. There was something about her that compelled me to open up without reservation. I hardly knew her, yet I found myself naturally willing to spill my guts before her. She was so charismatic, so kind, so inviting.

She was manipulating me.

Before I knew it, our talk was over and we were back in the lobby. For the next several hours, Scarlet had me shadow a random teenage leg mage who didn't speak a word of Nurian. She checked on us intermittently as we ran mundane errands, like fetching food and supplies for whoever needed them. Throughout the day, I eagerly caught glimpses of her in action, running the show. I noticed how she could be as fierce as she was sweet. She could snap between the two divergent personas in a millisecond, depending on what the situation required. No, she didn't have a split personality. She was just a soldier, through and through. The mark of the military was on her, that much was clear. She was ever-vigilant, ready to strike. Her intensity was almost scary, coming from someone so deceptively dainty.

Night fell. Nurtic approached me for the first time since our arrival.

"I've got a present for you." With a flourish, he handed me a scroll. "Your first assignment, reporter Ree."

I danced inside. I did it! I made it in! I was a World Revolt journalist!

"Scarlet wants you to draft an article using *these* stats and facts as your springboard." He tapped the parchment. "You can branch out, of course, just as long as the sources you find are legit." He beamed at me, causing my pulse to quicken. "And, once edited and approved, your piece will be translated into a dozen different languages and posted on the front page of the *Fire and Ice*."

My jaw literally dropped. That was easily the most trafficked Campaign website. "She wants *me* to write for the *Fire and Ice*?" I squeaked.

"Yes. Regularly. Which also means, after tonight, you won't be staying at Headquarters, anymore; you'll be at Fourth Cabin with our other top journalists."

My head spun. Me, an essayist for the most widely-read anti-isolationist publication in all of Second Earth. "I can't believe this. I must be dreaming."

"Well, you better wake up real fast—Scarlet wants your first piece by the end of our fall break."

I gulped. We were leaving the day after tomorrow.

"Is that going to be a problem?" he pressed.

"Oh, no, of course not," I quickly answered. "That's why I'm here, isn't it?"

He offered me his huge hand. "Welcome to the World Revolt, Linkeree."

He used my real name but, at this glorious moment, nothing could've bothered me. I took his hand and shook it, vigorously.

It was scalding hot.

"Nurtic, have you checked your temperature, yet?" I asked.

There was a pause.

"Yes."

"And?"

"Look, Ree, I don't feel sick."

"So, you *do* have a fever! I knew it."

"I said I'm okay, really—"

"What is it?" I insisted.

"One-oh-five," he resigned. "But, I feel perfectly healthy." Oh, my word. Wasn't that nearly high enough for a heatstroke or something? "And, I've been meaning to ask you," he continued, "since I have no other obvious symptoms, why did you even suspect I was sick, yesterday?"

"You give off heat like a radiator."

At that moment, the probable truth hit me like a stack of books to the head. It made no sense at all, but the similarity was uncanny: Nurtic's warm sandy tint resembled a magical aura, except dimmer.

But, how!? He wasn't Conflagrian!

"Ree, everything alright?"

"Yes," I lied. There was no way I could share what just crossed my mind; he'd call me crazy. "Uh, I was just thinking about… my talk with Scarlet, this morning."

His face lit up. "So, what do you think of her?"

I wanted to say how impressed I was by her intelligence and charisma. I wanted to say that I understood why armies would follow her to the ends of the earth. I wanted to say how thrilled I was to be working for her. But, instead, all that managed to escape my lips was, "Pregnant."

The grin melted off Nurtic's face like an ice cube in a cup of hot chocolate. "Yeah, it's a boy."

"I'm really surprised," I went on. "I mean, she's in the middle of leading two major rebellions. And, she's what, seventeen?"

"Yeah."

"I sure hope she has a good support network. Like, where's the father?"

"He died," Nurtic spoke through tight lips, "in the Second Infiltration, serving alongside her."

His words traveled slowly from my ears to my brain. I felt like I swallowed a hunk of hairy taro root, without chewing.

It was Commander Cease Lechatelierite.

"Scarlet's child is… covalent?" I whispered.

Nurtic nodded. "That isn't public knowledge, by the way. But, once the baby's born, the truth will be kind of obvious and Scarlet's life will get even more complicated. So, please keep quiet until the birth; she still has about three months of relative peace."

"Of course."

My stomach churned. My mother and father made international headlines when they married and had mixed children. It was all a pretty big controversy; everyone knew they only got away with it because of their political power.

But, covalence would be a far bigger scandal than any stunt my parents pulled. And, Scarlet's son wasn't just covalent, he was the offspring of the legendary Leader of the Ichthyothian Resistance and the Conflagrian Multi-Source Enchant. The child's many enemies, allies and responsibilities already awaited him. Growing up with such peculiar parentage during these turbulent times, the poor boy didn't stand a snowflake's chance in the Fire Pit at a normal upbringing. In fact, it'd likely be a challenge just to stay alive at all, evading kidnap and assassination.

Nurtic's grim facial expression told me that he'd already followed my same frightening thought-process, a thousand times.

NURTIC LEAVESLEFT

It was Sunday night and I'd just returned to Conflagria from a daylong smuggling job along the Anichian coast. When I entered Headquarters, I found a very exhausted and sweaty Ree, looking rather Conflagrian in a loaned burgundy robe. She sat cross-legged on the floor amongst rumpled parchment.

"It's finished," she breathed, wiping her face in her tattered sleeve. "My article is finally done."

I smiled. "Good job."

"What do I do, now?"

"Take it to Fourth Cabin. A moment ago, I ran into Prunus Persica outside and he said that Fair Gabardine is on her way over, now. When she gets here, she'll walk to Fourth with you and help you get settled in. The tenants there should have a tarp ready for you. Go get some rest, do some homework. Just be sure to come back by noon tomorrow so we can head to UVA."

Ree nodded, looking both relieved and nervous at the same time—a combination I hadn't thought possible.

"You okay?" I asked. "Coping with the heat alright? Had enough to drink?"

"Oh, yes, I'm fine," she said. "I think coconut water tastes like dirty shower runoff, but it's better than the river sludge everyone here guzzles by the barrel. I also had a few sips of that berry wine stuff, until I realized that drunkenness probably wouldn't pair well with my writing assignment."

I laughed.

"So, what're you up to, this evening?" she asked.

"I'm just going to have a quick talk with Scarlet, then I'm off to bed. I'm really tired from my flight." I thought grimly about the physics homework I didn't have the energy to finish tonight.

"Oh, okay."

"Fair should be here, any minute. I'll see you tomorrow, alright, Ree?"

"Sure. Have a goodnight."

I knocked on Scarlet's door. She opened up, right away.

"Hey, Nurtic," she chirped.

"Hey." I closed the door behind me.

She perched on her tarp, wearing only her brown vest and pleated skirt. It was the first time I'd seen her without her signature floppy red robe, since the World Revolt began. Her bulging belly contrasted starkly with her overall frailty. She looked more like a starving child with tapeworm than a pregnant woman starting her third trimester.

"Scarlet, how much do you weigh?" I asked, sitting beside her.

"I don't know. Why?"

"I'm not totally sure about this or anything, but aren't you supposed to have gained like a dozen or so pounds, by now—about as much as a college freshman who eats in dining halls daily?"

"You're a college freshman." She grinned. "Have *you* gained a dozen pounds, yet?"

"I've been in school for less than two months. You've been pregnant for six. If you don't eat enough, I don't know... your baby could be born underweight or something."

She blinked. "Come on, Nurtic, look who his parents are. He's probably going to be underweight his whole life, no matter what."

I shrugged, unconvinced.

"And, you're like Tincture calling the sun orange," she chortled, poking my ribs. "It's been half an age since you and Fair were marooned; you should really be a lot farther along in your recovery."

How exactly did she flip this conversation around? *Her* health was the issue here, not mine. I wasn't the one sustaining a second human life.

"Anyway, while I don't think you've packed any freshman pounds yet," she went on, "you *have* been gaining something else that I've been meaning to talk to you about, all weekend."

"What's that?" I batted my lashes, jokingly. "Has the desert sun blessed me with a bronze glow, already?"

She laughed again, rolling her enormous eyes. "You were tan even when we lived in the arctic. That's not what I'm talking about." Leaning forward, she took a deep breath. "Nurtic," she spoke firmly, "I think you're developing an aura."

I froze.

"An aura," she repeated, loudly. "You know, a colored wavelength."

I continued to stare.

"Ree was actually the one who brought it to my attention," she plowed on. "During our chat on Saturday, she mentioned something about you having a 'warm sandy haze.' She's right. Cease started developing an aura, too." It was the first time she called Lechatelierite by his first name, in front of me. Moreover, it was the first time she ever willingly brought up the topic of her dead husband, since we parted ways in June. "I didn't know it was possible for a visible frequency to twine to an infrared one, until Cease came along. By binding to my wavelength, his eventually changed from infrared to black. The same thing is happening to yours now, except it's a sort of yellow-beige color."

Now, how would I respond to *that?* I was terrified by the thought... but, also, rather touched and elated I was apparently close enough to Scarlet for something like this to happen.

She touched my wrist. "It's a little early to tell what your source is, but your superhuman dexterity and the fact that your hands could even dwarf Ambrek's inclines me to believe you're predisposed to hand magic."

Hand magic. My freshman age just kept getting stranger and stranger. I knew college was the time for self-discovery and all, but *this* was certainly more than I'd ever bargained for. *You're a wizard, Harry.*

"Cease never actively cultivated his powers, but I could tell his source was his throat," she added, nostalgically.

Really? Lechatelierite's skillset was so wide, I wondered how Scarlet could be so confident about that. I sort of considered myself a one-trick pony—I had strong eye-hand coordination, which aided in pilotry—but, Lechatelierite was a jack of very many trades. I never really considered his voice to be his most remarkable trait. It was true that, whenever he delivered an order, disobeying seldom felt like an option, and not just because he held formal authority. When he spoke, powerful conviction always overcame me, even when I didn't agree with his stance. Yet, I never attributed that to the might of his tone, but the bizarre mix of trembling fear, tremendous respect and fierce allegiance he seemed to effortlessly incite in the hearts of his men by simply being... well, himself. How large a role did his vocal mastery subconsciously play in everyone's perception of him?

"Once your aura grows strong enough, you can start training," Scarlet interrupted my thoughts. "I think Dex Nahd, a hand mage at Tenth Cabin, would be a suitable teacher for you. He's smart and patient, and he used to be a System soldier before the Crystal's end, so he speaks some Ichthyothian. I could get a hold of him for you."

Whoa, hold your horses, Scarlet! "Training?" I echoed, dumbfounded. "You want me to get mage training?"

"Why not? You're developing the muscle; why not exercise it?"

"Because… well… I… um…" Because this was totally nuts!

She sighed, heavily. "Characters in fictional stories are always so thrilled to learn they have superpowers. Yet, when it happens in real life, people freak out. Why is that?"

I looked away, dizzy.

"I'll give you some time to digest it." She toyed with a lock of hair. "Let's just say, you're still taking the news way better than Cease. The topic made him real mad, for some reason. I only ever brought it up because he was *literally* liable to set off spectrometers, but he told me to shut up and never mention it again."

Did he, now? My chest tightened. I understood why any Nordic would feel intensely unsettled by the idea of developing an aura—I sure did—but, to respond to the news with an angry ultimatum seemed unnecessarily hurtful and over-the-top. After all, Lechatelierite's changing frequency was a byproduct of his emotional proximity to Scarlet. Surely, he couldn't have hated *that*, considering he married and impregnated her within an age of meeting her. I thought back to my broken viola and, for the umpteenth time, wondered just how much crap Scarlet must've put up with while she and Lechatelierite were involved. From the bits and pieces I'd heard and witnessed thus far, I gathered that Scarlet endured unfettered rage, yelling, violence, manipulation and manhandling.

His whole life, Lechatelierite was never shown compassion. Forced to suppress his humanity since infancy, he was taught that love was detrimental and toxic. While this certainly didn't let him off the hook for mistreating Scarlet, it did explain why he apparently had so much trouble with conducting a romantic relationship. There was no way someone so emotionally damaged—a victim of a lifetime of serious abuse, himself—would naturally know how to give or receive love in a healthy way. I understood that Lechatelierite was attempting to overcome several enormous emotional hurdles when he decided to pursue Scarlet. What I didn't understand was why someone as headstrong and smart as Scarlet would tolerate being anyone's punching bag.

Since early childhood, every aspect of Scarlet's life was an uphill battle. As the ages passed, her road only seemed to grow bumpier. I thought of love as the only force in the world powerful enough to ease most any burden. I couldn't think of anyone who needed that kind of relief more than Scarlet. Yet, even with love, she couldn't catch a break. Even there, she managed to acquire more scars.

The thought of anyone compounding Scarlet's pain made me furious. But, there was nothing I could do now about her troubled past but treat her kindly while optimistically hoping that, despite it all, Lechatelierite still made her happy somehow—that, in the end, she was still glad to have loved him. I could only hope that their relationship wasn't the twisted, chaotic, dysfunctional disaster I suspected it was. At the very least, I knew that Scarlet didn't see Commence's existence as a tragedy. Though the timing was poor, she saw her son's life as cause for celebration. She cherished him, tremendously. So, at the very least, her crazy circumstances produced one joyful outcome.

I wished I could make her happy the way I hoped Lechatelierite once did. But, it wasn't my place and it wasn't our time. What Scarlet needed from me now was friendship and hard work. Anything more would only salt her still-fresh wounds.

* * *

I awoke in the middle of the night to the sound of agonized whimpers piercing through the wall. Immediately, I jumped up and ran into Scarlet's room. And, I found her doubled-over on the floor beside her tarp, crying and shaking.

"Scarlet!"

Dropping to my knees, I scooped her up. Her stare was wide, wet and glossed over. What was this? A seizure? A stroke? Something to do with the baby? I stroked her cold, clammy white face.

Of course. I'd seen this happen to Fair several times while we were marooned together: Scarlet was suffering an attack of the System mind-control. I couldn't believe it. These days, mental attacks were commonplace amongst the Reds, regardless of age or physical distance from the Fire Pit. But, Scarlet was supposed to be immune. If the Multi-Source Enchant wasn't safe, was any mage?

"Scarlet," I hissed, voice loud, "stay with me. Please, Scarlet. You can fight it; I know you can! Come on!"

She shook her head, vitreous gaze pleading for help.

Help. Aside from holding and reassuring her, how could I possibly help? Whenever this happened to Fair, the only thing that ever *really* helped in the end was borrowing more energy from Scarlet's aura, to which hers was twined.

Aura. Scarlet said that *I* had an aura. An aura attached to hers. My heart drummed against my Adam's apple.

Could I possibly use it now, to help her? Was I strong enough for that?

There was only one way to find out. I placed my hands—my supposed powersource—on her head, scrunched my lids and willed my photons to surge into her scalp. And, lo and behold, I could feel my frequency obey. How in the world did I know how to do that? It happened almost... naturally. Where did the instinct come from? Moreover, how could I even sense my wavelength in the first place when I had no idea how spectrum was supposed to feel?

Scarlet's body visibly relaxed as the light returned to her eyes. She was herself, again. The danger had passed. For now.

I lay her in bed.

"Th-that hasn't happened to me before," she panted, voice laden with dread, "not since my hair actually touched the Crystal itself."

"You scared me half to death, Scarlet," I whispered, exhausted beyond belief by my brief magical exertion.

"If even *I'm* at risk, then Conflagria's got less time than I thought," she moaned. Then, she stroked my elbow and breathed, "Thank you for pulling me out of that, Nurtic. I don't know what would've happened if you weren't here, tonight. You and Fair seem to be the only ones really twined to me, these days. I may have countless political followers, but I still don't exactly have a vast spectral support network. You know, real friends."

Inhaling, I met her gaze and solemnly said, "Scarlet, I think it'd be a good idea to reach out to Dex, after all."

She gave me a small sleepy smile. "I'm glad you want to train." She squeezed my hand. "I can tell already that you're going to be a fantastic mage."

And, with that, her lids fluttered shut. She looked so peaceful as she slept, arms nestled around her belly as though trying to hug her unborn son. I pulled her ragged blanket over her tiny frame and left the room, closing the door behind me.

ARRHYTH LINK

Monday, December third.

Today, I'd head to Conflagria. Since Seven was coming with, Inexor wasn't. The two of them took turns traveling abroad, leaving the fleet under the other's command.

Scarlet audio-called my PAVLAK, just as we were taking off. "You and I are no longer the only fluent Star speakers on the team," she greeted me. "We have a new Orion essayist."

"Really? Who?"

"A couple days ago, Nurtic brought her from UVA."

My stomach disappeared. "Linkeree?" I breathed. *My sister* joined the World Revolt?

"That's right."

Wow. "Are she and Nurtic still on the island? Will I get to see them today?"

"Maybe," Scarlet replied. "They only got here on Saturday, but they're leaving today at noon." Noon! Not a second to waste! "Their fall break is ending."

Nurtic always stayed in Conflagria for far more than two nights at a time, regardless of his course-schedule. "So, what, can't they just skip some school?"

"They have an orchestra concert tomorrow." Scarlet sounded irritated. "Apparently, marks in that class depend heavily on performance attendance. The World Revolt already shot most of Nurtic's grades to hell; I don't need to make him flunk Music, too."

I winced. I never thought I'd see the day Nurtic would receive anything less than a perfect score in a class. Linkeree also always got straight 'A's.

"I wonder if my sister knows what she's gotten herself into," I murmured.

"She better, by now. She's already in too deep for us to let her out alive." I sure hoped Scarlet was only kidding. "But, her job will be a lot less physically demanding than Nurtic's, from here on out. Nurtic travels more than any of us. Ree's a journalist."

"And, I'm a translator," I chuckled. "In a single weekend, Linkeree has outstripped me, already." That's my little sis.

"Not really. You're our primary Orion liaison."

"Which makes me the most hated man *in* Oriya," I mumbled.

"No, that's your dad."

I gave a hollow laugh. "So, Ree and Nurtic are leaving Conflagria in a few hours. When are they due back?"

"December seventh."

Ugh. I was supposed to return to Icicle on the seventh; our schedules were reversed. I had to find a way around that…

"If you're thinking of screwing with your calendar, you can forget it," Scarlet read my mind. "We've got a solid system worked out; emergencies are the only reason I'd ever let you or anyone mess it up."

Wait, what? Now, I was getting pissed. Real pissed. This was so unlike Scarlet. It seemed more like something Lechatelierite would do. Scarlet was supposed to be the compassionate one. She wasn't a base-raised zombie— she was supposed to care about people's relationships and feelings.

She'd changed a lot since Lechatelierite's death. She was more like him, now. The side of him I didn't like.

"I know how it feels, Arrhyth," her tone suddenly grew softer and more Scarlet-esque, "to be separated from everyone you ever loved. That's what war does to relationships; it tears them apart." She exhaled. "But, Arrhyth, it also creates new ones. I have a new family, now. My Reds. The Diving Fleet. My fellow Tri-Nation-Campaigners. And, soon, a son. Yes, I've lost a lot, no doubt. But, in the process, I'm also gaining a lot. So are you."

And, with that, she hung up. It was true; despite the Laws of Emotional Protection, some of the closest bonds I'd ever formed happened right here at Icicle, in the wake of tragedy.

But, no one could replace Linkeree. I wanted to see my sister, dammit. Today.

"Step on it, sir," I growled to Seven, at the helm.

"This isn't a semivowel or a flivver," he retorted, fingers drumming the joystick. "There's no pedal."

* * *

We arrived in time to see two white figures hop aboard a grey convertible. I ran toward them, waving my arms and hollering like a little kid. Two tinted visors swiveled toward me. Then, the person in the passenger seat—Linkeree, no doubt—threw off her harness and helmet, jumping out of the cockpit and into my waiting arms. Nurtic clambered after her, flipping his visor open and grinning his head off. Seven stood several feet away, watching with stony eyes, obviously put-off by the whole gushy scene.

"Look at you, all dressed for battle!" I exclaimed to Linkeree. She looked a lot like Scarlet in her skintight diving suit. Delicate. Frail. "I can't believe you joined the World Revolt! Did Nurtic here talk you into it?"

"Actually, it was entirely Linkeree's idea," Nurtic said. She nodded, proudly.

"Whoa, wait a sec, *what* did you just let him call you?" I gasped. "Is Nurtic your new brother or something? Have I been replaced?"

I watched as Linkeree playfully shoved Nurtic, giggling like I'd just made the funniest joke she ever heard. Nurtic said they weren't dating but… well… in my opinion, there was something about them that seemed to click. I thought Scarlet and Lechatelierite clicked too, long before the truth came out. I even shared that thought with Dither once, but he just rolled his eyes and made snide remarks about how Scarlet shouldn't touch the likes of Lechatelierite with a mile-long glacier-thawing lance. I made Dither eat his words when Inexor found their marriage certificate, months later. My comrades often treated me like the fleet clown but, the truth was, I had good intuition.

"Actually, I don't *let* Nurtic call me that," Linkeree chuckled. "He just does it anyway, sometimes, to spite me."

I shook my fist at Nurtic in a mock-threatening manner. Then, I asked Linkeree how she liked her new job.

"It's a real challenge already, I'm not going to lie," she answered. "But, I enjoy it tremendously. I never thought *my* work would circulate the globe!"

I delayed their departure by an entire hour, catching up. The whole time, Seven waited with folded arms and pursed lips. We probably would've chatted even longer if Fair Gabardine didn't barge out of Headquarters and literally drag me away. Seven looked relieved as he followed us inside.

"They have a long trip back followed by early class in the morning," Fair shot, yanking my wrist. "Nurtic hardly ever sleeps, anymore. I don't want tomorrow's headlines to read, 'UVA Students Crash and Drown After Pilot Snoozes at Helm.'"

"That's too long for a headline, and Nurtic won't drown," I objected. "He's a professional diver."

"Yeah, well, what about Ree?"

"Ree is one of the best civilian swimmers I ever—"

"Hi, Arrhyth, Seven," a voice interjected.

We wheeled around.

"Hey, Scarlet." Her arms were loaded with scrolls. "My translating homework?" I asked.

She nodded. "Due Wednesday." She handed them over then turned to go.

"Hey, wait a sec," I called after her. "When am I going to get those Conflagrian-language lessons?"

She froze.

"You promised, remember?"

Fair scowled at me. "Scarlet doesn't have time for stupid crap, Link, so buzz off and get on with your assignments."

"No, it's okay," Scarlet said, brushing Fair's arm. "I can do it if Arrhyth really wants to."

"When will you get the time?" Fair growled.

"We'll make time. I mean, if Nurtic and I can make time to chat every night he's here, then…" She shrugged.

Fair's white brows met her hairline. "Is that so?"

I stared at Scarlet's burning cheeks. What was so shocking about that? She and Nurtic were World Revolt co-leaders, after all. Of course, they'd need to touch base regularly.

That's when I realized that Scarlet didn't say 'talk' or 'touch base.' She said '*chat*.' So, their nightly conversations weren't necessarily about work.

Back at Icicle, I always got the impression that Nurtic irritated the living photons out of Scarlet. I never thought they were true friends. Either their friendship only really ignited with the World Revolt, or it existed back at Icicle and my instincts failed me, after all.

* * *

"Wow, maybe, I should be asking *you* to translate our Conflagrian articles from now on," Scarlet breathed. Night was falling and we were wrapping up our first Conflagrian-language lesson. "You're doing an incredible job!"

I yanked a curl. "Am I?" I thought my progress today was mediocre at best. Conflagrian was hard to pronounce and the letters were impossible to draw. Everything sounded like vowels and looked like squiggles. I felt lost.

"Are you kidding? You were able to repeat my every word, without a hiccup."

"So, I can echo sounds I don't understand. So, what?" Scarlet was typically hard to impress; what on earth was going on, here?

I got the answer, soon enough.

"You should've seen my sessions with Cease, in preparation for the First Infiltration," she laughed, rolling her eyes. "I think it took him about three hours to learn to say, 'I would like a torch of fire,' without forgetting half the sentence or inserting Ichthyothian words. Not to mention, his accent was *awful*. It was terrifying to think that our entire mission depended on his ability to recite a couple lines without screwing up."

Her joviality stunned me. While she and Lechatelierite didn't have much of a marriage—maybe, eighteen hours, if that—he was still her dead husband. Her dead husband, the father of her unborn child and probably the only man she ever had time to love, thus far. She was able to roll her eyes and laugh at him?

She was getting over him, I realized. She was able to think of him without falling apart. She was able to speak of him cheerfully, invigorated instead of sorrowed by his memory. She was finally coping with his loss in a healthier way. I smiled. Lechatelierite would've been happy to see that.

LINKEREE LINK

After only three days in the desert, I was already exhausted out of my mind. Between my continual bellyache and my inability to decide between roasting in a robe or freezing in a diving suit, I barely ate or slept, all weekend. Nurtic told me not to be discouraged by the rough start, though; he believed I'd adapt to the inhospitable environment, sooner or later. He said, after a little while, you just sort of go numb.

Only twenty minutes into our return-flight, I was out cold. Sometime later, I got startled awake by a loud snapping noise.

"What's going on?" I asked, sleepily.

Nurtic didn't respond. Not with words, anyway. The plane suddenly lost a few hundred feet of altitude, causing my stomach to jump up my esophagus. Instinctively, I screamed.

"Ree, please!" Nurtic shouted.

There came another series of earsplitting pops. Nurtic, uttering some foul words I'd never heard him use before, abruptly wrenched his joystick to the left, sending us into a wild spin. I clung to my seat cushion, whimpering.

When we stabilized, I squeaked, "Nurtic, are we under attack?" And, what would happen if I threw up in my helmet?

"What do you think?" he growled.

A rumble shook the sky as a wooden jet with orange and olive-green markings darted much too close to our hull. Nurtic whipped around, opening fire… and the craft detonated *right above us*. I gnawed my tongue until it bled. I'd never witnessed a real-live explosion before. It was nothing like the nice neat puffs in the war movies; it seemed to fill the whole atmosphere, like a hurricane. Debris billowed in all directions. As the clouds cleared, Nurtic began weaving through the grid of enemy planes, changing course twice per second. The sky and sea kept swapping places, horizon twirling like a baton. This was far worse than any rollercoaster ride. I couldn't believe Nurtic was in control, at all. How could he tell where we were going? It seemed like he was just jerking us around. I scrunched my lids shut, forcing myself to breathe deeply. Inhale, exhale. Inhale, exhale. It didn't help. I wound up gagging and vomiting in my helmet anyway, foam absorbing the warm globs.

My eyes opened. I needed to focus on something static, to keep the motion sickness at bay. At first, I tried to concentrate on the back of Nurtic's helmet, but that didn't work because the man didn't sit still for a millisecond. Ignoring his PAVLAK's projection, he seemed to look anywhere but forward, turning his head this way and that. His heavy breathing resonated through the intercom.

"Th-there's too many of them," he choked. "I've never fought an entire fleet by myself, before. I can't do this!"

"Don't say that. Yes, you can." I hoped I sounded reassuring. In truth, I was so scared, I'd accidentally used my catheter... except I wasn't even wearing it properly.

"The entire System Air Fleet," he wailed. "Linkeree, I'm so sorry for bringing you out here! I never should've let you get wrapped up in this World Revolt mess! Oh, God, please help me; I don't want to kill my best friend!"

"Nurtic, concentrate!" I somehow managed to cry, finger poised over the eject button. "Relax!" Relax? Was I kidding!?

"Oh, God, please help me!" he shrieked again.

Upon joining the Tri-Nation Campaign, I knew I'd be commuting regularly across dangerous warzones. But, my fear was moderated by Nurtic's stellar piloting record. Yet, now, with terrifying dread, I realized that the flying champ was panicking. Staring at my knees—since I couldn't close my eyes without feeling sicker—I began to pray. A scrambled stream-of-consciousness zipped through my brain. Unable to think of my own words for long, I started to silently recite an excerpt from psalm eighty-nine.

O Lord, God of hosts, who is mighty as You? We barrel-rolled. *With Your faithfulness all around You?* We swerved, violently. *You rule the raging of the sea.* A deafening boom resounded. *When the waves arise, You still them—*

Sea. Waves. Of course!

"Nurtic, can the enemy planes go underwater?" After all, he did say they were from the Air Fleet, not the Water Forces.

"N-no."

"But, we're in a convertible, right?"

There was a stunned silence, followed by, "Ree, you're a genius!"

With that, Nurtic pressed his joystick flat, sending us straight into the white-capped waves. After a few more minutes of rapid descent, he declared we were finally in the clear.

"I've fought outnumbered before," he breathed, "but, never like this. Never a whole fleet, at once. We would've died if you didn't speak up, Ree. Thank you."

"Oh, don't thank me," I chortled, thinking about the psalm.

"And, I'm sorry for yelling at you."

"It's okay, really."

I noticed that he called me by my real name while freaking out. Well, that was fine by me. I figured, in times of crisis, we were all family.

"Are you alright?" he asked.

"I puked in my helmet but, other than that, I'm okay," I replied, nose wrinkling. I decided not to mention my little bathroom break. "You?"

Apparently, Nurtic had no such reservation: "Let's just say, I'm glad this suit has a nice big catheter."

I realized I was still straining forward, death-gripping my seat cushion. I forced myself to let go and lean back. I couldn't believe I'd just caught a glimpse of combat.

"So, that's what battle's like?"

"That's not what it's *like*, that's what it *is*. Except, I'd usually have an army. An army on my side, I mean." He exhaled. "I do have a great co-pilot, though," he added, cheerily.

"Not co-pilot," I corrected, glad he couldn't see me blush. "Passenger."

SCARLET JULY LECHATELIERITE

December fifth. The World Revolt was roughly a month underway.

Our team of computer hackers—Seven and Inexor at the forefront—worked around-the-clock to break through the Order's never-ending succession of online barriers, so we could continue posting media. Our work was eclectic. The Magic Wars and the Ichthyo-Conflagrian War sure provided our writers and filmmakers with plenty of fodder. We infiltrated System strongholds to capture footage of Red warriors and Nordic soldiers in bondage. We taped several violent street-skirmishes between System authorities and innocent villagers. We broadcasted some old footage of last spring's Spectral Hurricane and the relief effort that followed, making it clear as day that all three nations impacted—the Order Authority included—had to breach the Isolationist Laws just to pull through. And, of course, we put out countless articles that attacked the theory of isolationism on every possible scholarly level.

Literally overnight, Ree's first published essay, 'Fire and Ice, Unite,' went viral. 'What does the world gain from shutting out extraordinary nations like Nuria, Ichthyosis and Conflagria, whose collective economic capital, diverse resources, brilliant minds and miracle-making wonders could revolutionize humanity?' Ree wrote. 'Instead of turning a blind eye to the Ichthyo-Conflagrian War, an effective world government would actively labor to eradicate it, freeing the Nurro-Ichthyothian Alliance to channel its scientific genius toward progressive endeavors like the establishment of manned space programs. I cannot possibly be the only person on Second Earth who believes that, throughout history, space exploration was the epitome of human courage and innovation.'

'The very existence—and budding success, I daresay—of the Tri-Nation Campaign proves that the Second Earth Order has failed to do its job,' read another one of Ree's stellar pieces. 'If isolationism breeds uninterrupted international peace, how come the planet is literally cleaving in two at this very moment?'

Well, in all honesty, Second Earth wasn't quite 'cleaving in two.' So far, out of seven-hundred nations, two-hundred-twenty-five submitted themselves to voluntary blacklisting. Which wasn't bad, considering how young the World Revolt was. But, was a third of the planet enough to carry the Tri-Nation Campaign beyond the impending death of the Red Revolution?

LINKEREE LINK

December fifteenth.

I was supposed to head back to Conflagria with Nurtic on December seventh, staying on the island until the seventeenth. But, the problem was, I could hardly emerge from under my covers anymore, let alone traverse the hemisphere.

Since returning from fall break, I'd fallen ill—tremors, nausea, vomiting, muscle weakness, diarrhea, headaches, the list went on. No doctor could determine what I had or how to make it go away, so they just blamed everything on my 'third-world travels' and told me to wait it out.

Each day, various peers brought over my school assignments. Mostly bedridden, I had plenty of time to knock them out, along with more research for the World Revolt. This evening, I was thoroughly startled to find Shawn Sordid at my door, arms folded across his massive chest. I didn't recall asking *him* to fetch me any work…

"Hey, Ree," Shawn said, for once not calling me 'Link-Link.' "Can I come inside?"

Without waiting for an answer, he barged right in.

"What's up?" I asked, uneasily.

He took a deep breath, toying with his jacket zipper. "There's… there's a new sci-fi movie coming out, tomorrow. It's, um, another remake of a vintage First Earth classic. You like those, right?"

I stared. Was he pulling my leg? Was this part of a twisted humiliation scheme?

"Like, if you're worried about making Nurtic mad or anything," he babbled on, "well... I mean... it's not your fault he's never around... and, um, you're not really his girlfriend, are you?"

This was for real. I nearly fell through the floor. Shawn Sordid was asking me out on a date. Was *this* why he still hated Nurtic so much, two full months after the cafeteria incident? Of all things to envy Nurtic for, was Shawn jealous of his proximity to *me?*

"Sorry, Shawn, that's really nice of you, but I'm not interested," was all I said. I didn't use my illness as an excuse or pretend I was too busy, because that'd just foster false hope. Outright rejection may've seemed harsh at first glance, but in the long run, it was actually far kinder than faux alibis.

Hands stowed in his pockets, he turned to go. "Alright, then. See you 'round."

"Yeah, see you," I echoed, closing the door behind him.

SCARLET JULY LECHATELIERITE

December seventeenth, seven o'clock.

Today, Nurtic would return to UVA where he would stay, uninterrupted, until his end-of-semester exams in February. On the brink of flunking out of college, he needed to focus exclusively on his studies for a little while. He didn't want to stay away from Conflagria for quite *so* long, but I insisted. I'd already turned every aspect of his current day-to-day upside-down; I didn't need to ruin his future, too.

From my bedroom window, I now watched him prep for departure. Kneeling beside his plane, he tossed his back-pack up into the cargo-bay. I spontaneously decided it was worth the exposure-risk to run outside for one last good-bye, especially since I wouldn't see him for two months. Two months! Tincture, I missed him already.

When he noticed my approach, his head banged into the lowered trunk door. Before he could stand, I threw my arms around his neck. He hugged me back with those long, lanky limbs of his, burying his face in my hair, the way Cease used to.

"Thank you, Nurtic," I breathed.

There was a pause.

"For what?"

"Saving my life."

He pulled away, expression quizzical.

"Me and my son," I swallowed, "we wouldn't be here today, if it weren't for the food you always left for me at the train station, all those ages ago." His sandy brows disappeared beneath his bangs. "I would've starved to death, without it. Without you. But, I never thanked you."

With that, I gave into the sisterly impulse to kiss him right on the dimple. He froze, flushing furiously.

"You're welcome, Scarlet," he finally whispered, giving me a quick peck by the ear. Cheeks still crimson, he shut the cargo-bay, got to his feet, climbed into the cockpit and took off.

I watched his plane disappear into the horizon, already counting down the days until his winter break.

Back inside, I was met by a rather smug-looking Fair.

"I see what's going on here," she teasingly sang. "I've seen it coming for miles."

"I have no idea what you're talking about," I replied, tiredly.

Her eyes rolled. "Come on, Scarlet. You can tell *me*."

"There's nothing to tell."

Her fists zipped to her hips. "Really?"

Anger pricked my scalp. "Yes, really." How dare she! I was yet to give birth to Cease's child!

"For Tincture's sake, Scarlet, are you honestly denying the way Nurtic looks at you? The way he acts around you? He cares about you, as more than just a friend or comrade. I'm willing to bet he loves you."

My lids scrunched shut. "I know," I whimpered. "I wish he didn't."

"Really? You don't care about him, too?"

"I do, but not like that. Not like Cease. I don't know, it's just… different. I need more time to heal, before my heart can remotely go there again."

How familiar those words sounded! I said something similar about Ambrek, last age. And, now, I had to ask myself the same question as I did then: once my grief over Cease became a little less excruciating, could I fall for Nurtic?

Heart hammering against my ribcage, I realized I couldn't rule out the possibility. Nurtic was the definition of a good guy. He was kind, compassionate, strong, loyal, altruistic, brave, I could go on. And, yes, he was attractive—anyone could see that, except perhaps Nurtic himself. I already loved him, deeply. Just, not romantically. I was still too traumatized by Cease's loss for new romance to be a possibility. But, the desire would return at some point, wouldn't it?

Face stoic, I stayed silent. And, for once, Fair let me be.

SCARLET JULY LECHATELIERITE

December twenty-second. The winter solstice. The day Cease would've turned nineteen.

I had the cabin to myself, tonight. Nurtic was away until February and Fair was currently visiting Prunus's stronghold—but, not on business. That was fine by me. The Red Revolution and the World Revolt was already depriving them of most aspects of a regular relationship. They deserved whatever shreds of happiness and normalcy they could find.

Shivering beneath my tattered blanket, I turned on my side, wicker tarp creaking. And, under my breath, I sang 'happy birthday' to Cease. I doubted anyone openly wished him that, his entire life.

When I finished the song, I realized my throat wasn't tight and my eyes weren't wet. Stricken, I lay still, wondering what it meant for me to be able to think about Cease without totally drowning in misery. Was I heartless? Cold? Calloused?

No. In fact, if Cease knew how badly I'd been handling his loss thus far, he probably would've grown livid—at himself. Weren't his last words on his deathbed, 'I'm so sorry'? I'd mulled over that cryptic sentence at least a thousand times since he spoke it but never really understood what it meant. Until now. Cease was apologizing for all the pain he knew his absence would inflict upon me.

"Well, Cease," I spoke aloud, to the ceiling, "it's my turn to apologize. I'm sorry I've let your memory drag me down instead of lift me up, all these months. I know you'd hate yourself if you saw how poorly I'd been managing my grief, thus far. But, the truth is, it's not your fault, but mine. Because, you never meant me any harm. Quite the opposite. In your own crazy, messed-up way, you made me insanely happy."

And, with that, I broke down into tears. Because, for the first time since the Crystal's end, I truly realized, with both relief and terror, that I could be a whole person again. That my life—and my son's—didn't end with Cease's. That I could dare to remember Cease's face and touch without feeling hopeless and haunted. That I could actually... *enjoy* his memory.

After crying hard for about twenty straight minutes, I wiped my face dry and lay a hand on my stomach, feeling a fresh wave of excitement for Commence, only about eight weeks from his own birthday. Lids scrunched, I began to drift into a deep sleep. My first peaceful sleep in months. Because, I was a whole person again.

No, I was two.

AMBREK COPPERTUS

It was December twenty-second of the ninety-fourth age.
The winter solstice. The darkest and coldest night of the
seventh era, thus far. It was eighty-seven degrees.

Since my premonitions began a few months ago, I lived
in fear of a crime I never committed, a crime I couldn't even
identify. The agony of it all was unspeakable. Excruciating.
Unbearable. So, tonight, I decided to find and confront the
wellspring of my nightmares, once and for all. Scarlet July.

I didn't wish to harm her. I only wanted to talk to her.
Tell her what I was afraid of. Reason with her. Because,
I figured, the only surefire way to prevent any unidenti-
fied horrors from transpiring would be if we *agreed* to it.
We would decide, right then and there, to let bygones be
bygones, forever. We'd confirm that, since she lost Cease
and I lost Crimson, the score was even. We'd vow never to
willingly interact nor seek personal revenge again. Despite
everything that went down between us in the past, I was
sure she'd consent to this. Her compassion and empathy
were her most beautiful attributes.

The sky was a deep muddy brown. The coarse sand, still
warm from the afternoon sun, raced beneath my feet. I felt
lighter already. Tonight, I'd sleep soundly for the first time
all age, because I'd know I'd never dream of Scarlet July
again. She was about to forgive me. I'd apologize, and she'd
set me free.

Apologize. Did I really regret my actions? No, not all of them. I wasn't sorry for my allegiance to the System. I wasn't sorry for serving my country. I wasn't sorry for fire-bombing the Nurian Trade Centerscraper, restoring the Core Crystal and avenging Crimson's death. But, what I *did* regret was the amount of pain everything wound up causing Scarlet. It grieved me that someone like her— sweet, pure, delicate—had to suffer so much because of what I did. Because of what I *had* to do, for all magekind.

At long last, I arrived at Red Headquarters. The guard at the door was out cold; I quickly broke his neck and tiptoed inside. I wasn't looking forward to facing Fair Gabardine and her hot temper. Though, I knew she'd stand down and let me talk to Scarlet—albeit, while tied up with diffusion rope—if Scarlet asked her to.

Their bedroom door was open; fireplace light danced on the far wall. And, below it, lay a half-rolled floormat. Empty. So, Fair wasn't home. Scarlet was by herself. I couldn't believe my luck.

Holding my breath, I crept inside. And, when my eyes fell on Scarlet's sleeping frame, I discovered she wasn't alone, after all.

She was pregnant.

My breath caught in my throat. So, *this* was why she'd been in hiding. Chest quivering, I advanced on her, sensing the unborn baby's budding frequency. It was a boy. His aura was iridescent. It was red.

And, black.

The child belonged to Cease Lechatelierite.

Second Earth didn't need another Lechatelierite.

Instantly, all desire to beg Scarlet's forgiveness vanished. I sure as hell wouldn't bow before a woman carrying the covalent child of my sister's killer. Scarlet was contaminated. Defiled. Dirty.

Shaking with rage, I seized her collarbone and easily snapped it in two, tearing her flesh. Sticky crimson soaked my hands. She awoke then, her earsplitting cries filling the whole cabin. I staggered back, staring at my stained palms in terrified disbelief. *This* was it—*this* was what happened in my premonition! This was what I set out tonight to prevent!

I dropped to my knees beside Scarlet's tarp, my sobs accompanying hers. Everything was red. Her clotting aura felt far too weak for self-healing. It was only a matter of minutes before she'd bleed to death, taking her child along. It took me a few moments to realize that she wasn't just shrieking incoherently—she was saying something distinct. "My son! My son!" she cried, over and over until she suddenly fell silent. My world stood still. It was all over.

I pulled her flaccid form onto my lap.

"Scarlet!" I yelled, hysterically. "Scarlet, I'm so sorry!"

Miraculously, her eyes fluttered open. She was still alive! But, for how long?

"Scarlet?"

She slowly reached out and touched my face with trembling fingers. And, through the spectral web, I felt my thoughts autonomously travel to her mind, as though vacuumed. Without speaking a word aloud, I almost involuntarily told her about my premonition and how it haunted me unceasingly until I found myself here tonight, desperate to prevent it, only to become an Oedipus, after all. I told her that she was my betrothed, that she was supposed to be mine, that none of *this* was supposed to happen. I told her how I wished, day and night, that the System never deported her, sending her up north where she'd change into someone she never should've been forced to become— someone who'd fall for a Nordic she never should've met.

So, Scarlet told me—also through the spectral web— that she believed everything happened for a reason, that this was the life she was meant to lead and these were the trials she and I were meant to endure, even if we didn't always understand why. And, the warm look in her watery eyes told me that she had no intention to die with the poison of unforgiveness in her heart. The tenor of her gaze was almost… loving.

Impossible.

"Why?" I croaked. "How?"

"Because, I know," she whispered, blood dribbling from her lips, "even then, even now, you aren't truly lost."

And, then, her wavelength abruptly demanded that I take my sword to her belly, slicing her baby free. I stared.

"Please, Ambrek," she whimpered, guiding my hand to my hilt, "save him."

I set her on the floor, drew my sword and held it out before me, blade glinting in the firelight. Could I really do it? Could I splice her stomach?

Could I rescue the son of my sister's murderer?

"Hurry!"

Yes, I could do it. I would. Not for Cease. Not for Cease's spawn. But, for Scarlet.

I hadn't a clue how, but she stayed conscious and alert as I got to work. Blood and amniotic fluid sloshed everywhere as I retrieved the fetus and cut the umbilical cord. My own flesh seared whenever I touched the boy's skin. Why?

Small as a doll, he was obviously at least a couple months premature. But, there was nothing little about his voice. He bawled like a throat-mage, his silver-green gaze terrifyingly astute. Call me crazy, but I thought I saw hatred in his lime-slice stare. I shivered, glancing away. How absurd. I was imagining things, projecting my guilty conscience on an innocent and ignorant newborn.

I wrapped the tiny baby in Scarlet's blanket and held him to her chest. The expression on her face was indescribable as she beheld him for the first time. She pressed her flushed cheek against his pale one.

It was all too much for me to bear, but I forced myself to stand my ground. The kid was dependent on me now, until I figured out what to do with him.

Tincture, what the hell would I do with him?

"Take him to Nuria. To the Alcove City Hospital," Scarlet answered my unvoiced question. She divulged where she hid the keys to her Nordic plane, freshly refueled by her recent Ichthyothian visitors. "Give him to Qui Tsop."

"Why Nuria?" I asked. "Who's Key Sop?"

She didn't answer.

"What about Ichthyosis?" I pressed. Wouldn't it make more sense to hand baby Lechatelierite over to the Diving Fleet?

"No! Not Ichthyosis. Promise you'll take him to Nuria, Ambrek, please. Give him to Qui Tsop. Nowhere and no one else!"

"I promise, Scarlet," I breathed, alarmed. "What's his name?"

"Qui already knows," she wheezed, "so, you don't need to."

That sentence was like a stab in the heart, but I accepted it with a single nod.

And, with that, Scarlet gave her son one final adoring look, whispered, "I love you," and closed her emerald eyes for the very last time.

I cried for the next fifteen minutes straight, the child occasionally joining in, until a glint of silver on Scarlet's chest caught my eye. I reached for it. It was a triangular medal, suspended on a black and blue ribbon. It was clearly some sort of award from the Nordic military. I wondered why Scarlet would wear it after all these months; she wasn't the type to treasure the praise of man.

Of course. Because it probably once belonged to Cease Lechatelierite.

I removed it from Scarlet's neck and gently tied it around the baby's slight wrist. He stared at his first possession with fascination, already attached. Then, cradling him in my arms, I got to my feet and headed out into the night, leaving Scarlet's shell behind.

Scarlet July's earthly life was over; her physical body was now nothing but an ethereal wisp of red on a dirty wooden floor. But, I knew, her legacy was far from over. Like a phoenix rising from the ashes, she brought something new into this dark world, to carry her iridescent torch.

SCARLET JULY LECHATELIERITE

I beheld the beautiful face of my dear son, amazed and overwhelmed. I never thought love this strong was possible. All of Commence fit comfortably in Ambrek's palm. It was astounding that a child so small could be conscious. Not only conscious, but alert. Watching. Moving. Thinking. I longed to cradle him in my own arms, but I couldn't move them anymore. My entire body was numb.

My life tried to flash before my eyes, but I prevented it, preferring instead to stay in the here and now. With weird satisfaction, I realized I couldn't have been the one the prophecy spoke of after all, because every damn thing I touched always turned to dust.

Suddenly, my sight got filled with grey-green eyes beaming from a flushed face that was so easy to confuse with Cease's—he looked maybe seventeen or eighteen. Was this a premonition? Was this my Commence, all grown up? Or, was I hallucinating—regurgitating a memory of Cease, modified by my desire to know what would become of Commence in the future? Well, I didn't have time to worry about that. All I could do now was enjoy what I saw. He was absolutely stunning—my husband, son and I, all blended together. True covalence. I was happy that face would be the very last thing I'd ever see. Because, in him, I saw hope and beginning, even as I faced my own untimely, abrupt end.

"I love you," I said, to both of them. And, I closed my eyes.

ANAPES PATRICI

The news spread like wildfire around the world: Scarlet July, the Multi-Source Enchant and Tri-Nation Campaign Leader, was dead. Her mangled corpse was found on the floor of her own bedroom. And, to make matters all the more shocking, she apparently had been pregnant. From all the circulating crime-scene descriptions and pictures, it was obvious that the attacker was after the unborn baby. Indeed, the infant's body itself was missing. But, considering how poorly the C-section appeared to have been done, how premature the fetus must've been, and how unsanitary the conditions were for such an invasive procedure, it was assumed that the child couldn't have possibly survived.

It didn't take a shrewd detective to connect Scarlet's assassination to the sudden disappearance of Ambrek Coppertus. Under normal circumstances, slaying the Red Leader would've made Ambrek a hero among heroes, in the eyes of the System. But, these weren't normal circumstances. Scarlet had one last trick up her sleeve, even in death.

By now, the System should've had complete control of the spectrum. But, since the night Scarlet died, our work was, mysteriously and abruptly, undone. Now, no matter how hard we tried, we could no longer seize a single photon. It seemed as though the threads *themselves* were resistant to our manipulation. It was a spectral phenomenon unlike anything ever encountered before: the spectral web simply refused to bend to the calibration of the Crystal. It had a will of its own.

The mystery didn't stay one for long. We could all feel the answer in our auras. Every lifeline was now entwined with strands of red. Every mage's magnetic field bore a new rosy tint. The Red Leader's aura, the strongest aura in spectral history, managed to retain its sovereignty after its host's death. It now lived in the web, as the keeper and director of all magical channels.

Scarlet Carmine July, the Multi-Source Enchant about whom the prophecy was written, had beaten us once and for all, in a way no one could have imagined.

FAIR GABARDINE

Nurtic returned to Conflagria on the first day of his college winter break, as planned. Upon his arrival, he showed us on his PAVLAK how poorly the planet was reacting to the assassination of the World Revolt Leader.

In life, Scarlet strove to keep her image hidden from the media. But, now, in death, graphic shots of her butchered body seemed to be everywhere. 'Heart-wrenching,' 'traumatizing,' 'terrifying' and 'tragic' were just some of the descriptors used by journalists around the globe. I thought those words weak, compared to reality.

I was the first to behold the crime scene. Walking into Headquarters at the crack of dawn on December twenty-third, I laid eyes on Scarlet's fly-infested corpse. Immediately, I turned on my heel and ran all the way back to Prunus's cabin, screaming like a wounded throat-mage. Of all the horrors I'd seen in my warrior's life, this was, by far, the worst. I was unable to eat, sleep, walk nor talk to anybody for days. I stayed in bed like a sack of taro.

As time passed, I was surprised to find that it wasn't just Scarlet's death that upset me, but also that of her baby. I never wanted Scarlet to have that child, but I found myself mourning him nonetheless, simply because she loved him with all her heart and would've given her life for his. And, so, I cried for him, for my best friend's sake, and because if I didn't, no one else would.

No one but Nurtic Leavesleft.

Nurtic arrived on February seventh and—unable to stand the environment that so strongly reminded him of the woman he obviously loved—promptly left for Nuria, the following morning. A few days later, we found out that he'd crashed upon arrival at UVA. The incident couldn't be traced to any external cause. He wasn't attacked, he didn't run out of gas, his plane suffered no in-flight issues whatsoever. The cause of his accident was completely unknown. And, it was a spectacular one, at that—he slammed into a row of parked crafts, totaling his own and landing himself in the hospital with serious injuries. It was a miracle he survived.

And, now, for the rest of Second Earth, it was the Book of Judges, all over again. Nurtic once told me about that story, about how Israel rapidly relapsed into chaos, every time their good leaders died. Likewise, in the weeks following Scarlet's death, the Tri-Nation Campaign unraveled. By mid-February, over half the revolting nations had rejoined the Order. I knew it was only a matter of time before the rest would follow. The only thing that fell apart faster than the World Revolt was the Red Revolution.

Ichthyosis also appeared to be following Israel's example. Inexor divulged to me that the Trilateral Committee had reinstated the Childhood Program, and there was nothing the Diving Fleet could do about it. And, Cease Lechatelierite, the man who tore the program down, wasn't even an age in his grave.

There was only one thing preventing the worldwide state-of-affairs from being considered a complete disaster. Scarlet's aura had done the impossible; the spectral web was now permanently preserved from the System's abuse. Not a single mage on Second Earth could ignore his or her frequency's new red tint. In death, Scarlet gave us the only possible answer to the seemingly-insurmountable Crystal restoration problem.

But, she didn't do it alone. Scarlet July finished what Cease Lechatelierite started. Cease made the initial change to the web, which Scarlet now maintained. In isolation, each of their sacrifices would've accomplished nothing in the end. But, together, they managed to rescue Conflagria from the System's spectral thought-suppression, forever.

Most people, myself included, believed that this was the fulfillment of the prophecy. In death, the Multi-Source Enchant took from the System—the fallen children of Second Earth—what wasn't rightfully theirs: absolute control. Scarlet Carmine July was the one, the prophet, after all.

NURTIC LEAVESLEFT

It didn't take long for the World Revolt and the Red Revolution to go to hell. Scarlet was irreplaceable. No one else on Second Earth had the tactical genius or linguistic talent to take her place. Not even Cease Lechatelierite could've done it.

I still believed that humanity would be saved from isolationism. Someday. Clearly, mankind was neither ready nor willing to fix its problems, yet. Though most disagreed with me, I didn't believe that Scarlet was the prophet after all, because I didn't think she accomplished what this world needed most. And, that was okay. She'd done more than enough, for her people and mine. One day, the true Multi-Source Enchant would arrive and finish what she started. I hoped I'd live to see that day, but I wasn't holding my breath anymore.

My service as a soldier was also through, for good this time. I was a fulltime college student again. Or, at least, I was supposed to be. On my way home from Conflagria on February eighth, I started sobbing. Hard. So hard, in fact, that I couldn't keep a proper eye on my instruments or windshield. So, I crash-landed on the runway, at UVA. Badly. I rammed right into a line of parked planes. Yes, parked.

Upon impact, I broke literally dozens of bones and tore a whole lot of flesh. My craft was totaled. Throngs of students rushed to the scene, Ree included. I saw her push through the crowd, crying hysterically. I wished I could tell her that I was still alive so she'd calm down—it was heart-wrenching to see her so upset—but, of course, I could neither move nor speak. I had to be cut out of the cockpit, strapped to a stretcher and rushed to the university hospital. I lost consciousness somewhere along the way.

I went inpatient for weeks, after that. Among many other things, I got metal rods in my legs. Countless people told me that I was lucky to have survived at all. I told them it had nothing to do with luck.

During my recovery, I kept busy with schoolwork. Or, at least, I tried to. I couldn't concentrate worth a damn. All I could really think about was Scarlet and Commence. Dead. 'Just another lost child of war,' the Reds said of Commence. Apparently, burying kids was nothing special to them, these days.

But, Scarlet's son was already someone special to me. I long since loved him, as I did his mother. I felt like I lost two family members on the winter solstice of the ninety-fourth age.

Ree came to visit me at the hospital the moment she was allowed. She sat at my bedside for hours as I drenched her shoulder with tears. I wept more that day than I did in ages, but I honestly didn't care about embarrassment. Nothing really mattered to me, anymore.

To preserve my sanity, I reminded myself constantly that, at the very least, I did get to bid Scarlet a proper farewell, the last time I saw her. I would always remember her thin arms around my neck and her gentle kiss on my cheek.

* * *

By the end of March, with the help of some crazy medical tech courtesy of the Diving Fleet, I'd mostly recovered from my injuries. My physical ones, anyway.

For my parents' sake, I visited Alcove City as soon as I was well enough to. Today, my first day home, I took a long walk through town. It was snowing, but I didn't wear a jacket. Nuria's snowfall seemed so pathetic compared to Ichthyosis's. The flakes were dusty and thin, like Conflagrian sand. After extensive exposure to both weather extremes, I hardly felt temperature anymore, anyway. I was numb.

I passed the train station now and, through the frosted glass, caught a glimpse of the arcade in which I'd spent so many afternoons, back before I became a soldier. I saw a group of boys playing boisterously—they were having a grand old time, blowing up digital submarines and ending only electronic lives and laughing at this artificial death. Their joy hurt me, offended me. It reminded me of the days when life was still beautiful. Empty, but beautiful. One of the kids noticed me through the window and waved. I ignored him and continued down the icy sidewalk, hands in my pockets and eyes downcast.

QUI TSOP LECHATELIERITE

The Red Leader was dead. Which meant, so was my grandson. I was truly alone in this world.

But, not for long. I now lay on my deathbed, accompanied by a nurse who couldn't care less.

There came a knock at the door. She opened up. It was another nurse. 'Hope Cede,' her nametag read. She carried a preemie in a blue blanket. The kid was restless and ruddy and small as a doll. He had auburn fuzz sticking up on his head and eyes like enormous crystal orbs.

My breath—or, what was left of it, anyway—caught in my chest. Hope Cede brought the boy close to me; my trembling hands struggled to stroke his rosy cheeks.

"Who is he?" Hope asked me. "I was passing through the lobby when a man dressed in a strange colorful costume just walked up to me, placed the child in my arms and said your name. I tried to talk to him, but he wouldn't engage. He turned and left, on the spot. Took off in an aircraft. I didn't know what to do but call the police then bring the baby here, to you. Who is he?" she asked, again.

I said nothing. Medical bills, tanking stocks and messy lawsuits consumed any inheritance Commence might've gotten. I had nothing good to leave him. He'd only gain debts, enemies and burdens, if the world knew he was the heir to Finis's capsizing corporate empire… not to mention, the offspring of the two most famous—or, infamous, depending on your perspective—military leaders to walk Second Earth. I wanted him to grow up free from the world of war, in an adoptive home, under another last name. He did nothing to deserve his family's terrible legacy.

"Who is he?" Hope repeated. "Where did he come from? Why would a stranger tell me to bring him to you?"

Ignoring her, I concentrated on beholding the child's beautiful silver-jade stare and flushed face. He was so small, yet so attentive. Precocious.

My lids grew heavy.

"Does he have a name, Mrs. Tsop?"

I supposed it couldn't hurt for Commence to grow up with his rightful *first* name. The name Scarlet chose for him. As long as his surname remained a secret, he'd stay safe. Right?

"C'mmm . . .ence," I wheezed.

"Ence?" Hope echoed, watching me closely. "Ence what?"

"C'mmm . . . ence," I choked, once more.

I could tell from her raised brows that she still didn't understand, but I lacked the strength to correct her again.

And, with that, I began to slip into death's slumber, a smile lingering on my lips as baby Commence—the sole continuation of the Lechatelierite bloodline—wiggled on my lap.

Wasn't this what I always wanted? To have a family. To die a grandmother. Despite all the terrible ends every Lechatelierite met, one new beginning remained. Who would've thought this fresh start would rise from the ashes of war? I didn't know how on earth the boy managed to survive his mother's grisly assassination and I didn't have time to wonder about that. I supposed it was never too late to start believing in miracles, after all.

EPILOGUE

The boy wound up at an orphanage. The organization was tragically under-funded, only accepting baby 'Ence' because they were too pious to turn away a child so small and sick. The facility was managed by the Nondenominational Church of Alcove City; most of its staff were international missionaries who were either still in training, in-between trips or retired from the field. In seven ages, a certain war veteran would find himself there for work.